CHRIS WOMERSLEY

CAIRO

Quercus

First published in 2013 by Scribe Publications Pty Ltd, Victoria, Australia
Published in the UK in 2014 by Quercus Editions Ltd
This paperback edition published in the UK in 2015 by

Quercus Editions Ltd
55 Baker Street
7th Floor, South Block
London W1U 8EW

The quotations on pp. 128 and 212 are from *Maldoror and the Complete Works of the Comte de Lautréamont* (tr. Alexis Lykiard, Exact Change, Cambridge, 1994). The quotation on p. 232 is from *The Standard Edition of the Complete Psychological Works of Sigmund Freud* and used with the permission of the Institute of Psychoanalysis, London. The quotation on p. 249 is by Ern Malley: lines from 'Durer: Innsbruck, 1495' from *Collected Poems* (ETT Imprint, Sydney, 1992), courtesy the publisher and the Estate of Max Harris.

A CIP catalogue record for this book is available from the British Library

PB ISBN 978 1 84866 394 7
EBOOK ISBN 978 1 84866 393 0

This project has been assisted by the Australian Government through
the Australia Council, its arts funding and advisory body.

This project has been supported by the City of Melbourne through the Arts Grants Program.

10 9 8 7 6 5 4 3 2 1

Typeset by Scribe Publications Pty Ltd

Printed and bound in Great Britain by Clays Ltd, St Ives plc

For Reuben

Good artists copy, great artists steal.
Pablo Picasso

PROLOGUE

I DREAM OF CAIRO STILL. THE DREAMS ARE SO VIVID THAT, ON occasion, I wake sweating, disoriented, expecting to see honeyed light glancing off the floorboards and curlicues of dust pirouetting lazily through the morning air; to smell sweet, stale smoke and the tang of vetiver cologne; to hear the grumble of trams, and the *pock* of tennis balls being struck in the shady courts across the road. There is the acrid taste of last night's whisky in my mouth. The melancholy breeze of a simple piano tune trickles through an open window. I am filled with a sensation so much richer and more flavoursome than love, and it is this: love's ardent promise.

They are all present in the dream, as vital and alive as I remember them being in life: Max and Sally; Edward and Gertrude; James; Caroline and the awful Eve; even my Aunt Helen, although she had died some months before I moved into her apartment block. Maria is in the background somewhere, muttering her telegrammatic sentences, as is Mr Orlovsky. And there is Queel, turning, turning always with a glass in his hand.

Also apparent in the dream is a quality of both anticipation and foreboding, that watermark that can only be discerned in retrospect. These dreams are like dispatches from history; I almost cannot believe what is happening there, how fierce and how

1

beautiful it might be. To go back might be the best thing in the world, but it is probably the worst.

The dreams are all different, but in each of them there recurs one sequence: I am standing before a wall in what might be a dilapidated palace of some sort, on which is painted an exquisite mural, similar to that on the wall of the Teatro Olimpico in Vicenza. In my dream, however, the mural is of an archway, beyond which a dim and tangled forest fades into the distance. Arranged across the horizon is a line of mountains, a pink and dusky sky, clouds like puffs of smoke rising into the air. I stare at the mural in wonder for some time.

Gradually, I realise that a door (the size of a postcard) in the bottom left-hand corner is opening very slowly. Tiny fingers curl around the frame, fingers the size of a child's but simian in appearance; the knuckles are defined, and there is the hint of fur. The crowd of which I had sensed myself a part has fallen away. I am seized by dread. So slowly does the door move that I can't stand it. There is no sound. At last, the tiny door hangs open on its hinge. There is now no sign of the person or creature who pushed it from the other side, but it is clear to me, with the irresistible logic of dreams, that I am expected to pass through into the place beyond, and that what lies in store for me is in equal measure beautiful and terrifying.

Despite all that happened at Cairo, I am disappointed upon waking from such scenes to discover the dream was only that; a breath of a summer and winter long since past. I know that one can never return, but that doesn't prevent me from sometimes being overpowered by longing at the most inopportune moments. Only last week, when shopping for shirts in the city, I halted mid-conversation with a sales assistant (cuff of the potential purchase crisp and gently abrasive between my thumb and forefinger; young woman's kindly smile, a smudge of lipstick on her teeth) to ponder what Sally Cheever might make of my choice — whether she would approve — before realising with a jolt that she left my life long ago. Years, in fact.

There are other things I remember, things so bizarre that even now, all these years later, I wonder if they happened at all, wonder if they weren't simply the product of a youthful, fevered imagination — forever associated with the smell of turpentine and oil paint; a recurring piano motif; a pistol shot; mocking laughter; my first disastrous love.

But now I am middle-aged. It happened suddenly, this ageing, almost without my knowledge and certainly without any effort on my part. I have tufts of black hair on my shoulders, mild aches in my joints. Most likely I have lived more years than remain to me. I reconsider my position on God, in case; a fumbling in the dark, like a child grasping for his blanket in the middle of the night, crying out for someone, anyone.

I imagine the three of us from a distance. Max, Sally and I. Sally stands clutching the collar of her red jacket at her chin as Max, with one arm draped over her shoulder, throws back his drink with obvious satisfaction and, perhaps, with triumph. Sally looks at the ground in front of her while Max's sweeping gaze takes in the red and orange lanterns from the previous summer that are scattered about like the seeds from a large and exotic tree; the tubs of mangy herbs; the tops of the elms in the park across the road. And there I am with my glass of champagne, stepping forwards to kiss Sally on the cheek and to shake Max's hand. The expressions on our faces are hard to read, and I'm too far away to hear what is said. There is laughter, Max's laughter, floating across the evening air.

There are times in life that score us forever, seasons or days that cast the die of our personalities so completely that it is against such periods the remainder of our lives is measured, just as there might only be a single photograph of us ever taken that captures one's true essence. Now that I am older I find I am living two lives: my present one with its daily requirements of nourishment and warmth; and that other one, back there, when I lived with nothing and had nothing, but learned everything. I know I can never return and wouldn't wish to, were I given the chance. And yet, and yet.

Like paintings, people are taken at face value but contain a host of secrets for those who know how to tease them out; the task of the art connoisseur is akin to that of a trial judge sorting lies from the truth. There is instinct and there is science. Were you truly painted by so and so? In what year? With which materials? In essence: are you what you claim to be?

But I became an author, of all things, and although I never intended to write about that time, now there is no choice. When younger, I was free to imagine my future at will, idly, and it was a pleasant and dreamy act. But that future has gone, and now the past crooks a finger to summon me. *Come here*, it says. *We have a score to settle.*

Any memoir is a kind of confession. Here, then, is mine.

ONE

I STAGGERED FROM SPENCER STREET STATION WITH MY BULGING green suitcase and stood on the footpath, bewildered in the city light. It was January, 1986. I was seventeen years old. The railway station loomed behind me like an infernal machine into which people vanished, heads down, all business. I had been too anxious to eat much that day and felt light-headed, even faintly delirious. The pavement was baking through the soles of my shoes. The air smelled of hot chips, of vinegar, of car exhaust. A lone taxi honked. A skinny boy sauntered past with a boom-box on his shoulder, the music blasting from it distorted into sheer incomprehension.

It was too late to turn back, but I experienced a swooning feeling of solitude that was unfamiliar and utterly exhilarating. *Anything could happen to me here*, I thought. *And no one would know.* This realisation provided me with inexplicable comfort. I am never happier than when on the verge of an experience; it is, often, victory enough.

It was warmer in Melbourne than Dunley, and I had broken out in a nervous sweat. Terrified that someone might perceive me for what I really was — a boy with almost no idea of the world beyond the country town where he had spent his childhood — I set off walking with what I hoped was a purposeful air. The suitcase banged against my calf.

I had gone two blocks and was in sight of the murky Yarra River before noticing I had headed in the wrong direction. I stopped in the bright sunlight and squinted about me, cursing under my breath. I blushed as I imagined the snickering and eye-rolling this error would have prompted in my sisters. But I was self-reliant to a fault, and the thought of asking anyone for directions appalled me, so I ducked into a side street and retrieved my wrinkled street map.

In those days, that lower part of Melbourne was deserted on Saturday afternoons, an arrangement of blunt concrete canyons abutting the docklands. A gritty wind scuttled along the footpath, bringing with it cigarette butts and a crumpled chip packet. I closed my eyes to the dust. Upon opening them a few seconds later, I was startled to see a man bearing down on me with a peculiarly intense and rollicking gait. He was about twenty metres away and getting closer, talking and gesticulating. 'Get out of here,' he was yelling. 'Get away.' His voice echoed off the buildings.

He wore very tight trousers and a green pirate blouse. His hair was long, his eyes were wild and his feet were bare, but the most alarming aspect of his get-up was his lips, which were tattooed a deep blue. I looked around, unsure if I should pick up my suitcase and attempt to outrun this bizarre apparition or whether such a move would merely antagonise him. I had read in *National Geographic* that it was fatal to try to outrun a grizzly bear; preferable to back away slowly while maintaining eye contact. This wildlife knowledge was, naturally, of no use to me; we didn't even *have* grizzly bears in Australia. Not only that, but it was in this blur of trivia retrieval and frantic indecision that he was almost upon me. His bellowing had subsided to an indistinct but menacing mutter. I froze. My heels knocked on the brick wall against which I had backed. I might even have turned my head away in expectation of a blow, but he paid me no heed as he walked past and vanished around the corner into Flinders Street, leaving a waft of sweet perfume in his wake.

I retraced my steps and caught the tram at Bourke Street. Rattled after my encounter with the blue-lipped man and worried about missing my tram stop and ending up in the wilds of suburbia, I watched through the window, mentally checking off the landmarks as we went: Myer department store; Darrell Lea chocolate emporium; the cinema complex; and the famous Pellegrini's cafe, where my late Aunt Helen had taken me for lemon granitas on the few occasions I had visited her alone. So many shops, so many people. A group of boys in sharp suits were busking in the mall, crowds of onlookers. As the tram clattered up Bourke Street towards my destination, my heart began to beat wildly. Surely, disappointment could be the only result of such high expectations.

I alighted one stop past the Exhibition Building in Nicholson Street and waited on the narrow traffic island as cars whizzed by. On one side of the large, busy road were the Carlton Gardens with their tennis courts and stately avenues of elm trees. On the other side, almost hidden behind a hedge and an overgrown peppercorn tree, was the apartment block with its name spelled out in white metal lettering affixed to one of its red-brick walls: *Cairo*.

Passing into its shady gardens on that summer afternoon, I felt transported (as even now my recollections transport me) into another world. Dappled sunlight, the cool scent of bricks, the abrupt cessation of traffic noise.

I lugged my suitcase up the unusual cantilevered staircase and along the walkway to the apartment in which Aunt Helen had lived for so many years. The key turned easily in the lock. With trepidation, I opened the door and stepped inside. On the floor in front of me, spilling from the service hatch where it must have been placed, was a pile of unopened mail. Also in the hallway were three or four boxes of Aunt Helen's things that my dad had packed up to be thrown out.

The apartment was compact but even lovelier than I recalled. Light splashed through the large, floor-to-ceiling window of the main room. I put down my suitcase in the narrow entrance hallway and knew, if only dimly, that my life would never be the same.

Cairo had been a focus for so much of my imaginative energy that to find myself there was confusing. Although the apartment only had two rooms (four, including the bathroom and kitchen), I spent a bit of time on that first sunny afternoon prowling around opening and closing cupboards, peering in drawers, half expecting to encounter someone hiding in a corner. But, of course, there was no one in the apartment and there hadn't been for some months, as was evident by the stuffy air and layers of dust on the furniture. My father had come and cleared away many of Aunt Helen's personal items after her death, but there were others yet to be disposed of, household things made strange and strangely meaningful by her absence: books, photographs, an empty vase, a dish of loose change on the fridge.

Constructed in a U-shape around an overgrown garden, Cairo apartments were completed in 1936. With only two storeys, the thirty or so one- and two-bedroom apartments had been built with bachelors in mind, and the block retained many of its original features, including the service and rubbish-bin hatchways designed as modern, labour-saving features. A dining room at the rear of the block, which had once served meals, had been transformed into a milk bar long before I moved in. Three cantilevered concrete staircases provided access to the upper floor at the southern and eastern corners. Architectural flourishes were kept to a minimum, in accordance with the modernist aesthetic of the era. The apartments' front doors all had porthole windows and these, combined with the waist-high railing along the exterior walkways, gave one the impression of being on board a liner moored at the edge of the city, waiting for clearance to set sail.

Helen's apartment was sparsely furnished, but tasteful: a green sofa, an armchair, Persian rugs over the bare floorboards, a wooden table by the window, a coffee table with a pile of magazines, a low bookcase. On the floor was a record player with a stack of old records (the soundtrack from *Dr Zhivago*, *Scottish Military Anthems*) leaning against the skirting board beside it. A floorboard under a rug in the narrow hall squeaked when stepped on.

The bedroom contained a spongy double bed, a wardrobe and a bureau of drawers upon which, among the scattering of jewellery and desiccated cosmetics, stood a framed, black-and-white photograph of Aunt Helen at a party with one hand resting on the forearm of the corpulent, bejewelled actor Frank Thring, who lived nearby.

The kitchen led off the entrance hall and was dim and poky, not much larger than a galley. A window of frosted glass set high above the sink allowed for some natural light. The kitchen's shallow cupboards contained a profusion of teacups, packets of spices, noodles, tins of tomatoes, bottles of liquor.

Opposite the kitchen was the equally small bathroom with its glorious deep bath, a mirrored cupboard, tiles of the palest green. It smelled of musty drains and peppermint mouthwash. Spider webs fluttered in the corners; the sink bore a rusty tear-drop from the dripping tap.

There was an elegant balcony off the lounge room that looked over a side street. Standing on it in the blazing sun, I could see the balconies of my neighbours on either side of this apartment, but no one appeared to be home. A car drove past in the street below, trailing a cricket commentary in its wake. I stretched out, tore off a handful of leaves and dry buds from the peppercorn tree, and held them to my face. To this day I cannot open a jar of peppercorns without being plunged into that distant afternoon; it is an aroma (blunt, complicated; familiar yet exotic) that contains multitudes.

My assessment of the apartment didn't take long. Obviously, it needed to be thoroughly cleaned, but on that first afternoon I could do no more than lie on the couch, red satin cushion beneath my head, and gaze through the window at the swaying fronds of the peppercorn tree. Every so often, the thin curtain billowed out in the warm breeze like a woman's dress. I was exhausted, relieved, scarcely able to believe my good fortune. I imagined Aunt Helen lying here doing the same thing. I felt at rest, as if I had travelled vast distances to be here.

The heat subsided as the afternoon drew to a close. People came and went along the walkway outside. I sensed doors opening and closing, birds chirruping, voices, a woman humming an indistinct tune as she walked by, the vague sound less a melody than an enticing scent that hung on the air long after she had passed.

TWO

IT'S DIFFICULT TO PINPOINT THE PRECISE BEGINNING BUT, IF I were to try, I would need to start earlier than the murder and that infamous heist; back further than meeting the Cheevers and their intriguing friends; before moving into Cairo, even though those events might be the obvious starting points for what transpired.

Let's face it: the rot set in early. Much later, Sally (dear Sally) told me that without a past a person has no character, and she might have been right. Now, perhaps, I have too much character.

If I cast my mind back into the murky waters of that ever-receding past, I can picture myself late one afternoon on a low hill overlooking the football oval in Dunley, Victoria, population 3250. There I sat, young and prickling with desires and grievances I would be hard pressed to name.

It was the winter before I moved into Cairo. I was in my final year at Dunley High School, where I studied French, European history, literature, art history and English with an earnestness and dedication that now surprises me. I struggled through irregular French verbs; tried to decipher Eliot's *Preludes*; and pored over my 1970 edition of E.H. Gombrich's *The Story of Art* (in which Pablo Picasso still lived), with its grimy reproductions of great paintings, as if they might reveal to me another, better world. In a hard

11

country town like Dunley — where a man's worth was measured by his ability to stake a fence or identify the number of cylinders in a car by sound alone — this made me a misfit. In addition, I was scrawny and morbidly uncomfortable in my skin. I bit my fingernails with grim determination and often scrutinised myself in the mirror for hours, as if the clue to my character might be found on or behind the cold, smooth glass. *What do people see when they look at me?* I wondered. *How am I supposed to be in this terrible world?*

Adolescence is a swirl of superiority and crushing doubt. Nowadays the so-called experts fret over epidemics of low self-esteem in our teenagers but, really, it is one of the many necessary planks used for the raft that transports us from youth to adulthood. Without it, we are nothing.

I lived with my mother, Emily, who worked as a bookkeeper at Stockdale's law firm. My parents had divorced four years earlier. My father, Roger, a real estate agent, had married his colleague Barbara Moore, who was famous around town for her bouffant hairdo that made her look like a rather addled extra from *La Dolce Vita*, an impression augmented by rumours that Barbara had an addiction to sleeping pills. My elder sisters, Meredith and Rosemary — with whom I did not get along — were both married and lived nearby.

In addition to school, I worked one or two shifts a week as a waiter at Eddie's Cafe on Main Street. My life at that time was characterised by yearning; I would find myself standing (in my bedroom, at the kitchen sink, the back door at Eddie's) gazing through a window at the sky, wondering what might lie beyond, what adventures people were having in New York or Casablanca. Even now, the images that most readily come to mind when I think of my youth in Dunley are of the low, grey sky; the flat horizon; a plastic bag snagged on a barbed-wire fence. I hated Dunley and most of the people who lived there, including my family. Or at least I thought I did, which is perhaps the same thing.

On that afternoon, the trees were skeletal, empty of leaves, and the air had in the last few weeks taken on an icy quality. In a month or two, the oval would be mud, and the streets of the town would be more or less deserted after nightfall — apart from drunks staggering home after last drinks at the Great Southern Hotel, kids doing wheelies on their bikes, and the occasional police car cruising, shark-like, along Main Street. Dunley was always a mean place, but in winter it became a town lurking with sinister possibilities; the bitter cold stripped away any bucolic veneer the place had acquired during summer. The few tourists who visited for the bushwalking or a weekend away vanished, the sun struggled low on the horizon, and sharp winds sheared across the boggy fields.

That afternoon I was sitting with David Blake. David and I weren't friends in the manner in which I have subsequently come to understand the term; we had been thrown together in the way one might befriend another tourist in a restaurant abroad — for no other reason than you shared a common language and could moan about the public transport or the quality of the food. Isolated among Dunley's beer-swilling, ute-driving football players called Macca and Robbo, David and I needed each other.

We had become acquainted four years earlier, when the Dungeons & Dragons craze swept the school — or at least captured the interest of those students who considered themselves brighter and more imaginative than the others. At lunchtimes, a cabal of bespectacled, Monty Python-quoting nerds assembled in one of the spare classrooms to listen to Kraftwerk, throw polyhedral dice around, and debate the relative merits of the broadsword against the ability to render a troll immobile for twenty seconds. For an hour or so each day — and sometimes, if it could be organised, for a rainy weekend afternoon — we embarked on campaigns to villages called Riverweft or Dugshen, squalid settlements populated by scheming wizards and elves, encrusted with smoky

13

taverns in which one drank mead and gathered information for the onward journey to Nighthawk Cove, where (according to legend) a trove of treasure could be found.

I became mildly obsessed with the world of Dungeons & Dragons. For hours I pored over large books with the heft of grimoires that outlined the various monsters and the types of characters who might attempt to slay or woo them. I always cast myself as a Ranger (daring, handsome, heroic, physically powerful), the character perhaps most removed from my real self (plain, weedy, impractical, cowardly).

Older than me by nearly a year, David had finished high school and joined the ranks of restless teenagers in country towns with not an awful lot to do. He rode his (by now too small) bike around, trying to convey the impression he had an urgent task at hand when, in fact, he was going to buy milk for his mum; he smoked pot when his dole cheque came through; he saw movies at the Dunley Odeon during the day. To me, he exuded a kind of diffident, louche charm but, crucially, he was also the kind of teenager who had a sixth sense when it came to dealing with parents. He asked after people's ageing relatives; he could advise mothers on baking, discuss with fathers the shortcomings of Holdens. Parents adored him, and invariably considered him delightful and responsible for his age. Even my mother, who was by nature suspicious, thought David a 'very nice boy' and would rise, cobra-like, to his defence should a rumour swirl and threaten his pristine reputation.

David and I both despised the parochialism of Dunley, and over the years we had developed an elaborate fantasy of escaping the place, a plan that, like a many-roomed mansion to which we were constantly adding new parlours and wings, had expanded over hundreds of late afternoons. In essence, however, the plan was simple and embarrassingly familiar to teenagers the world over: as soon as I finished high school, we would get jobs at the local peach cannery and save enough money to travel to exotic countries. In many respects, the route of our adventure — even the specific countries to which we would travel — was unimportant and varied from month to month.

What remained unchanged, like some great palace steadfast in the shifting sands of the desert, was the desire to escape to a larger life and, for me, to become a wholly different — and far more interesting — person. To remain in Dunley would be to risk ending up like David's older brother Jason, who had transformed from one of the few vital students at Dunley High School to a pothead living in the leaky bungalow at his Aunt Milly's place near the railway station.

This, most certainly, was not for us. In our future lives, David and I would argue in Parisian cafes with beautiful, troublesome women who wore stockings and high heels; we would climb the pyramids at dusk; we would urge our faltering ponies through the snow of the Russian steppes. We would take risks; we would live. What a time of life is youth! To have all of that in front of you, unsullied by reality or — as in my case — by the shortcomings of one's character. Yet embedded in such dreams is, inevitably, an irresolvable tension: the persistent lure of elsewhere, the longing for other, better places.

Such a life was, for me, part of some vague, unarticulated plan to transform myself into a scholar — or an artist at the very least. Not that I had any obvious artistic talent; moreover, in my family such a thing was not encouraged. I suspect my ambition, if it can even be called that, was a matter of seeking to transform my clichéd alienated adolescence into a tale with a narrative roughly commensurate with biographies of actual artists I had read about. I sketched things on scraps of paper, as I had read Henri Matisse did; and, recently, acting on the advice of an author I had read about in the serious weekend papers (found abandoned on a table at Eddie's Cafe; my mother would never buy such a thing), I had begun to keep a journal in which I scribbled quotes from books or films and earnest observations about my oh-so-unique troubled interior life. *Love is a battlefield. L'enfer, c'est les autres.*

On that evening in 1985, the local footy team, the Dunley Tigers, were training out on the oval, and their hoarse cries were like those of drowning men as they barrelled about on the floodlit grass, their shadows circling and re-circling as they tackled and ran. Every so often, the team huddled in the middle of the ground to receive instructions from the coach, where their steaming breath plumed around them before dissipating in the night air.

David and I observed the footballers with the potent mixture of envy and scorn that is, I suspect, the default emotional setting of teenagers the world over. Many of those training on the oval were our classmates at school, friends even, but those bonds were gradually loosening as we began veering on our separate ways through life.

'They look like trolls, don't they?' David said as he riffled through his coat pockets and produced a packet of Marlboros. He lit one and inhaled deeply. 'Running around stinking, crashing into each other.'

I asked him if any jobs had come up at the cannery yet.

'Nah. Bugger all. They say things are pretty bad. I don't reckon they'll have anything all year.'

I doubted this but said nothing. In the past few months I had noticed a change in David. He was becoming impatient with me, querulous, reluctant to engage in discussing our plans even as their fruition grew ever closer.

We watched the Tigers practise kicking for goal from a variety of difficult angles. I recognised Spider Murphy, who insisted on trying to dribble the ball through from impossible positions on the boundary line in imitation of a Collingwood player famous for such a talent; Dale Freck, the butcher's kid, notorious for punching the maths teacher Miss Dawson after failing surds in spectacular fashion last year. The shouts of frustration and triumph — the phrases and intonation lifted directly from radio commentary of matches — drifted up to us through the thin air. *He goes for it and, aaarrrghhh, so close. Frecky shoots aaaaaannnnnddddddd, did you see that? What a goal!*

David smoked in monkish silence, popping out fragile, trembling smoke rings. 'I'm going to do an apprenticeship with Mr Wilson, starting next month,' he announced.

I felt as if the air were drained from my lungs. Graeme 'Sparky' Wilson was an electrician with his own business. We saw him driving around town in his van with a yellow light bulb painted on the side.

'I thought you said you'd *never* do anything like that in a million years, that you'd —'

'Shut up, Tom, will ya.'

I was wounded and couldn't help but stutter in a whining tone that appalled even me. 'What about our trip? What about the pyramids? Paris? I'll finish school this year, remember. Then I can start saving some money. I can get more work at Eddie's. Full-time. It'll only take me six months or so. An apprenticeship takes *years*.'

David jammed his cigarette butt into the damp ground where it sizzled before going out. 'God, don't you realise? Those things are only dreams.' His voice rose above my protests. 'Don't be such a baby. What else am I going to do? I need money, don't I?'

I thought of the stash under my bed — the maps on which we had scrawled proposed routes, the colour pictures of ancient ruins scissored from *National Geographic* magazines, the postcards we'd hoarded from the few people we knew who had travelled abroad (*Salut de Montparnasse!*) — and I understood at once, with sudden, humiliating clarity, that David had never intended to follow through on our plans. He had been humouring me for years. And now I was on my own.

David smoked another cigarette, then hopped on his bike and left with a curt 'See ya'. In retrospect I can recognise that he was as

17

disappointed as I was, but life lived backwards is of no use, is it?

I wouldn't be exaggerating to admit that at that moment, on a low hill in a wintry dusk, I had to resist the urge to weep with frustration. It was a betrayal of the most heinous kind. I wandered home through the empty town, taking the back way past Sarah Lumb's house. I dawdled on the other side of the street in the hope of glimpsing my latest crush but only saw her mother at the kitchen sink, brushing her hair from her forehead with the heel of one sudsy hand.

It was dark by the time I stepped through the back door into the kitchen. My sister Meredith was sitting at the kitchen table with a packet of Iced VoVos, flicking through an old *Women's Weekly*. She was wearing a woollen coat over her blue nurse's uniform. Meredith was ten years older than me, and although she lived with her husband Bill, she was often at our kitchen table or sitting on the sofa, drawn back by the sweet biscuits in constant supply at our house.

'Oh,' she said with a smirk, looking up long enough from the heartbreaking exclusive story of a soap star's marriage bust-up to register my arrival. 'It's you. Hi, Spaz. How's your existential angst today?'

I counted off on my fingers. 'That's a big word for you. Four whole syllables. But it's pretty good, thanks. How are you?' I waited a beat. 'Still barren?'

Meredith stiffened, and for a second I regretted bringing out the big guns so soon. In the four years of her marriage, Meredith had so far been unable to fall pregnant. That alone would have been bad enough — she had wanted to have children since she was a child herself — but her misery was compounded by the fact that our sister, Rosemary (younger than her by two years), had two children with her idiotic husband, Jason. This was a source of distress for Meredith and the main reason she could be found so often at our house, seeking solace from our mother and a packet of biscuits.

When it became clear she was not going to respond to my barb with the venom I anticipated, I opened the fridge and poured myself a glass of orange juice. On the table was the latest edition of *National Geographic*. The historical and the exotic had always exerted an almost irresistible pull on me, and the delivery of a new edition never failed to prompt in me a jolt of pure joy. It was addressed to my father (his late mother had given him a lifetime subscription years earlier), but they continued to arrive at our house with pleasing regularity. There were many dozens of these magazines in the back shed, stacked in yellow-spined piles. Over the years, I had spent hundreds of happy hours immersed in the last days of the Incas or the Ancient Egyptians. Learning about Pompeii, the Battle of Cajamarca, Pizarro, roomfuls of gold, garrotting; a world so far removed from my own that it glittered with an impossible, surreal magic. After an afternoon in the company of such feats and wonders, I would look up, dazed, neck sore, and the dim shed (heavy cobwebs in its corners, rusty tools on the bench) unnerved me, as if this real home of mine — not the historical dramas by which I had been entranced — were utterly foreign.

I tore the wrapper off the latest magazine and flicked through it. Photos of Amazonian Indians with red plates wedged beneath their lower lips, a Mexican boy being tossed from a bucking bull. Meredith watched me with an amused expression, and I sensed her formulating a withering riposte. But, to my surprise, she said nothing.

I rolled up the *National Geographic* and tucked it under my arm. 'What are you doing here, anyway?'

She made an inarticulate noise, wetted a finger with her tongue and turned a page. She had always been matronly, my sister, hunch-shouldered and plump. It was hard to see her running around after children. In fact, it was hard for me to imagine her anywhere but sitting right here picking over women's magazines and munching on an Iced VoVo. That we supposedly shared parents was not only unlikely to me, but downright distasteful. I watched her as I might a sorrowful creature in an exhibit and suddenly felt contrite. In an effort to be conciliatory, I asked her where our mother was.

She shrugged without looking up. 'Still at work, I guess.'

Mystic Medusa's horoscopes snagged her attention and she read for a few seconds, lips moving, eyes narrowed with concentration. What she gleaned evidently chimed with her and she leaned back, popped the final shard of her Iced VoVo into her mouth and nodded with approval. Then she wiped away the crumbs on her lip. 'What star sign are you again?'

I downed the last of my orange juice and put the glass on the sink. 'I can't believe you read that drivel.'

'Come on, Tom. Don't be so stuck up. It's fun. Everyone knows you only read those' — she pointed to my *National Geographic* — 'to perve on the topless African ladies. You're an Aquarian, right?'

I rolled my eyes. 'Yeah.'

'OK, the water carrier. Let me see. Well, it says here to beware of strangers promising great riches. And … that secrets you have been guarding will be revealed, whether you want them to or not. Sounds interesting. What secrets have you got, brother?'

'None.'

'Oh, I reckon you do.'

I flashed her my retard face and left the kitchen.

'Wait!' she shouted after me as I walked down the hall. 'It also says here that you're a complete and utter loser. See? I told you. Mystic Medusa is usually pretty spot-on.'

I went into my bedroom and collapsed onto the bed. Never before had my room, my life, my prospects been so desolate and so few. My window rattled in the wind. After a while I became aware of Meredith talking on the phone in the hallway. To block her out, I rolled onto my back, closed my eyes and placed the *National Geographic* over my face. What fresh hell was this?

Meredith droned on.

'… *And then we went to Sarah Lumb's place after school. She's such a spunk and I'm pretty sure she likes me but Billy told me he kissed her a few weeks ago at John's party* …'

Sarah Lumb? A spunk? Billy? I sat up, horrified. By now Meredith was leaning against the doorframe, my journal with its characteristic red cover splayed open in her hand.

'What else is there?' she went on. 'Oh yeah. This is great, this bit. A poem. Mystic Medusa said your secrets would be revealed.'

I jumped up from my bed and lurched across the room, but Meredith ducked into the hallway and I sprawled on the floor, cracking my temple on the skirting board as I fell.

'*By now it is night and the stars they shine like your eyes* …'

'Give me that!'

'… *and I wish … I wish …* Wait. Sorry, but it's hard to read your scribbly writing here.'

I lunged for the book again, but Meredith, although overweight, was nimble on her feet and she backed away with an agility honed by years of playing wing defence in netball. I heard someone at the back door.

'*Oh, Sarah. Oh, Sarah.* Oh, man, this is so great. *Oh, Sarah, I wish we could lie together.* Lie together!' Meredith doubled over with laughter. '*Like river reeds.*'

Again I ran at her, this time managing to wrest my precious diary away from her, tearing a number of pages in the process.

'What in the hell is going on?'

Our mother stood at the entrance to the kitchen, plastic shopping bags in her hands. The blue corner of a Weet-Bix box had nudged through the plastic and threatened to tear the bag. There

21

was a pause while Meredith and I caught our breath — something about our mother's demeanour made us stop in our tracks.

'Sit down, you two,' she said. She went into the kitchen and put the shopping bags on the floor, then faced us. 'I've got some bad news. Your Aunt Helen had a stroke and died last night.'

Just like that.

Aunt Helen, my father's younger sister, had for many years been a distant figure in our family landscape. Despite this (or, more likely, because of it), she loomed large in my imagination, a magical island glimpsed from the deck of the family vessel from which I longed so desperately to disembark.

Helen was a public servant and worked in the city. She knew interesting people. We saw her regularly when I was young, and as I got older she would take me back to the city alone to stay with her for a night or two. Her apartment was cluttered with books and knick-knacks and held a fantastic appeal for me. Helen treated me not as a mere child but more like the adult she assumed I would become. Unlike anyone I knew in Dunley, she was fascinated by the world at large. She had an encyclopedia and *Cole's Funny Picture Book*, to which I had unfettered access — even the rude bits. She taught me to play rummy and asked for my assistance doing the crossword. We spent time on the roof of her apartment block watering her herbs. She explained their names, held up their crushed leaves in her dry palm for me to smell. From her I learned how to tie a variety of useful knots, how to eat spaghetti properly, how to approach unfamiliar dogs in the street. No one else in my family ever showed me how to do anything, and this aspect of my childhood — of being left to my own devices — fostered in me an almost fanatical self-sufficiency, but also a quality of emotional distance; I am an easy person to like, but so much harder to love.

In any case, the infrequent visits to Helen's apartment had dried up about five years earlier. From that time, any mention of her name in our house or suggestions to visit her were met with an uneasy *We'll see* — a phrase that, as any child knows, is code for *Probably not*. She continued to mail gifts to my sisters and me for birthdays and Christmas, but Helen was no longer invited to family celebrations. She and my parents had fallen out, although the nature of their disagreement was never specified.

And in this vacuum of information there evolved a belief that Helen was, in fact, my real mother. I didn't construct this theory consciously but, rather, various elements combined over time in my childish imagination until they assumed the shape of truth fattened far from the sight of others. It was partly a consequence of feeling so disconnected from my family, a sensation that is, I have since discovered, so common as to be a tedious rite of passage. The constant bickering with my sisters, my mother's distance, my father's abrupt departure: these emotional sore spots I could salve with the application of this single thought. The idea that the people I lived with were not my actual family was not a source of angst for me but, rather, a trusted secret to which I turned at times of stress or familial conflict, as other children might a blanket or favoured teddy bear. I never asked my parents about my suspicion in any direct fashion, preferring to console myself that, yes, my family were awful and didn't understand me, but my own tribe were elsewhere, waiting to embrace me. In a way, this proved to be true.

I had no theory as to how I came to be in the Dunley family in which I was raised, but the details were unimportant and would not have borne close scrutiny; after all, how to explain the oft-told tale of Rosemary vomiting on the hospital floor when she and Meredith came in to visit my mother and me after my birth, or that crinkled black-and-white photo of my sisters sitting on a blanket in our garden cradling my one-month-old self?

Certainly Aunt Helen never gave me reason to think her simple kindnesses were different from those of any aunt. She enjoyed drinking Scotch, playing patience late into the night, and listening to dreadful Barbra Streisand records. Stories swirled around her: that she had once met a spy operating a radio transmitter out of a tree stump in Sherbrooke Forest; that she had been married for two weeks but, scandalously, refused to change her name; that she had a pistol hidden behind a skirting board in her apartment. After the disagreement (or whatever it was that prompted the estrangement), I had overheard my parents discussing her in our kitchen late one night and, although details of the conversation have long since evaporated from memory, I recall my mother and father — who argued over so many things in those years — agreeing that Helen was *a bad influence on the kids.*

Despite the recent lack of contact with her, news of Aunt Helen's death hit me hard. I retreated, wounded yet again, to my room. Rain pebbled against my windowpane.

From that day forwards, I was more determined than ever to escape that dreadful town. I formulated a new plan for getting away from Dunley and stuck to it with the wilful tenacity that only a teenager can summon.

Helen had died intestate and, being unmarried and childless, her Fitzroy apartment was left to her only living relative, my father. The place was small, ramshackle, and in a part of Melbourne's inner city deemed seedy and undesirable. My father was unsure whether to sell the apartment and, somehow, while he was deciding what to do, I got him to allow me to move in there. I told him I would paint the apartment and fix it up while I attended university in Melbourne the following year. By working away at the guilt he felt for leaving his family, I was able to convince him of the idea's inherent excellence. My mother's brother Mike was a GP who lived in Melbourne's eastern suburbs, and although I found him insufferable I promised to check in and have dinner regularly with him and his wife, Jane. In so doing, I persuaded my parents that I should move to Cairo.

All this took a few months, and involved careful and cunning arguments. In reality, though, my mother didn't have the heart for a struggle. I was the last of her children to leave home, and I suspect she was not sorry to finish that phase of her life. In the meantime I hunkered down and completed my final year of high school. My results were unspectacular, but good enough for me to enrol in an arts degree at the University of Melbourne, whose campus was a mere fifteen-minute walk from Cairo. I felt on the dizzy verge of real life at long last.

That final Christmas in Dunley was the most pleasant I had experienced since I was a child. It was a blazing day, thick with the sound of cicadas. We ate lunch among the rose bushes in my mother's garden. My sisters appeared genuinely moved at the prospect of their little brother heading off to bigger and better things; Meredith might have had a tear in her eye. Even their profoundly stupid husbands were on that day bathed in auras of Labrador-like, simple-minded goodness that was hard to begrudge. In the setting sun we played croquet with the neighbours. My father and Barbara came over late in the afternoon to wish me well and slip me an envelope containing five hundred dollars in cash. Such pre-departure bonhomie I have since come to mistrust; a place is never more appealing than when one is preparing to leave it forever.

In early January I caught a train to Melbourne. I had a suitcase stuffed with clothes and another canvas bag full of books. My offer of a place at the university was in my jacket pocket, along with the money my father had given me, plus three hundred dollars I had saved from my job at Eddie's. At last I was on my way.

THREE

I WOKE GRADUALLY, AS IF BEING HAULED UP THROUGH A TUNNEL towards daylight. To wake in a new room for the first time is always disorienting; it can feel as though one has been relocated during the night without consent. The realisation of where I was seeped through me but, rather childishly, I kept my eyes closed and luxuriated in that dim land between wakefulness and sleep, where anything might happen.

One after another my senses came to life. I became aware of unfamiliar bird noises, the almost subterranean grumble of a tram. My bed was cosy, perfumed with sleep. I imagined the city outside my window waiting for me, the magnetic draw of its charms. A car revved in the street; a man laughed.

But in the peace that followed I heard a different noise, perhaps a mouse moving around in the next room. I opened my eyes, as if to hear more clearly. A muffled thump, not loud but definitely caused by a creature much larger than a mouse. The dire warnings offered by my weird and unhelpful sisters gathered murmurously in my imagination: *You'll get killed in that Fitzroy; my friend Joan's sister once saw a bloke get stabbed there in broad daylight.*

I held my breath, drew the bedsheet aside as gently as possible and swung my feet onto the cold floor. Then came the squeak of that loose floorboard in the hallway. There was no doubt: someone was in the apartment. I picked up a teapot from the floor by the bed — if all else failed, I could hurl it at my intruder. I tiptoed as fast as I could across the room and hid behind the partly open door, teapot at the ready. More footsteps, now drawing closer. I waited. Dear God, perhaps my sisters had been *right*?

But, to my surprise, a young girl with pigtails walked into the room, wheeled around to see me standing there (clad only in ill-fitting pyjama pants), and demanded to know who I was and what I was doing.

'What?' I croaked.

'You shouldn't say *what*,' the girl said loudly, as if she assumed I were hard of hearing. She blinked and sniffed. She looked no more than five or six years old. 'My name is Eve,' she said, and took a step closer.

Still too astonished to speak, I cowered by the wall.

'Are you making tea? I love tea! This apartment has been locked up for ages. Since that old lady died.'

'Who are you?' I managed to say.

'I told you, already. Eve. E-V-E.'

As I would learn over the coming months, this declamatory manner of speech (like an annoying doll on which the volume cannot be reduced) was typical of Eve, who indeed was six years old.

I sidled across the room, placed the teapot back on the floor and pulled on a T-shirt, all the while observed by this child who was unperturbed at discovering someone lurking in an apartment that wasn't even hers to enter.

A woman's voice called her name and, preceded by the child, I wandered back into the lounge room. Hopefully, someone had arrived to take her away.

A dumpy woman wearing ghastly tracksuit pants and a

shapeless, navy-blue sweater, her own greying hair also in pigtails, hovered in the front doorway. Eve ran to her, then wriggled free from her cuddle and dashed back to me.

The woman — who was surely too old to be the mother of a child so young — chortled. 'Oh, Eve,' she said in a sing-song voice, 'you can't go into other people's apartments.' Then to me: 'Sorry about that. I'm Caroline, by the way. We live over the other side. I trust Eve has introduced herself.'

By now I had the teapot again in my hand and, for want of a more suitable response to this invasion, held it up as if acting in an advertisement spruiking the neighbourly qualities of freshly brewed tea. 'Yes. I'm Tom Button. Hi.'

'But he told me to come in! The door was unlocked, Mother.'

Caroline pursed her lips and addressed the girl. 'Are you telling the truth, young lady?'

Eve had drifted away from me and was riffling through a basket of my aunt's jewellery on the lounge-room bureau, but stopped to stamp her foot at her mother's query. 'Yes!'

Without invitation, Caroline stepped inside. 'Honestly,' she said to me, 'you shouldn't go around inviting girls into your apartment. It's highly inappropriate.'

I started to protest my innocence, but she ignored me and waddled over to stand beside Eve and join her in examination of the jewellery. I regretted not throwing the teapot at the child when I'd had the chance.

Ignoring me, they oohed and aahed over the various trinkets, Caroline giving her daughter an impromptu spelling lesson as they did so. 'Locket. Can you spell *locket*, Eve? What do you think it begins with? Locket. Locket. Oh, this tiny key is nice. It must be for a box of some sort.'

I tore open a packet of crackers and began popping them into my mouth. They were dry and tasteless. Out of the window I could see the peppercorn tree lit up savagely in the morning sun. As I watched, a magpie landed on a branch, lifted its tail feathers and expelled a shit as if in agreement with my unspoken misgivings. The creature reshuffled its feathers briskly, warbled and flew off.

After a few more spelling lessons, Caroline took Eve's hand and tried to coax her home for breakfast. The child, however, was having far too much fun. She wrenched free from her mother's grasp and collapsed to the floor with fury, where she pounded her tiny feet and fists on the boards. 'But I don't want to go! I don't want to go!' she wailed.

Caroline kneeled beside her daughter and tried to reason with her. Above the squalls of childish distress and the thumping of Eve's feet on the floor, Caroline said she would take her to the park to ride her bicycle. She asked her daughter to behave herself. She tried being more stern. All this was to no avail, and the crying increased in vigour. I was horribly uncomfortable, while Caroline was unruffled, as if I were somehow experiencing the embarrassment on her behalf.

In desperation, I held out the box of crackers. 'Would Eve like a biscuit, perhaps?'

Caroline flung out a hand as if I had offered the child a dose of arsenic. 'No, thank you. We only eat organic food.' She turned again to her daughter. 'Eve, if you promise to come with me now without any more fuss, you can have an extra taste of' — she lowered her voice — 'special milk when we get home.'

This was obviously some sort of parental trump card. The girl's tantrum was downgraded to sniffles in a matter of seconds. She sat upright in the glittering pool of jewellery and rubbed her eyes. 'Really?'

'Yes.'

'Do.' Eve sniffed. 'You.' Sniff. 'Promise?'

'Mummy would never lie to you, would she? Come along now.'

Eve stood and wiped her snotty nose with the back of one hand. Whatever special milk was, it had worked a treat. My uninvited guests dusted themselves off, packed away the jewellery and were gone almost immediately. I was left staring around my apartment as if in the aftermath of a storm. I closed the door and locked it before heading into the bathroom to shower.

After dressing, I sat on the sofa with a cup of tea and sorted through the mail that had piled up in the hallway in the months since Helen's death. In addition to out-of-date flyers advertising department-store Christmas sales, there were bills and half-a-dozen postcards from a variety of South American cities (*Hola de Buenos Aires! La Paz, the world's highest capital!*) sent by a person named Pat. The postcards were only semi-legible, written in a sprawling script, their most notable feature the effusiveness of the sign-offs embroidered with kisses.

Most mysterious of all was a letter addressed to someone called Max. The envelope was cream coloured. Its triangular, sticky flap had not been sealed but rather tucked into the body of the envelope, as if delivered in haste. It smelled faintly of perfume. I sipped my tea and balanced the envelope on my palm. I knew I would inspect the letter (for who could resist the lure of someone else's private correspondence, especially when it was as good as open?) but nonetheless played out a brief charade of indecision.

Eventually, I took out the single folded sheet. The letter was brief and written on unlined paper in an exaggerated feminine hand (loops and curls, large dots on the i's).

Dearest Max,
Thank you so much for last night.
I had a lovely, lovely time. You are so sweet. Call me soon.
xx D

31

Envious and mildly aroused, I stared for some time at what was evidently a love letter. It must have found its way into the wrong mailbox, but who on earth was Max? I re-read it.

Careful not to reveal any sign of the letter having been tampered with, I re-folded the sheet and slipped it back into its envelope. I gathered up all the junk mail to throw out, and put any other mail to one side. The love letter I placed into my shirt pocket.

I stood in my lounge room wondering what to do next. I needed to buy food and general supplies but was gripped by irrational anxiety. Where would I shop? Was I suitably dressed for this bohemian part of town? What if I got lost? It occurred to me with force that, aside from Uncle Mike and his wife, I was on my own. There was no one else to help me if things went awry.

Eventually, hunger got the better of me and, feeling brave, I stepped onto the walkway outside my apartment, carrying the junk mail. Halfway down the stairs I encountered a tiny, walnut-faced Greek or Italian woman dressed head-to-toe in black. She was shuffling up with a cane laundry basket grasped between her outstretched hands, like a beetle with a disproportionately giant crumb. A silver cross on a chain around her neck bounced about with her exertions. On seeing me, she smiled one of those smiles calibrated to demonstrate not only her effort, but also her strenuous attempts to conceal that effort from her fellow humans and soldier on.

Ever the polite country boy, I enquired if she needed assistance, but she shook her head.

'Oh no. I will be OK. Thank you, young man. Very kind.'

I gestured at my front door. 'My name is Tom Button. I moved into flat number twenty. My Aunt Helen used to live there. Helen Button?'

The woman made a face as if to imply this information could not have been more trivial to her had it been the results of a camel race in Dubai. I flushed with embarrassment and stood back on the sunny steps as she manoeuvred past and, for a second, we were wedged in such proximity that I felt it rude not to attempt further conversation.

'Beautiful day,' I said, as indeed it was; the sun shone and the sky was a flat, sheer sheet of blue. The garden was abuzz with insects and birds.

'Yes,' she said with a shrug. 'Summer. Good day to wash clothes.' Her basket squeaked against the metal railing. After re-adjusting her hold on it, she sighed, rested the basket on the rail and looked up at me. 'I been here twelve years.'

'Oh, right. Well, it's very nice here.'

The woman made a noise that might have been of agreement or not; it was hard to tell. Then she scrutinised me as if committing my features to memory. I had the disconcerting impression she was preparing to lunge at me, but she merely licked her lips and grunted again. 'Yes. Quiet. Except for bloody kid running around. You got no children?'

Although phrased as such, I realised this was not a question but a statement, which she did not wish contradicted. I shook my head and told her I was living alone, an answer she heard with an expression of grim pleasure.

Heartened by this exchange but unsure how to finish the conversation, I brandished my rolled-up junk mail and asked her the whereabouts of the bins.

She put her basket down, gripped my upper arm with surprising strength, and spun me around so that we were facing the main entrance on Nicholson Street. It occurred to me that she was one of those hardy European peasants I'd read about in *National Geographic* — a woman who would live to a hundred and fourteen, chopping wood and slaughtering pigs in her kitchen until the day she died.

'Round the side,' she said, jabbing with a bony finger. 'See there. The bins. Throw it in there, bah.' She released me and picked up her laundry basket.

I thanked her and was about to continue on my way when a thought occurred to me. I took the letter from my shirt pocket. 'Excuse me. I was wondering if you knew anyone called Max who lives here?'

She glanced at me with acute distaste, as if I had enquired about something intrusive — the state of her sex life, say, or the regularity of her bowel movements. Her eyes and mouth narrowed in concert. 'Cheever,' she said.

I showed her the letter but she made a dismissive gesture, accompanied by another *Bah.*

'So there's no one living here called Max?'

'Yes.'

'There is?'

'There, there. Place number twenty-eight. Max Cheever.' With her chin she indicated a first-floor apartment at the bend of the U-shaped block. She put her basket down again. Then she looked around to make sure no one was in earshot and grabbed my hand.

'You know what I saw one time?' she said.

'No. What?'

She made a disgusting movement with her mouth, as if whatever she prepared to say possessed a physical component she was endeavouring to locate behind her bottom lip. Her eyebrows arched. 'I saw one time those two doing very weird things with their pale friend. Late at night, at the full moon. Dancing over there in the park.'

She made a noise in her throat, a sort of grunt, perhaps attempting to impart some extra meaning to the episode she had witnessed. When it became obvious I was not registering this subtext, she crossed herself with her free hand and grasped my arm again so tightly with the other that my fingers began to lose all feeling. 'They were like devils.'

This was interesting. 'Devils?'

'Like little, little *devils*. And a bottle of blood.'

This was very interesting. I was speechless. The woman was mad. She gave me a final significant look and released me. 'Stay away from them. You a young man. They no good for someone like you. Parties and all that. Bah!'

And with that, she picked up her laundry basket and went on her way.

I was left to ponder the meaning of her dire warning, which only further piqued my interest in this mysterious neighbour. I returned the letter to my shirt pocket and stood on the stairs, tapping the rolled-up junk mail against my lower lip, trying to decide what to do. The apartment she had indicated looked no different from all the others: a yellowing door with its round window, disused service hatch, frayed doormat.

I retraced my steps back up to the walkway. At that time of morning it was shady up there, cool and peaceful. Through an open window I heard a radio playing pop music. Lining the walkway was an assortment of garden tubs with flowers and herbs growing in them. Parsley, thyme, mint, a burst of red geranium.

I removed the letter from my pocket and, on instinct, licked and sealed it. I waved it about in the air to dry it (I was nothing if not cunning in my naivety). Then I knocked on the door of apartment number twenty-eight.

FOUR

I WAITED FOR SOME TIME BUT THERE WAS NO RESPONSE. AS I was preparing to leave, I heard the thump of footsteps and a man calling out from within.

The door was opened by a black-haired, olive-skinned man in his late twenties. He wore blue trousers and a white shirt unbuttoned to reveal his hairless chest. A packet of cigarettes sat in his shirt pocket. He made no effort to hide his disappointment at finding me there. Clearly, he had expected someone else.

'Yes?' he asked.

'I'm sorry for knocking so early. I'm wondering if someone called Max lives here?'

The man seemed undecided whether to answer, then scowled. 'And who wants to know, may I ask?'

His abrupt manner caught me by surprise. I was shy at the best of times but now, more than usual, I struggled to answer.

'Well?' he said.

I held up the envelope. 'I have a letter for Max. I moved into number twenty, along here. The old lady said a Max lived here, so I thought ...'

'Who's it from?'

'I don't know. I didn't open it. As you can see.'

He made a face, snatched the envelope from me and squinted at it, taking his time over the single scrawled word. He sighed, and I smelled liquor on his breath. He appeared to be drunk, even though it was only nine-thirty in the morning.

From inside the apartment there came a drift of woozy jazz trumpet. Someone coughed, and I made out a man's voice, followed by an intimation of movement. A gaunt figure popped his head around the entrance-hall corner, then vanished so rapidly I wondered if I hadn't imagined him.

'It was with a pile of other mail,' I went on gamely, realising I had made a mistake in bringing the letter here; I should have thrown it out.

He turned it over. 'When did you say it arrived?'

'I'm not sure. It might have been there for a while. Although it was on top of the pile so it was probably recent. Are you Max?'

The man wafted the envelope under his nose, touched it to his lips. He glanced back over his shoulder, then eyed me with suspicion. 'Yes. I am Max Cheever. Luckily for you.'

This caught me off guard, too. After a short silence, I held out my hand to shake. 'I'm Tom.'

Max ignored my proffered hand. Instead, closing the door partly behind him, he lurched out onto the walkway.

'Listen,' he began, leaning in as if preparing to impart some confidential information. But then, changing his mind, he shoved the letter into his pocket and went back inside, slamming the door behind him.

Although disconcerted at being rebuffed in such a fashion by Max Cheever, I set about the rest of my day. The excitement of living in my own apartment was dizzying. I was desperate to explore my new city but felt overwhelmed by the choices available to me, so I opted to stay close to home.

I shopped for supplies in Smith Street and, after making a cheese sandwich for my lunch, set about cleaning the apartment with gusto. I put on my Pink Floyd record and rolled up my sleeves. My father had given most of his sister's clothes away; the wardrobe was empty aside from a few coathangers and an ancient winter coat that had been left behind. I scrubbed the bathtub and toilet, brushed away the spider webs that had accumulated in the high corners, and tidied up the few personal items scattered about. Although dusty, the apartment wasn't especially dirty, and it was small; it didn't take long to make it habitable.

Occasionally I found myself standing, rag in hand, stunned to discover myself on the verge of a life I had so often dreamed of. *Surely*, I would be thinking, *surely this has to go wrong somehow?* It was all too easy. I half expected to hear one of my sisters (Meredith, most likely) slopping up the stairwell with her overstuffed suitcase. *I've left Bill and decided to move in here*, she would announce in this awful fantasy. *Have you got any biscuits?* The thought made me shudder and prompted me to peek — quite irrationally — out the door every so often. Perhaps I should change the locks?

It was while I was organising the kitchen that I found a set of keys on a hook beside the doorway. I recognised them at once and laughed with delight. The blue Mercedes. Of course. I had completely forgotten Aunt Helen's old car.

I dashed downstairs and located it parked in a side street. I must have walked past it earlier on my way to the supermarket without noticing. A hubcap was missing, and it was covered in bird droppings and dry leaves. The left side mirror was cracked. Otherwise, it looked undamaged. I unlocked the driver's side door and sat inside. The interior smelled of sun-baked leather.

The steering wheel was hot under my palms and moulded to the grip of my fingers. Inside the glovebox was a mess of registration papers, pencils, a crumpled soft packet of Peter Stuyvesant cigarettes and a bottle of dried-up Liquid Paper.

When I used to visit her, Aunt Helen drove me around in this beautiful vehicle: once, to the Dandenong Ranges east of Melbourne for scones and tea; and sometimes to St Kilda Beach, where she would paddle in the shallows with her dress tucked into her underwear as I flung myself about clumsily in the gentle waters of Port Phillip Bay. Even as a boy I was aware of the car's special qualities, and a trip in it was always accompanied by a degree of fuss and pomp. Helen was a reckless driver who cruised through red lights, cut off cyclists and generally behaved like a dignitary who owned the road — all without the car suffering a scratch. 'The Krauts know how to make a car,' she would say warmly as (gimlet-eyed, chin tilted upwards) she careered front-first into a parking spot with absolute precision.

Sitting in the red leather driver's seat, I was once again overcome by my good fortune, even as it was tempered by the knowledge the car had come to me as a result of Helen's death. I tried the ignition and, miraculously, the car started. The Krauts certainly did know how to make a car.

I wound down my window and leaned back with my left arm flung over the passenger-side seat. I was wary of driving in city traffic, but for now it was good enough to sit in the fabulous car, dreaming of the places I could go. I imagined escorting girls around with the radio on, elbow on the window ledge, a cigarette between my fingers.

While adjusting the rear-vision mirror, I saw in its rectangular frame the figures of Max Cheever and the other man I had seen that morning in his apartment. They were walking on the opposite side of the street at a rapid clip, engaged in intense debate.

Max was gesticulating wildly, tossing his head to throw his hair from his eyes. His companion was very tall, extremely thin and wore a suit in defiance of the summer heat. He walked with his torso tilted forwards at the waist, as if so accustomed to accommodating the lesser height of most people that it had become an established part of his demeanour. Even at that distance, what struck me most about him were his eyes, which were of a pale, almost luminous, blue. The pair of them resembled charismatic aliens, both dangerous and alluring. Although it was unlikely they would see me sitting in the car, I instinctively slouched down in my seat as they drew closer. Still talking, they crossed the road in front of me and walked around the corner into Nicholson Street without noticing me.

I had never smoked a great deal, but I dislodged a cigarette from the packet I'd found, located a book of matches on the floor and lit up. The tobacco was stale; I had to force myself to enjoy it. I crouched there for a long time, thinking and smoking. I was deeply, fatally intrigued by them.

As fascinated as I was by Max Cheever and his friend, I had at that time much more pressing matters to address. My envelope of eight hundred dollars (by then stashed in a biscuit tin on top of the fridge) would not last me very long, certainly no longer than two or three months at the most. I wasn't paying any rent but I needed to buy new clothes, and the Mercedes needed some attention. In short, I needed a job. It was a daunting prospect. There was not much I knew how to do except wait on tables in a country cafe, but my former employer, Eddie, had written me a glowing reference.

With this reference tucked in my shirt pocket, I spent the afternoon walking the streets of Fitzroy, asking for work at a number of local establishments: the Great Northern Hotel, the Colonial Inn.

Eventually I entered a gloomy French restaurant called Monet, on Nicholson Street. It was three o'clock in the afternoon. The chef was a portly, moustachioed man named Marcel, who I later learned was Swiss. He was sitting at the rear of the empty restaurant with his maitre d', an effete Frenchman in a black suit whom he introduced as Claude. Both of them were smoking — Marcel a cigarette, Claude a pipe. Marcel read my reference, pursed his lips and took me out the back to the kitchen, where he showed me the industrial dishwasher and gave me a rundown of the hours. I was hired, with a trial shift scheduled for the upcoming weekend.

I retired to bed early but woke disoriented in the middle of the night. The anaemic glow from the streetlight through the peppercorn tree cast a shadow of restless leaves on my bedroom wall. I was wide awake, too excited to sleep.

Without bothering to turn on the lights I groped my way to the kitchen, where I poured myself a glass of water. The liquid was cool and refreshing. I drank and refilled my glass. My fridge whirred like an outmoded but determined robot. Having slaked my thirst, I was preparing to return to bed when I heard murmuring and footsteps drawing closer along the walkway outside my apartment. As the voices became clearer, I discerned they belonged to Max Cheever and his friend. They were obviously drunk, unaware of how loud they were talking.

'I mean it's not the bloody *Girl with a Pearl Earring*,' Max was saying in his toffy voice. 'We don't need Gertrude to equal Rembrandt, do we?'

'Vermeer,' said the other man.

'What?'

'Vermeer painted the *Girl with a Pearl Earring*, not Rembrandt.'

They stopped directly outside my door. As if compelled by an invisible force, I stepped into my hallway to listen. Through the porthole window in my front door, I could see the silhouettes of their heads bobbing around. They were no further than a metre away, and I felt a thrill not only at the illicit act of eavesdropping, but also at my proximity to them.

'No,' Max said. 'I don't think so.'

'I bet you one hundred dollars.'

'You're on. But who can we ask to be our referee? Who would know such a thing?'

'Gertrude.'

'Well, she can't be. She's on your side.'

'But she's the expert.'

'What about Anna Donatella? Let's ring her up when we get in.'

'Look, Max. I'm telling you. It was Vermeer. Everyone knows this.'

One of them belched.

'Bloody kebab,' Max said in a drunken whisper. 'Anyway, back to our girl. Back to old Dora.'

'Oh God. Dora. Yes.'

'This has fallen into our laps. Tamsin says it would be a cinch.'

'The art student.' His companion snorted.

'Yeah, OK. Maybe not a cinch, but she says they don't have any special security or anything. But listen, Edward. The thing is ...' Another burp, followed by a groan of discomfort or disgust. 'Think about it. For what we could get for her, it could be so simple.'

'That's easy for you to say, Max. You don't have to deal with, you know ...'

'I'm aware of that. Believe me, I am.'

'This isn't just some old Norman Lindsay painting of ladies with big tits sitting in a river. This is the towering genius of the century.'

There was the strike of a match and the dry crackle of a cigarette. I smelled smoke as I pressed my ear to the wooden door.

'I'll deal with them,' Max continued. 'I promise. Imagine that much money. This could be the making of us.'

'Or the unmaking.'

They started to wander away, and their conversation dissolved into an urgent sibilance of whispers, from which I could only make out fading words or phrases. 'Millions … Only one risk … A real crime not to seize this opportunity …'

I stood in the hallway until I heard a door slamming shut. Then just the wind through the leaves of the peppercorn tree. When I was confident they had gone inside, I opened my front door and peered out into the warm, jasmine-scented night. No one. A possum scurried along the railing, stopping to glare at me before going on its way. I closed the door and returned to my bedroom, where I sat on my bed, thinking about what I had overheard.

After ten minutes or so, I turned on the light and pulled out my yellowing copy of *The Story of Art*. I located the entry for the *Girl with a Pearl Earring*. Sure enough, Max was wrong — it was Vermeer who had painted it. I admired the colour reproduction, enraptured by its unearthly charm: her smooth face and eyes; those parted lips; that earring.

I switched off the lamp, lay back in bed and closed my eyes.

FIVE

ABOUT A WEEK LATER, AFTER BREAKFAST, I CLOSED THE DOOR
on my cool haven and made my way along the walkway with
some herb seedlings, a tin watering can, a sack of potting mix
and a trowel I'd found in a bathroom cupboard. I was intending
to rejuvenate Helen's plant tubs on the rooftop with some fresh
herbs.

Even at 8.30 a.m. I recognised the pensive, almost post-nuclear
hum of a Melbourne midsummer morning. Some people dislike
Melbourne in summer — and there's no doubt it can be a difficult
season, with its gritty northern winds, abrupt mood changes and
wilting public gardens — but for me it has always been the most
wonderful part of the year, and on that morning the heart in my
chest swelled, a balloon of pure joy. I was seventeen years old,
alone in the city, the world at my doorstep. Innocence, I have since
discovered, is a condition to be both relished and feared.

The rooftop was a concrete expanse, edged by a railing,
measuring ten metres by twenty metres or so and, in accordance
with the overall design of the block, in the shape of a deep U.
It was littered with a number of cracked and dried-out garden
pots, deckchairs and the detritus of numerous parties — grubby
streamers, bottle tops, butts and empty bottles. Although still

partly shaded, in an hour or two it would became unbearably hot up there.

To my surprise, I spied Max Cheever sitting in a tattered canvas deckchair on the far side. Although he was already in the shadow cast by the peppercorn tree, he sat in the richer shade of a large, rose-red beach umbrella jammed into a hollow pole possibly intended in the past to support some sort of structure, an awning perhaps. In front of him, his slender back to me, sat his friend Edward. Each of them held in one hand a fan of playing cards. On a rickety coffee table between them lay disordered piles of playing cards.

Max was talking in a wry, fluting voice: 'But, Edward, for God's sake, democracy has run its course. There's absolutely no reason why it should be the default position, any more than any other form of government. Take a look around the city one day. Better still, catch a tram in the morning with the peak-hour crowd and you'll see precisely what I mean. Those people are not only *allowed to vote* but are required by law to do so. And yet half of them have never even heard of — I don't know — Charles Dickens. All they care about is the hedge of their suburban house and Allan Border's batting average. They're reading novels by Jackie Collins. They think Rambo is a great guy. And you think *they* should be deciding who is in charge of the country? No. I'm sorry, but no siree. We need a better system, a sort of … aristocracy, if you wish. A benign dictatorship. The mouth-breathers cannot be trusted to know what's best for them. I wouldn't trust most of them to look after my *dog*.'

After delivering this tirade, Max lounged back in the low-slung chair with his right foot — sporting a blue espadrille — jiggling upon his left knee. He was wearing a white open-necked shirt, cream trousers and a frayed straw boater; the overall impression was of a scene transplanted from the 1920s.

Although a pair of sunglasses obscured Max's eyes, I was aware of his gaze sliding over to me, registering my presence and flicking back to the cards in his hand. These movements took no longer than a second, but I felt I had been, blatantly, appraised, found wanting and disregarded as unworthy of any acknowledgement whatsoever. He showed no sign of remembering me from the morning I dropped off the letter at his apartment. With eyes still fixed on his cards, he reached down beside his chair, picked up a teacup with a floral design from its saucer, and took a sip before replacing it.

'It's your turn, you know,' he said to his friend.

Feeling exposed as I stood on the rooftop in the opulent sheen of the morning sun, trowel in one hand and bag of potting mixture in the other, I hesitated. A trickle of sweat zigzagged across my ribcage. It was excruciating, akin perhaps to forgetting one's lines in the glare of the footlights. So thrown was I by the presence of Max and Edward that I forgot why I had come up to the rooftop in the first place. A tram ground past on Nicholson Street behind me, dinging its bell.

I have always viewed most human beings with the mixture of fear and puzzlement that I believe most people view lions, say, or other wild animals: they are mysterious creatures, sure of themselves and their place on the planet. I, on the other hand, have never been confident of anything and lurch from age to age, always hopeful that each new decade might bring me the knowledge of how to be in the world. It has taken me a lifetime to understand that most individuals are beset by similar insecurities, but it is now too late to use this to my advantage.

On that morning, my instinct, honed by years of discomfort in social situations, was to act as if I had suddenly recalled something vital (slapping palm to brow, chastising self) and retreat down the stairs, cower in the curtained gloom of my apartment and wait for a more opportune time to re-ascend to the rooftop, if I ever dared

47

do so again. But somehow, gathering to myself a fistful of courage I had never known I possessed — let alone gathered — I began poking around in the three large wooden tubs from which I had picked basil and oregano for Aunt Helen all those years before.

The actual tubs were in lousy repair, but perfectly usable. The same could not be said of their contents: any organic matter was no longer to be found. Instead I dug up more cigarette butts and bottle tops, along with aluminium ring-pulls and shards of broken glass, from the dry soil. This rubbish I put to one side before pouring the potting mix into the tubs and planting the seedlings of basil, thyme and parsley that I hoped would provide me with a bounty of herbs in the coming months. It was comforting to feel the soil under my fingernails and the trowel in my grip; it was an unimportant task, but at least it was a job I knew how to do.

As I toiled, I detected the clink of Max's and Edward's teacups as they were set on the ground, the murmur of languid conversation. Mostly they sat without speaking, absorbed in their card game. Now and again I chanced a look in their direction; they paid me no heed.

Potting the herbs was not arduous labour, but thanks to the sun, which by now had risen above the block of flats to our east, I was sweating profusely before long. I straightened up and realised, with some dismay, that the tap was located in the boiler room at the other end of the rooftop; I would have to walk right past Max and Edward to fill my watering can. In the twenty minutes it had taken me to clean out the pots and plant the seedlings, I had managed to quell my embarrassment, but the discomfort returned with vigour.

Just then, however, Max staggered to his feet, accompanied by the frustrated curses of his opponent. 'Well,' he said, 'rummy yet again, I'm afraid. I'm making a dash for *la toilette*. I have you where I want you, oh yes. And for the record, this victory will make it' —

he consulted a notebook, produced with a flourish from a trouser pocket — 'twenty-two to twelve in my favour.'

He then picked his way across the rooftop rather delicately, as if aboard a listing ship, and descended the set of stairs at the far side, whistling as he went.

Still unaware of my presence, Edward lit a cigarette and leaned back with his bare ankles crossed. The smell of his cigarette mingled with those of the peppercorn tree, the sun-baked concrete and the fumes from busy Nicholson Street. Gritty and exotic, they produced a perfume that represented the city and all its potential for good and ill, the very reasons I had worked so hard to get here.

I wandered over to the tap with my watering can. Sensing my approach, Edward made a gesture of greeting, hardly more than a flick of his cigarette, before hunching forwards to shuffle the deck of cards.

I filled my watering can as slowly as I could, then sauntered across to him, water sloshing over my right knee. On the ground, around the two chairs and the makeshift card table, were three plates on which slumped the burned-down stubs of candles. Indeed, the remaining candle of a three-pronged candelabra near my feet still flickered, its flame almost invisible in the morning glare. Milky splodges of dried wax were spattered across the rooftop.

Edward squeaked with surprise at my approach. He was the most extraordinary-looking person I had ever seen, and the memory of our first meeting remains vivid in my mind's eye to this day. He was aged anywhere between thirty and forty-five. His face was thin, almost elfin, with a pointed nose, a tiny beak of a mouth, and a hank of straight black hair (greying in places) tumbling across his forehead. He was dressed most inappropriately for the summer heat in an elegant, deep-blue shirt and black trousers, although his rather cadaverous demeanour was leavened by a child's digital watch on his wrist that bore the likeness of Papa Smurf. He blinked up at me with mild distaste in his raw-blue eyes.

'Yes?' he said, although I had not spoken.

His teeth were uneven and discoloured, as if he had recently gobbled some vile liquorice. He gave me the impression of a sinister uncle from a fairy tale, an impression that, as I grew to know him better, became unnervingly apposite.

'Sorry to bother you,' I said, my courage failing me even as I spoke, 'but I couldn't help but notice your card game.'

'I see.' He blinked, then looked around as if attempting to locate the other, even less interesting party from which I had become detached.

He sipped from his teacup, and I realised the teacups were not filled with tea at all but, thrillingly, whisky. A two-thirds-empty bottle of it stood on the ground beside the milk crate. He and Max were drinking whisky. At nine o'clock on a Sunday morning. From *teacups*.

'I'm Tom,' I said, aware of how provincial I must have sounded. 'Tom Button.'

'Tom Button?' he said with amusement, as if my name alone were reason for mirth. He wiped his mouth and set his teacup and saucer on the ground.

'I moved in downstairs last week. Flat twenty.'

He narrowed his gaze and pondered this. 'God. That wasn't you playing Pink Floyd the other day, was it?'

The manner in which he asked me this intimated that admission of such a crime would be tantamount to confessing involvement in the Holocaust. But would it be worse to be caught out in a lie? As I sought in vain for a witty rejoinder, I could almost hear the crackle of my capillaries blooming beneath the skin of my cheeks.

In an effort to draw attention away from myself and retrieve the situation, I indicated the deck of cards still in his hand. 'My aunt taught me to play rummy.'

'Ah.'

Idiot, I thought. *Idiot. Idiot.* 'She used to live here. Before she died, I mean. Helen Button. Maybe you knew her?'

'I don't live here.' He gestured with a flick of his bony wrist. 'I live in … Italy.'

I could think of nothing to say. Edward drew on his cigarette with practised languor — indeed, he fell asleep for a few seconds before jerking awake again. Not surprising, considering he had doubtless been awake all night drinking. Then he coughed and checked his Papa Smurf watch.

'Christ. Is it nine o'clock? This tournament has gone on for long enough, I think.'

'How long have you been playing?' I asked.

'Oh. Years.'

'No, I meant this tournament. How long?'

'Yes. I understood the question.'

I laughed and blushed all over again, but my embarrassment was quickly replaced with that familiar toxic mixture of spite for this person and desperation to earn his friendship. Accordingly, I pressed on. 'Anyway, if you need someone else to play with you …' I trailed off, my voice sagging under the weight of his indifference.

'I shall keep that in mind, thank you,' he said, and set about shuffling the playing cards again with his long-fingered hands. It seemed I had been dismissed.

After a pause, I walked over to the other side of the rooftop to water my seedlings. I packed up my tools and retreated, eager to escape. But to my dismay I encountered Max Cheever on the stairs, making his way back up to the rooftop. He looked distracted, deep in thought. The curled stairway was narrow; there was no way we could avoid each other. As we passed I mumbled, 'Good morning', which he ignored.

Halfway down, however, I had a thought. The situation might yet be retrieved.

'By the way,' I said. '*Girl with a Pearl Earring* was painted by Vermeer, not Rembrandt.'

Max stopped wearily, as if I were the last in a long line of querulous supplicants. He turned around and looked at me, perhaps noticing me for the first time. 'I beg your pardon?'

'The *Girl with a Pearl Earring*. I overheard you one night last week when you came home. I was in my kitchen getting a glass of water and you were talking loudly outside my apartment. I couldn't help but hear some of what you were saying.'

Max gazed over my head into the grounds of the Catholic school next door before allowing his eyes to alight on me. He resettled his sunglasses on his hawkish nose. 'You couldn't help it, eh? And who are you again?'

'Tom Button. From apartment twenty. Remember, I dropped that letter in for you.'

'Ah, yes.'

I pointed towards my door, a few metres away. 'You were standing right outside my kitchen window.'

He doubled over the railing to see. 'I thought that apartment was empty?'

'I moved in there a few weeks ago.'

'And I suppose you're an art expert, are you?'

I blushed. 'No, I mean I looked it up in a book.'

'In a *book*?'

'Um, yes.'

Max considered me from behind his sunglasses, as if deciding whether to believe me. He ran a hand through his floppy hair.

Then, without another word, he turned and mounted the stairs to the rooftop to continue his card game.

After my humiliation at the hands of Edward and Max, I withdrew to my apartment and sat on the sofa, trying to compose myself. I felt I had grievously erred in my efforts to befriend my new neighbours. I drank a cup of tea.

Eventually, I stuffed my dirty clothes into a large plastic bag and headed to a laundromat on Brunswick Street. While I waited for the machine to complete its cycle, I wandered across the road to Cafe Rhumbarella to have a coffee.

When I had finished my laundry I took it back to Cairo, and spent the remainder of the afternoon reading *One Hundred Years of Solitude* on the grass in the Carlton Gardens across the road. On my return home, I discovered an unaddressed envelope lying on my hallway floor. Its message was short:

Come to our place for dinner this evening
Apartment 28
8 p.m.

Yours,
Cheever

SIX

IT WAS WITH TREPIDATION THAT I APPROACHED APARTMENT twenty-eight that evening. The front door was open on account of the heat, as were most of the other front doors in the block. From inside I could hear music and voices. I called out.

Max jogged down the hall, cigarette dangling from the corner of his mouth, face screwed up against the smoke. He ushered me inside with a foppish bow. In stark contrast to our first two encounters, he was remarkably welcoming, saying how pleased he was that I was able to accept his dinner invitation. I was too overwhelmed to register very much of what he said but, talking effusively, he guided me by the elbow around a bicycle propped against the wall, along the hallway past the kitchen door, and into the lounge room.

The lounge was much larger than my own. It was packed almost floor-to-ceiling with such a profusion of furniture and *objets* that it resembled a wunderkammer. There was a sofa and some armchairs with faded floral designs; two bookcases crammed with books and files; piles of records; a waist-high, free-standing ashtray in the shape of a stern, rather Churchillian butler. A palm spread its fronds from a large tub by the curtained window. Persian rugs covered the wooden floor. Perched on a stack of magazines on a sideboard, a metal fan circulated the fuggy air and caused an elegant paper mobile consisting of the faces of famous composers to sway as if in time to music. The apartment's white walls were covered in photographs and paintings of all sizes, butterflies pinned to boards. In addition, there was a (distinctly moth-eaten) mounted deer's head that gazed glassy-eyed over the chaos.

The item that dominated the room, however, was an upright piano against one wall. On top of the instrument were reams of paper tied with ribbon, more books, a black-and-white group photograph ('My grandfather playing cricket with those ghastly Mitfords,' Max later told me), and a lamp with a red shade, the black stand of which was a statue of a wildly grinning Josephine Baker captured mid-gyration.

In contrast to the humble dimensions of my two-room apartment, Max's place contained poky hallways and numberless unseen rooms. Rather than a bright modernist living space designed for busy workers, the apartment felt more like the cramped under-quarters of a once-grand mansion. The labyrinthine effect was unsettling, and I struggled to reconcile it with the exterior of apartment twenty-eight, which looked pretty much the same as those of all the other apartments.

Adding to the busy ambience was a string quartet seeping from a set of speakers sitting on the floor. I was trying to absorb it all and keep one ear on what Max was saying ('Edward initially thought you might have been a police spy of some sort, but we haven't slept much in the past week so you'll have to forgive us') when a hitherto camouflaged figure extricated itself from the tableau and rose from a chair.

'Ah,' Max said, hesitating, as if taken aback himself at finding this man in his lounge room, 'this is James Kilmartin, poet extraordinaire. The laureate of Smith Street, we call him. James, meet our newest neighbour. From along the way there, I think …'

James and I shook hands and — as it was clear Max hadn't a clue what my name was — I introduced myself. James's handshake was soggy, apologetic. He wore a tattered black velvet jacket, a grubby white shirt and black trousers. A stud glinted in his left ear, and his feet were bare. Although James looked to be only in his late twenties, his hair — which I had initially assumed was blond — was, in fact, quite grey. When he sat down again, crossed his thin legs and lit a pungent cigarillo, he resembled an effete and rather mournful angel banished to live among mortals.

Max, meanwhile, had broken away to turn up the volume of the music in order to demonstrate some point. 'Here,' he said to James above the bickering violins, conducting with an imaginary baton in his right hand. 'Hear that? That gradual slackening there? Then the swirling. Da da da daaaa. Synthesis. There. That's what I'm aiming for in part eight of *Les Chants*. Not at all easy to do. No way, monsieur. Has had me stumped for some time, I must admit. That's Beethoven, you know. Number twelve in E-flat major.'

He closed his eyes and listened. 'No point fooling around with anyone else, is there? That's what I'm always telling Sally. Pop music, my God. Why would you even bother? Cole Porter, sure. Anyway, enough of that for now. I need to check on dinner. Tom, isn't it? Help me out in here for a second.'

Without waiting for my response, Max propelled me through a bead curtain into the galley kitchen, where pots bubbled away on the stove. Dirty pans and dishes filled the sink. A magnificent vase of wilting red roses stood on the bench.

He crouched to check whatever was cooking in the oven. 'I'm making pheasant,' he said. 'Roast pheasant with chestnut sauce. One must be meticulous with such a dish. Magnificent when it's done right. One of Oscar Wilde's favourites, I'm reliably told. Let's see … Excellent. Look at that. What do you reckon? Another fifteen minutes, I should say. Now, a drink? What's your poison? I tell you what — I'll make you a Tom Collins. Your namesake drink is perfect for summer weather. Basically gin and lemon, dash of soda. Sound OK?'

I nodded, staggered by his extravagant and reckless charm that laid to waste any misgivings I might otherwise have had about spending an evening in his company. He mixed my cocktail with dextrous efficiency, slamming cupboard doors, squeezing a lemon by hand and whisking his creation with a fork before handing the glass to me.

'Sorry there are none of those miniature umbrellas. But tell me, Tom, how is it?'

Up to that point, I had never in my life even heard of a cocktail called a Tom Collins, let alone drunk one. The concoction tasted of the brittlest, most verdurous perfume. It was redolent to me of the Charleston, of bons mots, of glorious failed suicides.

'It's fantastic,' I answered, cringing inwardly at my fawning eagerness to please my host by being myself pleased.

The record of the Beethoven string quartet playing in the other room died away, and into the ensuing lull burbled disconnected words of conversation. A woman laughed, said, 'Yes, perhaps ...'

Max became flustered. He grabbed my shoulder and drew me close. His voice sank to a whisper, and he affected the facial expression of one walking barefoot over broken glass. 'Ah. Now, Tom. Do me a favour.'

'Sure.'

He glanced at the doorway. 'We don't ever need to mention that, uh, *letter* you found at your apartment, do we.'

'No, I suppose not.'

'Do you promise?'

I perceived, dimly, a chink in his otherwise bluff armour, but was content to assume the role of the innocent. 'OK.'

His grip on my shoulder tightened. 'It's very important. In fact, let me be even clearer. Breathe a word of it and there will be trouble.'

My nervous giggle was curtailed by the suspicion, reinforced by his blunt stare, that perhaps he wasn't joking.

Before alarm truly set in, however, he snapped back to his previous genial self. 'Good. It might make things, ah, difficult for us, that's all. Now, do me yet another favour and look at that recipe up there. I can't recall how long they recommend cooking our fat friend.' He indicated a large, food-stained cookbook propped open on top of the fridge.

Relieved at the brisk change of subject, I did as he asked. 'It says … cook for an hour and a half at 180 degrees Celsius.'

'Excellent news!'

There was a wonderful fragrance, followed by movement at my right shoulder. I turned to see a woman standing in the hallway, which was gorgeously lit by the sun setting through the trees — hot wooden floor, glancing light, a mermaid breaching the shadows.

Although she was obscured by the jangling bead curtain, I recognised her as a woman I had admired many times around the neighbourhood. I had, in fact, seen her that morning at Cafe Rhumbarella reading a paperback novel and smoking thin, hand-rolled cigarettes. Up close, her loveliness was heart-stopping. I heard myself gasp but, fortunately, any adolescent embarrassment I might otherwise have betrayed was eclipsed by Max dashing across the tiny kitchen to pop his head through the beads.

He pecked her on the cheek. 'Feeling better, my love?'

The woman shrugged and smiled sleepily. She wore a cream dress patterned with large red hibiscus flowers. Her blonde hair was damp and marginally darker where it touched her neck.

'Sally. This is our new neighbour, Tom. Tom, this is my wife, Sally. Poor thing has been lying in a cool bath all afternoon. This damnable heat, you know.'

We exchanged greetings and shook hands. Again she smiled. Her body exuded an orchidaceous warmth. I felt the insistent tug of what I would recognise, in later life, as doomed romance.

'Dinner's ready,' Max said behind me. 'Tom, will you grab some cutlery from that drawer. Sally, take him up, will you. Are you prepared for a feast?'

Sally cocked her head and held out a hand to me. 'Come.'

To my surprise and my everlasting delight, that dinner took place on the Cairo rooftop. Somehow, Max had managed to transport a table (complete with white tablecloth, crystal decanter of wine and candelabra) and chairs up there. Strung up around us were half-a-dozen red and orange Chinese paper lanterns. The tower blocks to our east glowed in the late sun and, below us on the other side, trams and cars and people passed by in the street. I imagined passengers in planes far overhead peering down upon the magical scene, wondering who on earth we were and how they could possibly be invited to our exclusive party.

The first hour of that dinner is little more than a blur of sensory snapshots in my memory: chilled Sauvignon Blanc, Max tossing his fringe from his eyes, James's smoke rings disintegrating like ramshackle galleons as they sailed the length of the table, Sally's collarbone as luminous as coral. The pheasant (in reality a very fat chicken) was rich and juicy, so different from anything I had ever eaten before, and followed by buttermilk panna cotta (which was custard from a packet, tasty nonetheless).

Keen to impress my new friends — or, rather, desperate to avoid making a dolt of myself — I tried not to spill food on my shirt or interject with idiotic questions, although they were all so kind it was unlikely anyone would have taken umbrage, had they even noticed. The party was lively and intimate, presided over by Max, who was the most gracious of hosts, ensuring the conversation flowed as freely as the wine. I felt I was being initiated into an eccentric cabal and, of course, this was exactly what was happening.

At first it was difficult to keep up with the current of conversation, and I was relieved that not a great deal was asked of me other than to be an attentive audience. I tried my best not to ogle her but was fascinated as Sally laughed and played with her food. She was an expert at rolling cigarettes but, endearingly, smoked them like an amateur, tentative as she held each one between her slender fingers.

I sat beside James, who smoked cigarillos throughout the meal and filled me in — parenthetically, from the side of his mouth — with sly and precise wit on the details of friends and incidents they discussed. It would be a role he adopted for the duration of our friendship.

In the course of that evening I learned Max was composing a major musical work based on an obscure nineteenth-century French poem called *Les Chants de Maldoror*. His piece would, according to him, change the musical landscape in the way Schoenberg's twelve-tone compositions had done earlier in the century.

I discovered that Sally had been a singer in a local pop group, but that Max had 'rescued her from the dreadful nightclub scene in order to preserve her voice'. She now worked as a temp secretary in offices around the city — only until the completion of Max's opus, naturally, whereupon her career would be re-launched into stratospheric new artistic realms.

Max told me the apartment he and Sally shared below us had, in fact, been two neighbouring apartments they had transformed into one by removing the dividing wall, which accounted for its size and unusual design.

'Poor Sally was living here all alone when I moved next door nearly eight years ago,' he explained. 'But after we met and fell in love, I bought her place. We smashed out a few walls and made a much bigger apartment. Bit of vision is sometimes all it takes, isn't it? Damned planning people wouldn't allow it but we went ahead and did it anyway. Sometimes you have to make your own rules. That's one of the many problems with this country. No vision. Everyone is so bloody *ordinary*. The cult of the ordinary man. Even the prime minister wants to be an ordinary man, God help us. Who wants to be the same as everyone else? You don't want to be ordinary, do you, Tom?'

I hesitated, self-conscious in the spotlight of sudden attention. It was a good question, and an opportunity to make a case for myself that might not again be presented. I was already tipsy, but paused to sip my wine.

'No. I don't want to be ordinary,' I said truthfully, feeling defiant and alive as the words left my lips. To say such a thing was a kind of delicious blasphemy, for which I might well be strung up were it to become public knowledge in Dunley.

'Of course you don't! Tell me, what is it you wish to do? You're not an office-worker type, are you? And you're not a tradesman. You, sir, are destined for greater things. Come on. Don't be shy. Tell us.'

'Well, I'm going to study at Melbourne University this year. Literature and history. An arts degree.'

'What?'

'I'm enrolling in —'

'Yes, I heard you. I'm puzzled, that's all. A chap like you.'

'Max,' said Sally, 'leave him alone.'

62

But Max was not to be restrained. 'You know what they study these days? You think by going to university you might learn about Tolstoy or Camus? Virginia Woolf? The causes of the revolutions of 1814, the philosophies of Aristotle? No! They study *TV shows*. It's absolutely true,' he shouted, as if someone were attempting to speak over him, which none of us was. 'They analyse game shows and fashion magazines and this kind of thing. Advertisements. Ask anyone who goes there. It's all about bringing everything down to the level of the average Joe. There's that bloody ordinary man again. Instead of bringing people up to a higher level, they bring everything down. That way, everyone's a winner. No one gets upset. Don't want to hurt anyone's feelings now, do we. Ugh. And art has been infected, as well. Look at Edward.' He lowered his voice, as if Edward might be in earshot. 'Even *he* will admit he's not much of an artist, but the thing is you don't have to be these days. People still buy his stuff as decoration. His dealer is practically blind, for God's sake.'

Max shook his head and wagged a finger at me, but not unkindly. 'No. You misunderstand. I don't want to hear the line you rehearsed to tell your granny or the bloody careers counsellor. Listen to me, Tom Button. Who. Do. You. Want. To. *Be?*'

I felt myself blushing and was rendered mute by an image crowding my mind: that of my smirking sisters, their mouths full of biscuit crumbs. *Look at him, will ya. What a bloody wanker.*

'I want to be a writer,' I said at last.

'Aha! I knew it. Didn't I say that, Sally? Didn't I? You've got a bit of the novelist about you. Secretive, watchful. I could see straight away that you were one of us. But listen: you don't need university for that. It will ruin someone like you. Art and university almost never make good bedfellows. Just write a novel. In fact,' he said grandly, casting his arms wide like a net with which to embrace the table, 'stick with us and we will give you a tale to write.'

Foremost among Max's talents was that of making everyone he

encountered feel special merely by being in his company. In part, it was an ability to divine — like a palm reader — what people wished to hear about themselves. I did not yet know that such a gift had a more sinister property; an ability to draw forth those aspects of one's personality best kept under lock and key.

Rather, that night, such flattery filled me with a desperate sort of gratitude. To be honest, I was enchanted by their company. Their lives seemed hermetically sealed, untainted by the universe at large and not even subject to its natural laws. In contrast to those in Dunley, they had no qualms as to what the neighbours might think of them, their clothes, their habits or their opinions. They gossiped about friends, discussed modern art and advised me as to the easiest department store from which to steal underwear or gourmet food. They warned me about a neighbour named Fiona Plinker ('That connoisseur of Third World cuisines'), told me to go to St Mark's Church in George Street for food parcels if I ran short of funds, and revealed that sticks of marijuana could be purchased at the Turkish takeaway shop on nearby Brunswick Street ('Ask for Jimmy').

Max was a man of strong opinions on an endless array of topics, ranging from the government of the day, to the best way to cook turkey, to the role of the artist in modern society. He was perpetually on the precipice of a vital revelation or in the throes of explicating, say, the obscure animal motifs littered throughout the poetry of Arthur Rimbaud or how chess could provide an avenue to creative play *par excellence*, as it had with Marcel Duchamp. That night he held forth at length on the new phenomenon of video art, which, according to him, involved filming something tedious rather badly and sticking it in a gallery. 'Why not watch TV, for goodness sake? At least something *happens*.'

He reserved his most strident criticism, however, for modern pop music. 'Such stuff,' he said with a scowl, tossing a chicken bone aside. 'My Sally here was singing with some group — what were they called again? — when we met. Hideous bunch of perverts, they were.'

Sally rolled her eyes and ashed her cigarette. 'Oh, Max.'

'Oh, darling, they were. Do you remember the leather trousers?'

'Nick was nice.'

'Nice? Who the hell wants to be nice, for God's sake?'

'They're doing very well, as a matter of fact. They're going on *Countdown* later this year.'

'Well, I doubt the Smiling Anarchists —'

'Assassins.'

'— will be remembered in one hundred years' time. You, on the other hand, will be known throughout the world. You'll thank me, you will. And our children and our grandchildren will be so proud.'

There was an awkward lull, in which I heard the growl and spit of one of the candles guttering in its candelabra stem. I detected a shift in the night air, before Sally reached over and grasped his hand. 'I know that, Max. I do.'

After dessert and coffee, Max suggested we go on to a nearby cafe to play pool. Although it was approaching midnight, this sounded a splendid idea. I, for one, was eager for the party to continue, lest such a fragile balance of company and mood never again be achieved. It was, in any case, much too humid to sleep.

James, however, was reluctant. 'I don't know, Max. I can't be bothered walking down there, to be honest.'

Max was appalled. 'Oh, come on! It's only fifteen minutes at a brisk clip. It's closer than your place.'

'Then I might sleep right here under the stars.'

'But, James,' Sally interjected, 'you know you're always welcome to sleep on our couch. It's comfortable.'

Max refused to be dissuaded from his quest. 'Come on, James. The air will be good for us. It's a beautiful evening. A post-prandial stroll, eh? Let's call Edward and Gertrude.'

'Don't bother,' Sally said. 'They're staying home to watch the space shuttle lifting off. You know what they're like. They've been waiting for days for this.'

I cleared my throat. 'I have a car. Perhaps we could drive?'

All three of them looked at me as if I'd uttered something scandalous, and I feared I had undone my evening's efforts to ingratiate myself into their good books.

Max was the first to speak. 'You can drive?'

'Yes. I have my aunt's old Mercedes.' I'd had it serviced the week before.

Max slapped the table with his palm. 'That settles it. Let's go. You have no excuse now, James.'

We lurched into action. Ignoring Max's protests to leave the tidying up for tomorrow, we set about clearing away some of the dishes, negotiating the ill-lit outside stairs with armloads bound for Max and Sally's cluttered kitchen.

Going up and down the stairs took some time, and after one such trip, while hunting around in their kitchen for a tea towel with which to dry my hands, I noticed large spots of what looked like blood on the wooden floor. I crouched to investigate. The stains were unmistakable. Now alert to their shape and hue, I saw that the sink and bench were also stained with droplets of fresh blood. On the fridge door, too, another smear.

As James had returned to the roof and I was alone, I followed the drops. The bloodstains formed an erratic trail that led from the kitchen, along the entrance hall, and continued through the lounge room, where they became difficult to see against the swirling Persian carpets.

I hesitated — perplexed, intrigued — at the short hall that led into the other part of the apartment, the portion that had been a separate abode. The hallway was dim. A door to one side was presumably for the bathroom; and another at the end, closed, probably Max and Sally's bedroom. A hat stand tilted like a drunken scarecrow, laden with coats and scarves and hats. A stack of phone books, a telephone. The fan blew at my back, creaking with each slow oscillation.

Then the bedroom door opened, and Sally shuffled out towards me with one hand clasped to her face, shoulders hunched, as if in grief. She was unaware of my presence until she stopped to turn into the bathroom, whereupon she removed her hand, revealing the lower half of her face to be black with shining blood. Blood, too, on her dress. I gasped. Coolly, she glanced at me before entering the bathroom without a further gesture or word, closing the door hard behind her.

I stood there, struck dumb. A second later, Max came out of the bedroom. He was dishevelled and stared at me as if unable to recall who I was. Eventually, a dim light of recognition flickered in his eyes, and he approached, tucking in his shirt.

'Ah. Sally has one of her blood noses and won't be able to come out with us, I'm afraid. But let's go, shall we?'

'Is she alright?'

'What? Yes. Perfectly. Gets them all the time. Now, where's that other man? Where's James?'

SEVEN

ONCE MAX HAD REASSURED JAMES AND ME AGAIN THAT THERE was nothing wrong with Sally, we staggered downstairs to find the Mercedes and set off. The fact that I was, by this time, quite drunk was not considered an impediment to driving. Max and James were so awe-struck by my ability to manage a car that, after a few whispered concerns ('What on earth is he doing now?'), each of them sat as riveted as they might have done upon witnessing the voodoo rituals of Caribbean savages.

As it turned out, the cafe in question was only a few blocks away, and it would have taken us less than ten minutes to walk there. El Nidos was a Spanish cafe on Johnston Street with plastic tables and lugubrious, unshaven bar staff who looked as though they had been on duty for some months without a break. Although it was late on a Sunday night, the place was buzzing with couples both young and old — Spaniards from the local nightclub as well as students eager to keep carousing after the pubs closed. At the front was a bar that served coffee and pastries, while the rear section was reserved for half-a-dozen pool tables of varying quality and size.

Mournful Spanish guitar music played in the background. James joined a table of older men playing a card game that involved much gesticulating and slapping down of cards. Max bought me a specialty of the house — a Sol y Sombra, brandy and anise — which was mixed below the counter and served in short coffee tumblers.

Max and I played pool, forming a rather formidable duo that beat all comers. One of the benefits of growing up in a country town was the access it had afforded me to hotel bars equipped with pool tables. I was an accomplished player. Max flirted with a ridiculously gorgeous, black-eyed Spanish girl at a neighbouring table until her brother or boyfriend threatened him, a rebuff that Max accepted with good humour. We played pool for money and won twenty-five dollars, more than enough to cover our expenses for the night. It must have been two a.m. by the time we had seen off all competitors and sat down to divide the spoils. My lips were numb from the liquor, and I kneaded them with my fingers to coax some feeling back into them.

Max motioned for me to come closer. 'You know that night?'

'What night?'

'Last week. When you overheard Edward and me talking outside your apartment.'

'Oh. Yes.'

'What else did we talk about aside from that painting? What did you hear?'

The swerve in conversation took me by surprise. Our table was littered with dirty glasses and cigarette ash. The only people left in El Nidos were a group of long-haired drinkers on the far side who, at that moment, burst into uproarious laughter. A pinball machine in the corner bleeped. With effort, I thought back to their conversation of the week before, of what Edward had said. *This isn't just some old Norman Lindsay painting of ladies with big tits sitting in a river. This is the towering genius of the century.*

It was late and I was drunk, but I was conscious of what to

reveal and what to keep hidden; secrets had value and it was wise not to spend them unnecessarily.

'That's all you talked about, as far as I heard.'

'You're a discreet chap?'

I shrugged. 'I think so.'

'I see.' Max slung back the last of his drink and crossed and re-crossed his legs. He patted his shirt pocket for cigarettes, extracted one with his teeth and shook out another for me.

When we had lit up, he beckoned me closer. 'You're a good guy, Tom Button. Wise, et cetera. I knew as soon as I saw you that first time. In fact, I remember saying as much to Edward.' He sat back and drew on his cigarette, keeping his eyes sidelong on me, as if weighing up a serious matter.

Finally, he checked to see no one was in earshot and leaned across to me once more. 'Tom.'

'Yes.'

'How would you like to make some money?' He brandished the twenty-five dollars we had won at pool. 'Real money. Not like this.'

I nodded. Who wouldn't want to make some money? I had passed my probationary shift and had started working part-time at Restaurant Monet, but the job only paid eight dollars per hour — enough to support me, but not much else. If it weren't for the fact I was living rent-free, it was doubtful I could afford to live in the city at all.

'Afterwards we're going to Paris. All of us. We've been planning it for ages. There's a place in the south of France called Saint something or other — mind you, they're all called Saint something or other. A house big enough for everyone. Sally and I. We'll take James, even though he's being difficult about the whole thing. You could come with us, write your great novel. There are markets and castles, fields of lavender. All those French milkmaids. We're getting off this island. You can't make anything great in this country. Imagine it. *Koo Wee Rup Revisited, Breakfast at Dimmeys, The Wagga Symphony*? No one allows melancholy to take root here, and you cannot make great art without melancholy. It's as simple as that.

'You know, in 1942 Shostakovich composed his seventh symphony; the *Leningrad*, as it's now known. This was during the war and three members of the orchestra who were meant to play died of *starvation* before the premiere.' He shook his head in disgust. 'All the good people leave. This country is large and spectacular, but it's completely and utterly dumb. Beaches and bimbos. Here they worship cricket players and jockeys. And criminals. Which is often the same thing.'

Although I had no idea what he was talking about, it sounded glorious. I thought of David Blake back in Dunley and felt victorious, the sweetness only dampened by the fact that he was unaware of what I was doing. If only he could see me now.

Just then, James leaned across the table between Max and me. 'I think that's enough,' he said.

To whom James had addressed this warning (for it did sound like a warning) was unclear, but Max sat back and scowled up at him. His eyes contracted into surly slits. '*Que?*'

'I think we should leave now,' James said.

'Been propositioning the wrong man out the back again, James? These Spaniards, you know …'

James flinched before composing himself. He played with the sleeves of his black velvet jacket, tugging them over his wrists in a manner I soon learned was habitual.

'Come now, James. I've been telling Tom here about the delights of Paris.'

James opened his mouth to speak, before glancing at me and reconsidering. 'It's late, Max.'

'Run along, then.'

Again James paused, evidently reluctant to leave us alone, before addressing me. 'Bye, Tom. It was nice to meet you.' And then, to Max: 'Be sensible, won't you? No need to involve young Tom here in all of your mad schemes.'

We watched him leave. A waiter drifted past us like a sad-mouthed groper, stopping long enough to clear our table. We lapsed into scrutiny of the last of the pool players.

Max stood and brushed crumbs from his trousers. 'OK. Let's press on. I think breakfast will soon be in order, eh?'

Following Max's instructions, I drove back along Smith Street, several blocks away. He gripped my arm. 'Slowly, slowly. You're a very good driver, yes. Really very good. Here. Stop! OK. Keep the car idling. You can be my getaway driver.'

Max leaped from the car and riffled among delivery boxes in the doorway of a health-food store. He returned a minute later with a cardboard box of fruit. I checked the rear-view mirror as we pulled out again, half expecting to see some irate store owner pursuing us, but there was no one else about at that time of the morning.

This process was repeated two more times in the neighbourhood — we stopped outside a milk bar for some newspapers, and next I waited in the car while Max dashed into Chalky's, the all-night liquor store on Lygon Street, and re-emerged with a bottle of vodka and three packets of salt and vinegar chips under his coat. It made me uneasy. Like any bored small-town boy, I had indulged in a spot of petty crime — letting down car tyres, carving my name into the back of bus seats, swiping Choo Choo Bars from the local shop — but I was basically very law-abiding.

'It's terribly bad form to show up at someone's place empty-handed,' Max said, as if attempting to appease my unspoken

73

misgivings. 'Hence the little … heists. Keep going this way. Turn right here, please.'

He declined to reveal where we were going but directed me to the adjacent suburb of Carlton. We cruised along ever narrower, ever darker streets and alleyways until we pulled up in an empty lot hemmed in by abandoned warehouses. Weeds sprouted through fissures in the concrete. The ground sparkled with broken glass. I cut the engine.

'Here we are. There's some people I want you to meet,' Max said. 'Edward Degraves is a well-known painter around town. His work sells, whenever he can get organised to have a show.'

Still pondering the thefts, I didn't bother to mention that I had already met Edward.

'Did you steal all that stuff?' I asked. My question sounded more prim than I had intended.

He punched the car lighter. 'Well, yes, *technically*, I suppose I did steal this stuff. But try to think of it more like the redistribution of goods. How else are we to have breakfast? You know, I've been learning French lately. They have a word, *magouiller*. It means circumventing the law but not breaking it. Smart people, you know.'

The lighter popped out, and Max touched it to the end of his cigarette. His profile flared orange and he was wreathed in smoke, which he waved away from his face. 'Their laws don't apply to us.' He stepped from the car and gathered up his booty. '*Allons, mon ami*. Don't fade out on me now.'

And, arms laden with pilfered goods, Max strode across the busted concrete and approached a large steel door set into one of the corrugated-iron fences.

After a few seconds I followed him, almost tripping over an old bike in the darkness.

'Pull that cord, will you,' he instructed when I joined him.

There came a distant tinkling of a bell from somewhere inside and, presently, the door opened a crack. A beaky nose, sallow cheeks, then those unmistakable blue eyes. Edward Degraves lurched through the door in pursuit of a snuffling black pug that had tried to dart past us.

'Damn dog is always trying to escape,' he said when he had gathered it up and tossed it inside. 'Gertrude would kill me if he got out. Kill *you*, I should say,' he told Max.

Although he betrayed no surprise at finding Max ringing his bell at three a.m. — indeed, he was fully dressed in a white shirt and black trousers — I detected Edward was displeased by my presence.

Perhaps picking up on this, Max was effusive on the fundamental excellence of my character and, as we climbed the rickety wooden stairs, he kept repeating what a wonderful person I was. 'He's a great driver, Edward. Really very good. He even has his own car. We stopped and picked up a few things for breakfast. There's some chips, fresh apples from the health-food Nazis …'

The only sources of light upstairs were a tall, stooping lamp and a flickering television. Although the corners and walls of the warehouse space were almost invisible, I intuited the space was vast, as one might be aware, when camping, of an unruly wilderness stretching out beyond the glow of a camp-fire's light.

Edward clattered about making tea and coffee like a marionette butler, his movements slow but precise. He looked even more extraordinary than the recent morning (was it only yesterday?) when we'd met on the rooftop.

Max introduced me to Edward's wife, Gertrude. She was a tiny creature, with a nest of toffee-coloured hair drizzled about her head. The light from the television played across her pale face.

Gertrude smiled and shook my hand. 'Pleased to meet you, Tom. Why don't you come and sit on the sofa here. We're waiting for the space shuttle to lift off. Shouldn't be long now.' Although she spoke with rounded vowels that betrayed schooling of some quality, each sentence devolved into a nervous, high-pitched cackle that lent her the air of a rather demented aunt. 'We can watch it live on television without leaving the couch. Isn't that marvellous? Heh heh.'

Edward stalked over to us with trays of food and coffee. The tips of most of his fingers were discoloured with what I assumed was paint. He and Gertrude bickered over his selection of tea set; he hadn't put out the correct cups, according to Gertrude. Together, they were like the exiled monarchs of a kingdom imagined by Lewis Carroll.

We ate chips and watched the NBC *Today Show* broadcast from New York. The jolly weather guy was in a snow-blasted street somewhere in middle America, wearing ridiculous earmuffs that made him look like an oversized koala bear. Every ten minutes or so the friendly but deeply concerned anchors, Bryant Gumbel and Jane Pauley, crossed to Cape Canaveral to check on the preparations for the Space Shuttle *Challenger*'s lift-off. Much was made of the fact that this time there was a female schoolteacher on board, in addition to the six professional astronauts.

The cameras panned to the crowd gathered to see the take-off first-hand. A squinting man in a chequered jacket, picnicking families, kids smiling and waving tiny American flags. *And the weather looks terrific there and we should be set for a successful lift-off today. Of course it hasn't been all smooth sailing so far. There have been some problems ...*

'Damn lift-off keeps getting delayed,' Edward said to no one in particular. 'It was meant to take off last week but there was a problem with the ship.'

'The whole thing is a scam,' said Max. 'Even that moon landing was faked, you know. Filmed in some studio somewhere. I read an article about it years ago that said Stanley Kubrick directed the whole thing. No one went to the moon. Why on earth would you? It's only a pile of dust.'

'Don't be ridiculous,' said Edward. 'Why would they do that?'

Max rolled his eyes. 'For the money, the prestige, the knowledge that it could be done — the same reasons you fake anything. They won the space race, didn't they? Showed those blasted Russians a thing or two. This whole lift-off is probably faked.'

Gertrude indicated the TV, which was showing footage of a previous shuttle orbiting the Earth. 'Oh, Max. Don't be daft. How could you fake that?'

'Did you not see *Star Wars*? It's called special effects. Besides, it's all in the preconditions. Visions of Christ only materialise to those who already believe in that stuff. If people are desperate to believe in something, then they will. You of all people should know that, my dear.'

Gertrude shot Max a sharp glance, and there followed a strained silence. I enquired about the bathroom, and Edward waved a hand towards the dim recesses of the warehouse.

'There's a cadmium painting there of an angular jester.'

I could hardly make out a thing in the meagre light, only shapes and shadows.

He sighed at my obvious incomprehension. 'It's *red*. A red painting. The bathroom is to the left of that. Along that hall.'

I felt my way through the cavernous space, my vision adjusting as I went. The sound of the TV fell away behind me.

The spacious bathroom resembled one that might be found in a ruined Venetian palace. There was a dilapidated claw-foot bath on a black-and-white tiled floor, a crystal chandelier (minus a number of its glass droplets) and a couple of ferns tumbling from earthenware pots. A gilded mirror with carved cherubs lounging on its crest was large enough to reflect one's standing self. I went to the toilet and splashed water on my face to freshen up.

When I came out I noticed another room directly opposite. Through its part-open door spilled a shard of light and the alluring odour of turpentine and oil paint. Across the warehouse, which must have measured twenty metres from end to end, the figures of Edward, Gertrude and Max were deep in discussion, their faces illuminated by the television's jittery light. From that distance they resembled actors on a faraway stage. While I watched, Edward swivelled on his chair to look in my direction, as if ensuring I was still out of earshot. Although there was no way he could have seen me, I instinctively shrank back against the wall.

Unable to contain my curiosity, I peeked into the other room. It had to be Edward's studio. In the centre of the room was an easel supporting what looked like a half-finished work of red and green shapes against a cream background. To my eye, the abstract painting displayed little in the way of technique or imagination, although the colours, juxtaposed as they were, were startling. A reading lamp was tied with wire to the easel. Scattered across a scarred wooden workbench were tubes of paint, rubber stamps, spoons, bottles of liquid, spatulas, brushes, and paint-smeared jars and plates. A hairdryer rested on the bench tangled, squid-like, in its black electrical cord.

On a shelf above the bench were arranged at least twenty cork-stoppered bottles of differing sizes, their labels so smudged and stained that they were hard to read. There was phenol something or other, saffron, gum arabic, linseed oil, gelatine, vinegar. Pinned to the walls were colour charts, postcards and photographs, yellowing hand-written notes in an indecipherable scrawl, chemical formulae. Some looked like they had been there for years. In addition, there were various colour reproductions of artworks torn from magazines or books: a couple of portraits, one of a woman who wore a faint moustache; another showing a pair of women engaged in beheading a man with a sword, their faces set in expressions of stony pleasure. Only one of the reproductions was familiar to me, that of Pablo Picasso's lurid *Weeping Woman*, a painting much in the press lately on account of the National Gallery of Victoria's decision to purchase it.

Canvases both painted and bare were stacked on the floor against the wall, and there were at least a dozen others under the bench. For an impressionable country boy like me — who had for so long dreamed of an urban, bohemian life — such a studio was utterly compelling: its smell, the spring-loaded energy, a sense that things were created right here. The wonder I felt could not have been more exquisite than that of a surgeon's upon encountering his first wildly beating heart. The pug sidled into the room and began snuffling about my ankles like sea water around an outcrop of rocks.

I was preparing to leave when a painting lying flat on the end of the bench caught my eye. It was a rectangular canvas, taller than it was wide. It was a portrait of a woman seated in front of a wavering blue background with her arms crossed on her stomach. Her hands were lumpen against a dark dress and her face was misshapen, as if hewn from a difficult clay. Her brown hair was an indistinct bob. The woman's pose was defensive and in her eyes there nestled a challenge, as if she had sat for the portrait under sufferance. The paint was thickly applied. I peered at it, then back to the unfinished work on the easel. It was unlikely they were the work of the same hand. Neither was signed, as far as I could see.

A cough at my back startled me, and I wheeled around to find Gertrude hovering in the doorway. I had the overwhelming feeling that she had been observing me for several minutes. She was not even five feet tall, flat-chested, her body like that of a child's. Adding to this impression of girlishness was her habit of grasping the sleeves of her white top in her fists. She had worried at them so much that the sleeves were frayed.

She crouched to pick up the dog and held it to her cheek, whispering to it in a language that sounded alien to my ears. The creature was so fat, it was tricky for her to hold. Its hind legs dangled against her stomach.

I began to apologise, but she waved my words away with a bony hand. 'Did you meet my precious Buster?' she asked, scratching the pug beneath its chin.

The dog's yellow eyes half closed in ecstasy, and its growl became an insistent throb. It fell asleep. Gertrude looked from me back to the painting I had been inspecting.

'Max told me Edward was a painter,' I said to explain my intrusion.

She hoisted the dog. 'Yes, he is.'

I gestured around me at the paint-spattered bench, the walls covered in pictures. 'It's wonderful. This studio.'

She laughed, somewhat derisively, I thought. 'This is where it all happens.'

I indicated the portrait lying on the bench. 'Is that one of Edward's?'

As if on cue, from the far side of the warehouse drifted the raised voices of Edward and Max.

'No, no, no,' Max was saying. 'That's where you are wrong, my friend. Oswald was set up all the way.'

'They're always arguing, those two,' said Gertrude. 'Men. Always trying to prove they're right. As if they don't have enough already.'

She pointed at the colourful abstract painting on the easel. 'That one is Edward's.'

I hmmed in a manner intended to sound both perplexed and appreciative, a vocal equivalent of tilting one's head while touching a finger to one's chin.

'Tell me, Tom. Do you know much about art?'

'No. I mean, I studied it a bit at high school, but that's all.'

I thought of old Mr Johnson in his tweed jacket (staring dreamily through a classroom window, as if willing it to transform into those of the Chartres Cathedral), trying to infuse sweaty schoolchildren with admiration for the Renaissance.

'Which of the two do you prefer? Which do you think is better?'

'Are those the same things?'

She ducked her head as if to concede my point, but said nothing.

For me — unschooled as I was — there was no question which was the superior work. The abstract painting on the easel seemed to me amateurish and ill-conceived, a jumble of shapes without meaning. The portrait of the woman, on the other hand, bristled with sullen energy. Its clumsiness was its very blood and skin. I suspected, however, that I was on dangerous ground when it came to expressing a preference.

'I like them both,' I said.

'I can see you are very diplomatic, Tom. It's a good quality in a person.' She regarded me, and in that light her eyes were like green marbles. 'The portrait is by a man named Chaim Soutine. It's called *Woman with Arms Folded.*'

'Is he a friend of yours?'

She laughed, but not unkindly. 'Not quite. It's an, um, experiment, that's all. What do you think of it?'

'I think it's amazing. Beautiful.'

I inspected the painting more closely. Its surface was cracked and the canvas was torn at its edges. 'It looks old.'

She gave a gratified snort. 'Well, you can have it when we've finished with it.'

'What do you mean?'

'Oh, nothing. Nothing.'

I surveyed the studio again. 'What about that abstract painting on the easel. Edward's one. What's that called?'

Gertrude made a scornful gurgle in her throat. 'Who knows.

The actual work is not so important these days.'

She put Buster on the ground and lit a cigarette with a match. Smoke plumed from her nostrils. 'What matters is those artist statements. As long as you have one of those. Say it's about — I don't know — consumerism or your childhood abuse at the hands of evil nuns, and you will be fine. Mention intertextuality. The claim of what the work is about is more important than the work. Be a one-armed lesbian. Be a one-armed *Palestinian* lesbian. Make sure you're oppressed in some way — it's more authentic. Better still, get someone else to make the work for you. That way, you don't even have to get your hands dirty.'

It was a disdainful way to talk about her husband's work, and I felt uncomfortable. I glanced away, but when I turned back Gertrude looked ghastly. She had reached out to grasp the doorjamb and was bent over as if likely to collapse.

'Are you alright?' I asked, stepping forwards.

She nodded and grimaced. The episode passed after a few seconds. She stood up straight, threw her half-smoked cigarette to the ground and crushed it under her heel.

'I have a condition known as … Oh, it doesn't matter what it's called. A long and complicated name. Sometimes it catches up with me, that's all.'

'Is it serious? My uncle is a doctor. He lives in Melbourne. I could ask him to take a look at you.'

'Oh, no. That's alright. There's a specialist I've been seeing. There's some new treatment, they tell me. I'll be alright.' Her voice disintegrated into her trademark nervous giggle.

'Well, if you're sure.'

She nodded again, caught her breath. 'You're new in town?' she asked.

'Yes.'

'Tell me, Tom. Are you really a person who can keep secrets?'

I made no answer. Gertrude stared at the Soutine portrait on the bench. Her eyelids drooped and she seemed, momentarily, to forget me.

Then Edward was behind her in the doorway, thin arms flapping about. 'What the hell are you doing in here?' he said to me. '*Gertrude!* He should not be in here. This room is meant to stay locked at all times.'

'Oh, darling. You scared the life out of me. Tom here was very keen to see your work. What's this one called again?'

Edward glared at me wild-eyed, and inspected the studio as if checking nothing was stolen or damaged, before ushering us out and closing the door. 'I don't know yet. Come on. Quick. The countdown has started.'

The flight of the *Challenger* lasted under two minutes. The shuttle exploded into pieces like a lumbering, oversized firework against the hard blue sky. At first it was unclear anything was wrong. The audio was a direct feed from NASA Control, an engineer's staticky drawl. *There seems to be a problem. An explosion. The feed is down.*

We watched in silence, shocked and thrilled at witnessing the deaths of seven people live on television. White smoke fizzed off in various directions, a dozen zippers opening in the sky. Shots of faces in the crowd turned skywards with mouths agape, hands clutched to pale American throats.

After seeing a replay of the explosion for the umpteenth time, Edward said, with an ill-concealed and callous air of satisfaction, 'Well, I doubt they'd fake that.'

Some time later, the television was switched off. Dawn light slunk through the warehouse. Despite this, no one showed any inclination to retire for the night. Gertrude was curled in a chair leafing through *The Face* magazine with a picture of Grace Jones on its cover. Buster snored on a red satin cushion on the floor. Edward and Max continued an argument they had been having about the Kennedy assassination ('Edward, the word "assassin" does *not* come from sneaky Arab killers smoking hashish in the goddamn kasbah — you've been reading way too much William Burroughs'). I was exhausted and still drunk. It had easily been the best night of my life to date. I wanted it never to end.

As the room brightened, and hitherto unseen parts of the warehouse were illuminated, I became aware of a remarkable sight. Like a silent-movie buffoon I sat up and rubbed my stinging eyes. The vision, however, remained. From beneath an arbour painted across the portion of the ceiling adjoining the far wall, there rose broken, vine-covered columns lining an ancient Roman terrace, shrubs, stone urns, a family of gypsies resting in the shade. Beyond that was a large bay enclosed on its left by houses. The sky was pale blue, its clouds wispy and thin. On the horizon was a mountain shrouded in gauzy mist. The cry of distant gulls, sunlight glinting on water. A breeze caressed my face. I sniffed the air, expecting to detect a briny tang from the sea.

'Welcome to Naples, Tom.' It was Gertrude. She was standing directly behind me. 'Do you like it?'

'I think it's the most incredible thing I have ever seen,' I said, quite sincerely.

The trompe l'oeil stretched across ten metres of wall, floor to ceiling, the effect interrupted only by a low bookcase and a wooden chair in the right corner. If one studied the mural, one might also notice the vertical bump of a water pipe passing through a menacing-looking succulent on the left.

'Naples is on Italy's coast. The home of Caravaggio after he fled Rome accused of murder. The birthplace of pizza, believe it or not, and the capital of its own kingdom for a while. That mountain in the background there is Vesuvius, the destroyer of Pompeii. This is based on a nineteenth-century painting. Naples doesn't look anything like this now.'

'Have you been there?'

She gave one of her cackles. 'No. I don't leave the house much. But I don't need to go there, do I? Naples came to me. It took us five months. The morning is when it's at its best.'

'Are you a painter, too?'

Her eyelids fluttered. 'Not really. I used to be.'

Max and Edward's argument ran out of steam. Coffee brewed on the stove; spoons tinkled against cups. I lay back on the couch, unable to remove my gaze from the splendid view of Naples that had materialised before me as if at a genie's whim. I closed my eyes and imagined myself far away. I heard waves washing up on a distant beach, the hoarse laughter of sailors and whores drifting up from the port. Birdsong. Morning sun beat down on my face.

EIGHT

SOME HOURS LATER, I WOKE ON THE COUCH TO THE SOUND OF Edward reading aloud articles from the newspaper in a mock-newsreader's voice. He and Max were sitting at the laminate kitchen table. Edward crunched into an apple between stories.

It was already hot. Somewhere, incense was burning, and it filled the space with tendrils of sweet blue smoke. Gertrude was not in evidence. My brain pounded against my skull. The slightest movement sent pinballs of pain to the front of my head, where they careened about for several seconds before falling still. I closed my eyes again.

Edward rattled the newspaper. 'Listen to this, Max. *Police believe they could be hunting a serial killer following the discovery of a man's mutilated body in Moonee Ponds yesterday afternoon.* Goodness, that's only up the road. *Detective Sergeant Mulrooney of Victoria Police confirmed the gruesome discovery and said there was a possibility it was linked to a similar case two months ago in Brunswick.* Blah, blah, blah ... *"We may be looking for a serial killer," said Mulrooney.* But he's advising the community not to be alarmed. Yes, right. Listen to this: *It is believed that in both instances, the men had been strangled and there was suggestion of satanic rituals, although Detective Mulrooney refused to comment on this aspect of the case.'*

'The Moonee Ponds killer,' Max said with relish. 'Imagine that. How exciting.'

'Satanic rituals. What does that mean?'

'It means that some unlucky guy had his dick cut off.'

'What makes people think Satan is so interested in penises? Some weird religious thing, I suppose. Religious people are all obsessed with sex — who's allowed to do it, when they can do it, the *kind* of sex you're allowed to have. Ugh. Max, this apple has a worm in it.'

'Well, they're from the health-food shop. I told you that. They don't use pesticides.'

'Damn hippies,' said Edward.

'Hippies probably cut that guy's dick off.'

'I would not be in the least bit surprised. You know, I saw one the other day in Smith Street with dreadlocks almost down to his bum. No shoes.'

'Anyway,' said Max. 'Carry on.'

Edward scanned the newspaper. 'Car crash in Frankston, one woman injured. Some political stuff.'

The front-door bell rang. I sat up, startled. Edward crossed to the large windows and lifted one of the matchstick blinds, releasing into the room a burst of brilliant sunlight. 'Who the hell could that be?'

He stood there for a while before turning around. Edward looked from me to Max, then back to me. The bell rang again, more insistently this time.

'Who is it?' asked Max, now standing.

'It's Anna.'

Max was nonplussed, but Edward jerked his thumb at me. 'Take him to our bedroom and tell Gertrude to stay in there. They're with her, too.'

'Who?' Max asked.

Edward hesitated. He checked his Papa Smurf watch. 'You know. I suspect they've come to talk about … our friend Dora and whatnot.' Then, to me: 'Tom. This is serious. Don't make a sound. And don't come out until we come and get you, OK?'

Before I knew what was happening, Max had bustled me towards the other end of the warehouse. Edward and Gertrude's bedroom was on the other side of the studio and bathroom. We went in, and Max roused Gertrude. 'Anna is here,' he said, 'and she has someone with her.'

Gertrude sat up and squinted at Max. Her hair was tousled, and her eyelids were clogged with black make-up. 'Who?'

'Those, uh, *other* art dealers, I think. So Edward says to stay quiet in here.'

This explanation sank in. 'Oh, right. Let the men have their powwow.'

'Don't start on that.'

I became fearful. 'What's going on?'

Max shushed me and began backing out of the room. 'They're, ah, art dealers, as I said. But they're a very cautious tribe. Unusual people, you know. Very secretive. Best if you stay right here and be quiet for now.' He left, closing the door behind him.

Muttering like a disgruntled goblin, Gertrude vanished behind a screen to dress.

The bedroom was stifling, its air laced with the smell of ethanol and rot. There was a pile of leathery orange peel on one of the bedside tables, along with an overflowing ashtray, scraps of paper and a torn cigarette filter. The floor was covered in mounds of clothes. There was a bookcase in one corner crammed with paperbacks. Pinned to the walls was an assortment of about a dozen postcards from around Australia: Goulburn, home of the Big Merino; Coffs Harbour, home of the Big Banana; and, perhaps most alarming of all, Gippsland's Giant Worm. There was also a colour picture of Lee Hazlewood torn from a magazine, and a poster for the film version of *Lolita*.

Naturally, my curiosity about these mysterious visitors was inflamed. I opened the door a crack. In the kitchen area, Max and Edward were talking to a very tall woman who pulsated with intensity. She was facing the opposite direction, but I could tell she was wearing a bizarre black-and-grey robe that required constant adjustment. Thick black hair fell well past her shoulders. Chunky jewellery glinted at her wrists as she laughed at some witticism of Edward's. She towered over a ruddy, round-faced man whose belly strained at the edges of his buttoned-up blue suit.

Gertrude materialised beside me. 'Anna Donatella,' she whispered. 'The Cyclops.'

Just then, as if it had been choreographed, this Anna Donatella wheeled around and I saw she wore a black eye-patch across her left eye.

Gertrude and I shrank away from the door, before sidling back again.

'Who's the red-faced man with her?' I asked.

After a second's scrutiny, Gertrude pushed the door shut. 'That's Mr Crisp. Don't worry about him.'

'But why do we have to hide?'

She lit a cigarette and flopped on the bed, where she picked up a magazine. She said, without looking at me, 'You studied art, you say?'

'Only in high school.'

'Then why don't you name a few famous painters for me.'

I thought of my dog-eared copy of Gombrich's *The Story of Art*, its modest reproductions. 'Well, Michelangelo, I guess. Titian. Tucker, Caravaggio, Rubens, van Gogh.'

'Excellent,' Gertrude said, and I felt inordinately chuffed. 'But what do you notice about them?'

'Is this a test?'

'What do these painters have in common?'

I lowered myself into a wicker chair and at once regretted it: the chair was uncomfortable. I shifted my weight, tried to settle, to no avail, all the while trying to think of an answer to Gertrude's question. The chair creaked beneath me. I shrugged.

'It's not your fault,' she reassured me with a bleak smile. 'It's the way history is written. Some people are inevitably left out. All the painters you named are men. Great art is seen as the province of men. The common perception of the heroic artist is almost exclusively male. The history makers, the painters of record. They don't want to think a woman can do it equally well. They never taught you about Frida Kahlo or Georgia O'Keeffe, did they? Elizabeth Durack?'

I shook my head. I had never heard of them.

With a wetted finger, Gertrude swept over a page of her magazine. 'Or Artemisia Gentileschi, famous for, among others, her painting called *Judith Slaying Holofernes*. It's a Bible story about two women who slice off a general's head in two swift strokes.' She made an upward slashing motion with one hand, her other pushing against the meaty temple of her imaginary Holofernes, her gesture replicating that of the woman in the reproduction I'd seen pinned to the studio wall next door.

'Caravaggio did the same scene, and — surprise, surprise — his take on it is better known. Artemisia was raped by her tutor, then tortured during his trial, subjected to an *examination*. Charming. Thus is the fate of women encroaching on male turf.'

Gertrude's genial manner had fallen away to reveal something quite different, and I didn't know what to make of it.

'You said earlier that you used to be a painter?' I said.

Gertrude looked at me as if preparing to reveal a secret, before thinking better of it. She ground her cigarette into a saucer on the cluttered side table. 'Oh, don't worry about it. Sorry. It doesn't matter anymore.'

She returned to her magazine. The topic, it seemed, was closed. I went to the window and pulled the blind aside a fraction. Outside, sunlight shimmered on corrugated-tin roofs. Below in the abandoned lot was my blue Mercedes with another, newer car parked beside it. A bearded man wearing sunglasses lounged against the second car.

As I watched, he collected a handful of rocks and began lobbing them at a busted red bucket several metres from where he stood. His aim was not very good but, after three or four attempts, one of the rocks landed in the bucket with a thunk and clatter. The man, satisfied with his work, wiped his mouth and leaned back on the car.

I was growing impatient and wondered how much longer we would have to cower in the hot room. Max had said the visitors were art dealers, but I was baffled as to why it was so crucial that we hid. Gertrude's enigmatic outburst had done nothing to clarify the matter. The chap below in the abandoned lot crouched with one hand outstretched towards the long grass erupting from the broken concrete. Then I heard voices in the hallway outside the bedroom. I let the blind fall back against the window. Edward and Max were showing their guests into the studio.

'So this is where the magic happens, is it?' Mr Crisp said in a gruff voice. His remark prompted a round of nervous laughter and a number of muffled comments. More laughter.

From outside came a pair of dull cracks in quick succession: the driver in the vacant lot outside must have taken up rock throwing again, this time at an object more solid than a plastic bucket.

Max, Edward, Anna Donatella and Mr Crisp remained in Edward's studio for more than half an hour, during which time Gertrude and I remained still and quiet. Gertrude continued to stare at her magazine, but I could tell she wasn't reading it. Instead, her gaze flickered about with the ebb and flow of voices from the adjacent room as if she hoped to discern details of the conversation from particles of mere noise. The murmuring was punctuated by Anna Donatella's barking laugh.

When the tour finished, Gertrude and I watched through the window until we saw Mr Crisp emerge and greet his companion waiting below. The two men sat in the car and chatted for several minutes before driving away.

Almost immediately, Max popped his head around the bedroom door. 'Hey,' he said to me, 'come and meet Anna.'

I was happy to leave the stuffy bedroom, but puzzled at the change in Max's attitude towards my encountering the art dealer.

'But,' said Gertrude, 'surely it's better if …'

'Now, now. Don't be like that. She asked to meet Tom.'

I sensed, rather than saw, Max and Gertrude exchange a meaningful glance.

'I hope you know what you're doing,' Gertrude said as she slouched off to take a shower. To whom this was addressed was unclear.

I followed Max from the bedroom.

If possible, Anna Donatella was even more impressive up close. She and Edward cut short a whispered conversation as we approached, and she spun on the heels of her leather boots, in the manner of a robotic Gestapo agent, to fix me in her sight.

When we were in reach, she flung a swathe of her outfit across her shoulder. Max introduced us and she took my proffered hand. Her own hand was clammy, decorated with a range of treacherous-looking rings. Her eye-patch was made of black suede. She was, I guessed, about fifty years old. Anna drew herself up to her full (considerable) height and glowered at me as if I were an artwork she suspected of being not much good but was forced, reluctantly, to appraise. I was petrified, but after a few excruciating seconds, she relaxed her bearing and eked out a smile. 'Tom. So very pleased to meet you.'

None of us sat, but instead stood around the kitchen. What followed was a disjointed interview made all the more difficult by my hangover and the fatigue that pressed against the top of my skull.

I was flattered to learn that Max had told Anna about me. She appeared gratified to confirm that my family lived elsewhere and was also pleased to hear that most of the people I knew in Melbourne were, at that very moment, at Edward's place.

'And you know James Kilmartin,' she added.

'Yes, I've met James.'

'And that is your car parked out the back, is it?'

'The Mercedes? Yes.'

'What year is it?'

'1974.'

'Very nice.'

'Thanks. It was my aunt's.'

'It's reliable?'

'It was serviced a couple of weeks ago.'

'Registered? Roadworthy?'

'Yes.'

She busied herself in realigning her robes (or capes, or whatever such a profusion of fabric might be termed in the fashion world) before returning her attention to me. Because of her limited vision, she kept her head on an angle as she spoke with us.

After about another ten minutes of uncomfortable chit-chat, Anna said, 'I mustn't keep you any longer. You all look *very* tired.' Then she smiled again, having wrung more satisfaction from our conversation than I would have thought possible.

Max, who had been uncharacteristically quiet, spoke up

then. 'Yes. What say we trundle back to Cairo, eh? Sally will be wondering where on earth we are.'

I was almost too exhausted to think, and the prospect of my bed was an inviting one. After brief farewells, Max, Anna and I clomped down the stairs. Stepping out into the scorching morning was a shock. I reeled in the heat, clutching at my hungover head. In front of my eyes, weird and colourful shapes floated in the air like bats, and I waited to adjust to the glare before picking my way over broken glass to my car. Anna seemed unperturbed by the temperature, although she was dressed for more wintry climes. She inspected my Mercedes with a keen eye, but declined my offer of a lift and stalked away up the alleyway with a curt goodbye.

I unlocked the Mercedes (fug of roasted leather and metal) and turned to see Max hesitating near the warehouse door with a dazed expression on his face. His shirt was wrinkled, and there was a glaze of sweat on his forehead.

'What is that god*awful* noise?' he said, looking around.

I shuffled over to him and, after several seconds, made out the sound he was referring to. It *was* godawful, a sort of guttural squeak.

'It sounds like some sort of monster,' Max said with bemused horror. 'Perhaps it's to do with that space shuttle?'

And he squinted into the sky, as if seriously searching for the craft in which the mysterious creature might have journeyed.

A nearby clump of grass shivered: something was in there. Another movement, closer this time. Whatever it was, it was heading towards us. With an imagination grown hysterical with fatigue, I thought of giant urban rats made fierce on their diet of burgers and waste. An unwelcome memory of seeing the film *Alien* with David Blake at the Dunley Odeon (teeth and drool, the girl in the front row so scared that her box of popcorn flew into the air).

Max swore and grabbed my arm. We stepped backwards. I cast about for an object to use as a weapon and spied a brick nearby, but before I could wrest myself free of Max to retrieve it, a creature stumbled out.

It was Buster. He whined up at us pitifully. Max and I laughed with relief, before realising the pug was in some sort of trouble. He dragged his hindquarters along the hot ground; his head lolled. There was blood smeared on the fur around his haunches, and it was clear that his left hind leg was damaged. And that pathetic grunt, over and over, each sounding like it might be his last.

I crouched down. 'What do you think happened to him?'

'God only knows. He'll be alright. He's a pug. They'll survive a nuclear holocaust, don't you know.'

'But we can't leave him here.'

'Oh, I'm so tired,' said Max, picking at a loose thread on his shirt.

His lack of concern for the animal was bewildering. After a few dithering seconds, in which Buster attempted again to raise himself from the hot concrete, I dashed across to the door. I rang the bell a number of times and managed to rouse Gertrude. She was horrified to hear what had happened, bursting into tears on the spot. Barefoot, wet-haired and wearing a tattered red kimono, she scooped Buster up in her arms, comforting him as best she could in that weird language she had spoken earlier. ('Stupid dog only understands Esperanto,' Max informed me as we filed back up the stairs.)

Edward slept through the entire drama. Gertrude dressed quickly, and with Buster wrapped in a blood-stained pillowcase on her lap in the back seat, and Max begrudgingly providing directions, I drove as fast as possible to the veterinary hospital in North Melbourne.

We slumped in the waiting room at the Lort Smith Animal Hospital while Buster was operated on. The place reeked of urine and disinfectant, of terrified creatures large and small. Owners sat glum-faced with their pets in cardboard boxes or wire cages. A large marmalade cat meowed like an air-raid siren. From somewhere out the back came a relentless yapping. The waiting-room walls were covered with posters about pet care, and advertisements for doggy shampoos and grooming services. Cartoon fleas rubbed their gloved hands together as they prepared to feast on poor Fido's blood. None of us spoke. Max dozed with an unlit cigarette in one hand.

After an hour, the vet came out to see us, clipboard under her arm. She introduced herself as Trish. She was short, wide-hipped, dressed in pale-blue medical trousers and jacket. Her shoes scritched on the linoleum.

'Well, you'll be pleased to know that Buster is going to be OK.'

'Thank God,' Gertrude said, bony hand pressed to her chest.

'His back leg was broken badly so we've set it and stitched his wound. We'll keep him here overnight to observe him.' Trish consulted her clipboard. 'So you have no idea what happened to him?'

Gertrude, who had been sniffling all this time, shook her head. 'We have no idea. At least he's going to be OK. Could he have been attacked by another dog?'

The vet contemplated us, as if she suspected us of withholding information. 'I doubt it. The wound is not consistent with a bite, or none I've ever seen.'

'Maybe he was hit by a car?'

Trish pursed her lips. 'This might sound crazy, but it looks to me like Buster might have been shot.'

At this, Max, who had been half comatose in one of the moulded plastic chairs, sat up and began paying attention to our conversation. An overweight woman beside him mouthed *Goodness*. Others in the waiting room glanced up from their year-old magazines.

'I can't be sure and there was no bullet left in him. He was very lucky, but it looks like a small-calibre bullet might have penetrated his upper thigh and exited.' She patted her own meaty thigh in demonstration.

After filling out various forms and arranging a possible time to pick Buster up the following day, we trooped back to my car.

'Well,' I said when we were all seated, 'I guess we'd better go to the police station.'

Max, in the passenger seat beside me, shook his head as he lit a crooked cigarette with the car lighter and exhaled. 'No, no. No police.'

'But we can't let someone run around shooting pets.'

I turned and appealed to Gertrude in the back seat but she, too, shook her head. 'No, Tom. There's no need to do anything like that. Can we go home, please? I'm so tired. The main thing is that Buster will be alright.'

Although I didn't understand their reluctance, they were both so resolute that I shrugged and let the matter drop. By then it was nearly midday. We drove through leafy Carlton streets. Near the university, fresh-faced teenagers swarmed around clutching knapsacks. They wore colourful clothes and shrieked with excitement as they crossed Grattan Street.

Max snorted. 'Look at the damn fools.'

I gazed through the car windows at these young people — ostensibly my peers — from whom I felt so distant.

'He hardly ever goes outside,' Gertrude was saying, returning to the problem of Buster and his injury. 'I don't even know how he got out today.'

'Those art dealers,' I said, slowing the car to allow a pair of pretty blonde girls to cross the road. 'Buster must have snuck out the door when your art dealers came over this morning.' Neither Max nor Gertrude responded to this comment, and I felt compelled to fill the pause that followed. 'But who on earth would shoot a dog?'

In the rear-vision mirror I saw Gertrude nodding as if the puzzle were beginning to make complete sense to her. She lit a cigarette with a tight flourish. '*Art dealers.* Of course.'

A few days later I was doing my laundry at Bert's laundromat in Brunswick Street. In my laundry bag I was surprised to find a sheaf of papers I recognised as the various enrolment forms for my university degree. Somehow they had ended up with my dirty clothes. Examining the documents, surrounded by the busy thrum of machinery, I calculated that the date nominated for me to enrol had been the morning I'd spent at the veterinary hospital with Max and Gertrude.

I had completely forgotten to enrol. Some of the young people thronging around Carlton when we drove back from the hospital would perhaps have been my classmates, had I remembered to select my classes and begun the course I had moved to Melbourne to study. My panic and confusion were temporary, replaced by relief as I imagined Max's pleasure at discovering this. It had been an oversight, but I was not unhappy at the outcome.

As these thoughts were coalescing in my mind, a tiny woman I knew to be one of Fitzroy's homeless population poked her head through the door and unleashed a twitchy smile upon me. I smiled back.

Encouraged by this, but darting her eyes about (for Bert was known to be most unwelcoming to vagrants), she came inside and sidled up to me.

'What have you got there?' she asked in a croaky voice.

'These? Some forms. For the university.'

The woman regarded them with disbelief, as if they might be the precise papers she had been seeking her whole life and whose loss had precipitated her current misfortune.

She shuffled about on the spot. 'Can I have them?'

I held up the enrolment forms. 'You want these?'

'Yep.'

Such an impudent and unexpected request demanded an equally surprising response. I considered the forms for a few seconds before handing them to her. Why not? After all, they were most likely of more interest to her than me.

As I watched her leave with them tucked under her arm, I imagined (with something like satisfaction, but not quite) a professor calling my name in a classroom, glancing over her spectacles at the ensuing silence and striking a line through my name.

NINE

THOSE FIRST FEW WEEKS OF 1986 WERE, UNTIL THAT TIME, THE happiest of my life. I explored my new neighbourhood — with its noirish, junk-strewn alleys and raffish share houses, jazz music and conversation drifting from their backyards. Many of the storefronts on Brunswick Street were former sweatshops, now boarded up and disused. There were two or three cafes, a laundromat, half-a-dozen pubs, a milk bar, and a smattering of fashionably shabby second-hand clothing and bric-a-brac stores. The local population was made up mainly of students, recent migrants, punks and drunks. Its patron saints were Sylvia Plath and Jack Kerouac. An old man with a Qantas bag walked about loudly weeping; girls wore cool sunglasses, boys winklepickers; the air was fragrant with hair gel, cigarette smoke and coffee.

I bought myself clothes designed to hide my country-town origins and attempted to pass myself off as a local, adopting a look of contrived carelessness. Before leaving my apartment I spent extravagant amounts of time smoothing my unruly hair in the mirror and making sure my demeanour was correctly calibrated. I took up smoking. More than once, I locked the door behind me and was about to leave the grounds of Cairo when I was overcome by self-consciousness, whereupon I was compelled to return to my apartment and change a shirt I suddenly feared would invite unspoken ridicule. I perched in the famous Black Cat cafe (waiters so laid-back they barely served at all, Tretchikoff prints on the wall, Coco Pops available all day) to drink coffee. For a time, life was as exquisite as a dream.

In subsequent weeks, I met some of the other tenants of Cairo. In addition to a couple of architecture students, there was old Mr Orlovsky from flat eleven, directly opposite mine, who looked as though he had dressed in the winter of 1974 and never changed again. His tie was spattered with gravy stains, as were his trousers. He was ever so tall, kindly and doddering but had the alarming habit of lurching forth — rather like an unfashionable Frankenstein's monster — from the deep shade of the garden when I entered through the front gate, and bombarding me with questions about recent news or sporting events and cryptic reminiscences.

This might have been fairly harmless but for the fact that he was, on account of ill-fitting dentures, difficult to understand and prone to a stutter that made even the most rudimentary chat rather a trial. In addition, he tended to spray the damp, un-swallowed portions of his lunch into one's face when speaking; to meet his gaze while talking, in accordance with basic social etiquette, was to risk a speck of masticated bread in the eye.

The man had fought in the Korean War, and the experience left him on the constant lookout for the devious machinations of any 'Orientals' he encountered in his rare sorties into the world outside Cairo's front gate.

Somehow, most likely on account of my gender, Mr Orlovsky had got it into his head that I was as fascinated with Test cricket as he, and never missed an opportunity to discuss with me the intricacies of team selection for the following year's Ashes series, a topic about which I knew almost nothing.

'That bloody Gower,' he would say with a heavy sigh, 'he's a lively one, eh?' Or: 'What about that Allan Border? Move him up the batting list?' There would follow an incomprehensible guttural remark or question to which I would make a sound (of agreement, of despair, of amusement) hopefully commensurate in tone with his own. Cricket bored me to tears, but after a number of these one-sided conversations, I had not the heart to reveal this and stooped to perusing the sports pages for names and figures I could mention to pass myself off as tolerably knowledgeable.

The ancient Italian woman who had warned me about Max Cheever was named Maria and, although I didn't run into her often after that initial meeting, I was aware of her peeking through her screen door as I passed her apartment on my way to the clothes line. Her television was on most of the time, and it was not uncommon to hear the scene-chewing emoting of daytime TV soap stars emanating from her apartment, borne on a flavoursome waft of spaghetti sauce or minestrone.

There was the child Eve, who could be heard rampaging through the block at all hours, spelling out everything that fell within her sight, her screams bookended by her mother's indulgent chuckles. Although Caroline seemed to me a far cry from an intellectual giant, she home-schooled her daughter according to some specific methodology designed to fashion the girl into a genius. Most mornings the child could be heard torturing her violin or spelling out the names of flowers or animals in the garden. 'Magpie. M-A-G-P-I-E. Wattle. W-A, wait! Don't tell me! W-A-T-T-U-L.' She was like a bird pecking shrilly at the language, tearing it into bite-sized pieces with gamine fury.

Since our encounter on that first morning, Eve had started knocking on my door and trying the handle at all hours of the day. Rather pathetically, I took to pretending I wasn't at home during the hours she might be up and about; it was easy enough because it was difficult to notice signs of life inside the apartments from outside, unless the door were open. Even so, I tended to stop what I was doing and shrink against the wall at the sound of her voice or the slap of her bare feet along the concrete walkway.

I couldn't, however, always be as vigilant as I wished and, in addition, I had to leave my front door ajar on hot days to facilitate a breeze through the apartment. Thus, Eve became a semi-regular visitor, perched on my green sofa with a cup of milky tea and a surreptitious sweet biscuit, imperious as a tiny Mogul empress issuing instructions and demanding answers to obscure questions ('When dogs close their eyes do they see the same reddy darkness that we do?' 'When is the future?').

There were other people I saw only occasionally and whose names I never learned: a stern New Zealand couple next door, who kept strict nine-to-five hours and were so self-contained they might have been a cult of two; an old woman who lived alone on the ground floor with her black cat called Belle; a single, middle-aged man who always wore a grey trench coat and carried a briefcase. Others I saw not at all, their presence only hinted at by the discovery of clothes drying on the washing line at the back, or bags of rubbish piled by the overstuffed bins.

By this time I was working three or four days a week at Restaurant Monet, mainly the night shift, which began at six in the evening and ended at midnight or one a.m. The work was hot and greasy, but satisfying. I scrubbed pots and pans. I rinsed plates and glasses and sent them through the dishwasher. I emptied the rubbish bins and did basic food preparation — chopping parsley, dicing meat for stews, cleaning prawns and the like. At the end of each shift I mopped the tiled floor and wiped the benches.

The other staff were mostly European. In addition to Claude, there was a lugubrious Italian waiter, Michael, prone to cursing in foreign languages and lamenting the eating habits of Australians when he swept into the kitchen to deliver an order. 'Australians,' he would say. '*Porco dio*. No *fucking* idea. Take away table three, please.' Marcel, who it turned out was both the chef and the owner, refused point-blank to cook steak any more than medium rare. He drank beer throughout the afternoon. Sometimes he threw pans to the floor or launched into long, drunken rambles about his days as an apprentice chef in Switzerland ('Five o'clock in the morning, winter, we would milk those cows, almost nude!') or how the Nazis should have been given the chance to finish off the Jews in Europe. His cantankerousness seemed — at least in part — an affectation and was, in any case, thrilling to me. They treated me as one of their own, allowing me a glass of beer or Pinot Noir at the end of the night, whisking out Zippos to light my cigarette, inviting me to discern notes of pepper or pencil shavings in the wines I sampled. I felt grown up, a part of the city's machinery.

When I wasn't working I spent as much time as possible with Max, Sally and James. We formed a quartet that roamed far and wide in my old Mercedes — from the hedge mazes of the Mornington Peninsula to the surf beaches of the coast. Sometimes I would come home from work to find a note had been slipped beneath my front door, on which would be written instructions (*Our place 7 p.m. tonight* or *Meet us at the corner*).

We went boating on the Yarra River at Studley Park, and for my eighteenth birthday in mid-February we picnicked on smoked-salmon sandwiches at Hanging Rock. We spent Sunday mornings trawling through bric-a-brac stalls at Camberwell Market for clothes and records. We played rummy and bridge late into the night. It was a period when many of my lifelong personal characteristics were forged — for better or (it must be said) for worse. Being with my new friends appealed to two contradictory aspects of my personality: that of wishing myself distinct from the mass of ordinary people while, at the same time, satisfying a human need to belong to a group.

During my childhood in Dunley, there had been no one I sought to emulate in any way. I held my father in contempt and was largely ignored by my mother and sisters. The thought of becoming a local baker like 'Crusty' Brown or a real estate agent like my father and his second wife distressed me almost more than I could bear. Aunt Helen had been the closest to a mentor I might ever have had, but the family rift had put paid to that relationship. And now she was dead. It wasn't until I met Max and his friends that I realised, with a fierce jolt of recognition, that these were the people I had been longing to know my whole life; my lost tribe.

To me they were fabulous, magical beings, capable of anything. They could do no wrong. If, in my more insecure moments, I wondered why they should befriend a gauche bumpkin such as me, I quickly banished the thought. Self-preservation is a necessary trait, particularly when one is young. There was the fact of my owning a car, but even now (stubborn rather than innocent) I refuse to believe they were interested in me purely for the part they hoped I might play in their sinister and dangerous scheme.

Max knew an inordinate number of people. It was rare to go anywhere with him — whether to the twenty-four-hour pool hall in Carlton or a filthy pub in Port Melbourne at six a.m. — and for him not to know at least one person, usually many more. Despite his archaic views about the need for a ruling intellectual aristocracy and such nonsense, he was at ease talking with anyone, whether they be loutish drunkards encountered at the Albion Hotel or attenuated classical violinists sipping ginger beer through a straw at an art opening. I was even startled to encounter him one afternoon at a tram stop in Brunswick Street, engaged in a complicated but genial transaction involving a carton of cigarettes with the blue-lipped vagrant (whom he introduced as Peter) who had so frightened me on my first day in the city.

I saw Anna Donatella several more times, usually at exhibition openings at dingy artist-run galleries, where we drank nasty white wine from plastic cups while musing over the latest offerings from an artist committed to presenting modern anxieties in original and disturbing ways. She never behaved in a manner that could be described as friendly (she would volunteer the type of smile typical at funerals, subdued, as if pleased to see me but aware of the constraints of the event).

I was also introduced to Anna's French assistant, Queel, her so-called 'good eye' when it came to the appraisal of artists for representation. He was a short, toadish chain-smoker in his mid-thirties who always looked both guilty and immensely satisfied, like a swimmer pausing to relieve himself in a pool. He wore ill-fitting suits and a cravat. His face was shiny, his fingers hairy and short.

Despite his obvious physical shortcomings — perhaps because of them — Queel exuded a malign sexuality and was always accompanied by a woman of barely credible beauty. At first I assumed it to be the same one, but over time I realised they were, in fact, different women who looked very much alike: tall, blessed with abundant cleavage, long-haired, clad in knee-high boots and miniskirts. One was rumoured to be a Russian pole-vaulter; another to have shot a lover during the course of a torrid affair.

Where such women gathered when not pouting on the corner sofa of an inner-city art gallery was a mystery. One might be forgiven for assuming they lived together in a fortress out of sight of regular mortals; it was impossible to imagine any of them walking down the street in daylight to buy a bottle of milk. I never heard them utter a word. It's not that they didn't speak; rather, their conversation consisted solely of whispering and giggling with

Queel. My single attempt at talking to one of these women was met with mute but deadly scorn, as if I were a servant egregiously overstepping the bounds of my employ.

Although they attended gigs and gallery openings, Edward and Gertrude almost never ventured out with us during the day. On the two or three occasions we managed to persuade them to accompany us, they did so under sufferance ('Ugh, that sun is *very* bright. Is it always like that?') and were either listless or else preoccupied, borrowing coins to make phone calls and suddenly remembering other places they needed to be.

As expected, Max was pleased when I told him of my decision not to pursue a formal tertiary education. He accepted it as a personal triumph. I know now that, despite their manifold personal shortcomings, Max, Edward, Gertrude, Sally and James provided me with not only companionship, but also a far more eclectic education than I would have received at university. They each possessed in their way the naive certainty (previously unknown to me) of their right to hold an opinion on virtually anything.

For me — brought up within the fearful, cloistered domesticity of a country town — it was immensely liberating. They shared their interests, plied me with records to listen to, books to read, and artworks to consider. Their unalloyed enthusiasm saved their arrogance from being insufferable, and it was during those months, through being in their company, that I discovered a way of navigating society, and a political and aesthetic perspective that has remained with me. It was through being with them, because of them, that I became myself.

One night, after finishing work late at the restaurant, I climbed the stairs to the Cairo rooftop. It was late summer, and the air was fragrant and mild. I gazed out over the eastern and northern suburbs, past the tower blocks suffused in their own chemical glow. On the eastern horizon, stars merged with the twinkling lights of houses. Below in the street, a man called to his dog. Hands in pockets, I patrolled the rooftop as if it were the battlements of a castle, and I its contented but watchful king.

On the far side, away from Nicholson Street, I became aware of a sound distinct from the traffic noise and the restless murmur of the city. It was Sally humming to herself, perhaps after taking a shower. I listened for several minutes, feeling privileged and dishonest. *My Funny Valentine.* I imagined her drying herself with one foot on the edge of the bathtub, hair across her face, the curve of her unseen back.

I leaned on the railing and inhaled the city's warmth. *At last*, I thought. *I have made it at last.*

TEN

THOSE MONTHS ARE SO CROWDED WITH HAPPY MEMORIES IT IS as difficult to individuate them as it might be to pick out a specific face in a crowd: there is Edward in his trademark frayed dark suit, wilting beneath a parasol on the boardwalk of Brighton Sea Baths one blindingly hot afternoon, features pinched with distaste as an ancient woman (skin as leathered as that of an Egyptian mummy) saunters past wearing nothing more than a G-string; of James cruising regally along Brunswick Street on his ramshackle bicycle with a cigarillo jammed between his teeth; Gertrude cackling at a caustic joke involving nuns; Max gesticulating so excitedly that he knocks a stack of dirty plates to the floor of his tiny kitchen, before drawing me close to whisper that 'Schoenberg was able to see through walls, you know'.

There is, however, one memory that surfaces with more frequency, for reasons that will become clear. It was late March. Summer had by this time drifted into autumn. High, gauzy clouds and the clatter of dry leaves along the road, the wind a friendly Labrador nuzzling at one's heels.

James and I were at Max and Sally's cluttered apartment one overcast weekday morning. Max was in a generous mood, playing the piano for us, the cuffs of his white shirt kept free of the keys with armbands. A cigarette burned in an ashtray on the lid of his instrument.

Sally sat cross-legged in a lounge chair, smoking her hand-rolled cigarettes, swinging a foot idly in time with the music. As so often happened, I found my gaze drifting over to her, as if my response were calibrated according to hers. I had watched her, nose buried in a tattered paperback copy of *I Capture the Castle* but alert to everything around her, the golden hairs on her forearms glowing like a miniature field of wheat in the light; strolling with a distracted air, as if unsure of her destination; lounging on a rug and picking at grapes in the Carlton Gardens, a massive, floppy hat shading her features; riffling through a rack of clothes in a second-hand shop.

Embarrassed to realise James had noticed my staring, I shifted my focus, hoping to give the impression that I had instead been admiring a sketch hung on the wall behind her.

Max rarely played any of his *Chants* for an audience but he liked, as on this day, regaling us with a variety of standards. He had treated me to many similar displays, and it was clear he took great pleasure in performing. As his fingers strutted and crept up and down the keys, his eyes would close, and across his face would pass an expression of rapt concentration. Despite the physical effort he expended (shoulders hunched in a tight shrug, head bobbing in time, even standing to navigate difficult sequences), it was while playing that he was at his most relaxed. He was a talented pianist and a natural performer, segueing from the pot-holed jauntiness of George Gershwin's *Sweet and Low Down* to a Beethoven sonata to a mordant cabaret tune.

At times he altered the tempo or volume to elucidate for us some details of a work or its composer. 'And this elegant bagatelle,' he would say, turning his head, 'was written by Erik Satie. A Rosicrucian in the late eighteen-hundreds, you know. House composer for the Order of the Rose Cross in Paris. Drawn to the occult.'

James, however, was in a foul mood. 'For God's sake,' he muttered, under his breath but loudly enough for the room to hear, 'just play the thing, will you.'

Although James was on the whole a genial person, these swerves in temper — provoked by what, I had not yet ascertained — were not unusual. There had been a number of times when he refused to be agreeable, a dangerous frame of mind in which to encounter Max, who relished needling him when these touchier aspects of his friend's personality arose.

That day was no exception. Max shot him a pointed look. 'Now, my dear. Don't be like that.'

'I don't think we need your carry-on, that's all. Play the damn tune.'

'You don't have to stay here if you don't enjoy it. You're welcome to run off and play with all your other friends.'

'Max,' Sally warned.

'Oh, that's right — you don't *have* any other friends.'

The theme of James's friendlessness was one to which Max returned now and again, and the barb found its mark: James twiddled his earring and lapsed into a sullen, embarrassed silence.

It was not long after that Max, having wandered unwittingly into an improvisational dead-end, stopped to light a cigarette and mop his brow with a handkerchief. He acknowledged our applause with a gracious nod before launching into a left-handed vaudevillian rag.

After a minute or so of this, his voice adopted the gravelly intonation of a sideshow barker. 'We live in dangerous times, ladies and gentlemen. A senile religious zealot is in the White House, his finger on the nuke-you-lar trigger. Let us not forget that we have never been closer to the end, and let us not forget also that it is in such times that life is at its sweetest. We are at the pointy end, no doubt about it. Don't fear the end, my friends, but embrace it. We will sing while the bombs fall. And now, gentlemen — you, too, James — allow me to introduce the incomparable Sally Cheever, who will break the hardest of hearts. Sally is set to become the greatest of her generation and you, ladies and gentlemen, will have the privilege, the honour, the *downright satisfaction* of seeing her here tonight. In the future, you will be able to say you saw Sally Cheever sing in March 1986 and your friends will weep with envy. That is, if we have a future.'

By this time Sally was standing beside him, smoothing her blue dress with one hand, her other resting on the piano lid.

She was usually reticent, so I was surprised by the alacrity with which she had leaped to her feet at Max's introduction. She arranged her hair. Her hips swayed ever so gently along with the introductory riff, which trailed away to be replaced by hesitant, meandering notes in search of their doleful key.

By the time these notes had found their key — independently, it seemed, of Max, who now slumped, inconspicuous, at his stool — Max and Sally Cheever's apartment had transformed into an ill-lit Parisian boîte with sawdust underfoot and the prick of absinthe in the air.

Sally cleared her throat and began to sing the wonderful Leiber and Stoller tune *Is That All There Is?* in a voice that, like an exotic scent, had a blend of textures, some silken, others faintly tubercular. Although I knew she was a singer, I had never heard her perform; my eavesdropping from the rooftop scarcely counted. During her rendition, each and every part of her body acquired its own eloquence, from the curl of her neck to the arch of her foot, the straight lines of her nose. Her clavicle, her milky wrist. One of her upper front teeth — the left — was cracked, which gave her smile a rare, flawed quality. She wore no jewellery aside from her wedding ring, no make-up apart from deep-red lipstick. The overall effect was electrifying.

While Max kept playing, Sally pushed away from the piano and wound her way to where I was sitting. She stood before me, one hip cocked, hand outstretched until I put my hand in hers.

'It looks like the only way a girl can get to dance,' she said with a faux aggrieved smile, 'is by asking for it herself.'

I was alarmed, but rose to my feet. What else could I have done? Until then I had hardly danced in my life, but dance we did for a minute or two, Sally and I, slowly, tentatively, until she detached herself and went back to stand beside the piano.

Relieved and disappointed, I resumed my seat and lit a cigarette with trembling hands. I had broken out in a nervous sweat. At eighteen years old my heart was as keen and clumsy as a puppy, and my experience of women was scant. I developed crushes on terse, scarlet-lipsticked women who worked in the city's record shops; on girls waiting at tram stops. I fantasised about women I spied sitting in bookstores or alone in cafes. But on that day I fell deeply in love with Sally Cheever, the woman destined to haunt me for so many years to come.

My growing familiarity with my new friends did nothing to lessen their mysterious appeal; if anything, intimacy with their peculiarities only enhanced their allure.

I spent the most time with James, because we were the only single people in the group. As he had on that first evening on Cairo's rooftop, he assumed the role of a sort of Greek chorus, filling me in on the personal histories of the Cheevers, whom he had known the longest.

Both Sally's and Max's childhoods had been troubled. Sally, he told me, was originally from Sydney and had a younger brother.

Her mother died when she was a girl, and afterwards her father converted to a ghastly evangelical religion that indulged speaking in tongues and other kitsch displays of devotion, including beachside camps at which suitable marriages between young parishioners were orchestrated by church leaders and parents. It was from one of these weekends that Sally absconded when she was about seventeen, winding up in Melbourne, where she found temp work as a secretary and singer in a local band.

Her father remarried and made a show of enticing her back to the family, but was more or less grateful that his most irksome child was no longer around to embarrass him in front of his new friends. She met Max two or three years later when he moved into Cairo, and they had lived together ever since.

Max's parents had been killed by Cyclone Tracy while they were holidaying alone in Darwin, when he was a teenager. Max and his elder sister, Edwina, had been raised by an aunt ('A creature straight out of Roald Dahl,' according to James) who returned to England once she had discharged her duties in regard to her niece and nephew. Edwina had moved to America and, although they didn't see each other often, she and Max exchanged regular letters.

In addition to his modest inheritance, Max had made a decent sum of money about ten years before, when a song of his became an unexpected hit in Europe and was used in worldwide TV advertisements for Volkswagen. There had even been a time when it looked likely that a Swedish version of the song would be nominated as that country's Eurovision entry, but there were complications over Max's nationality and the idea was scrapped. James couldn't recall the song title but sang a portion of it for me (*We will go on and on, our song will still be sung, forever* ...) and, with a thrill, I recalled the advertisement of which he spoke, and had a flashback to watching TV while lying on the carpet in our lounge room (swooping aerial shot of yellow Beetle whizzing along a mountain pass, grinning blonde, sunset over snow-capped peaks).

Although it made him wealthy for a time, Max was most ashamed of this brush with popular success, and James advised me never to mention the song or the advertisement in his presence. It did explain, however, how Max had managed to buy the two apartments and combine them to make his and Sally's current residence — not to mention affording him the time to devote to his magnum opus without having to work at a 'day-job' to make ends meet.

James knew so much of Max's personal history because they had attended the same high school. It was, he said, the sort of alternative high school fashionable among parents who considered themselves to be of a liberal, artistic disposition — an establishment at which students were allowed to smoke in the common room and call the teachers by their first name, but where discipline was non-existent and very little actual education took place.

'Max couldn't read until he was fifteen,' James told me late one night.

'What? *No.*'

We were sitting around the filthy laminate kitchen table in his apartment and eating Paddle Pops, having attended a party in a nearby warehouse. James's apartment was behind a shop on Smith Street, accessed through a door of frosted glass beside a barber shop, where — if the curling, black-and-white photographs in the window were indicative — Gene Pitney was still the height of fashion, and older men favoured hair from a can.

The apartment was ugly and chaotic, its crummy kitchen benches piled high with old takeaway food containers encrusted with the remains of curry, with dirty dishes and boxes that formerly contained frozen sausage rolls. The kitchen's linoleum floor was the deep shade of green most often found in hospital wards. James lived alone and subsisted almost exclusively on a diet of junk food, frozen desserts, alcohol and cigarettes, most of which he shoplifted from local supermarkets and grocery stores.

James licked his chocolate Paddle Pop and slouched over the table. He was drunk. Ice-cream had stained his mouth, giving his smile a half-cocked, sinister edge, like the Joker from *Batman*.

'Absolutely true. Well, he could write his name and a few other things besides, but for ages he couldn't read anything much more sophisticated than Dick and bloody Jane books. He only made it through high school because I helped him so much. I wrote half his assignments.'

'But what about all those books in his apartment?' I said. 'He's quoted long passages of things to me, talked about what he's read —'

'Let me guess: a few lines of Nietzsche, perhaps a bit from Walt Whitman, a stanza or two from his beloved *Maldoror*?'

I was puzzled by the bitterness that had crept into James's voice, taken aback also by the reassessment of Max's erudition that this information entailed.

'Have you ever seen him *read* anything?' James asked, keen to press his point.

I thought about this for a few seconds, sorting mentally through snapshots of our acquaintance. I recalled Edward reading the newspaper aloud to him that first morning at the warehouse, and I'd observed him doing that since. And I thought back to the day that I'd met Max when I'd delivered the letter that had erroneously been put through my mail slot. Had I actually watched him read? Perhaps not.

'But he sent me an invitation asking me to dinner that first night I met you,' I told him.

James shook his head. 'It would've been written by Sally. If you've still got it somewhere, look at the hand it's written in and you'll find it's a woman's handwriting.'

This prompted in me, not for the first time, a stab of affection for Sally. I imagined her labouring over the invitation — hair tumbling into her eyes, lips pursed in concentration — and relished the illusion she had written it expressly for me.

James wiped the back of his hand across his mouth and tossed the clean Paddle Pop stick aside. 'Don't get me wrong, Max is no fool. He does have a fantastic memory and a capacity to absorb and understand information. Knows recipes by heart, can quote chunks of Shakespeare. He can read now, but not terribly well. Sally does most of that stuff — pays bills, reads and writes the letters to and from his sister and so on. He reads music, knows complex rhythms and musical schemes, can hold symphonies in his head. A few years ago he and Sally got hold of a home-schooling guide from the 1960s and devised a curriculum to compensate for Max's abominable education. Haven't you noticed that most of the stuff he goes on about is — how should we put it — outdated?'

Now that I considered it, many of the poems Max quoted *were* idiosyncratic (he had, for example, a few days earlier regaled me with all fifty-five lines of Tennyson's *Charge of the Light Brigade*, complete with exegesis). I had assumed his and Sally's arcane traits were merely an endearing affectation, but at that moment I understood they formed part of a more comprehensive worldview, in which much of the second half of the twentieth century had not yet taken place.

James leaned over the table in a manner I recognised as preparatory to imparting a confidence. 'You know what I call him? *The Undercheever*. Do you like that? Do you? That bloody masterpiece he's been working on for years, that *Maldoror* or whatever it is. He has these piles of notes sitting on his piano, but they're the same bundles of paper that have been sitting there forever. Most of what he plays are segments of other works that he strings together. He can get away with it because none of his friends know enough about classical music to pull him up. He does have an extraordinary memory, which is why he seems to know so much. Sally reads to him almost every night. She's an excellent reader, can do it for hours on end. Novels, textbooks, history books, you name it. She read *Lord of the Rings* to him, for God's sake. That must be a zillion words long. Full of creepy hobbits and wizards.'

That explained a mystery that had been bothering me for some time. While taking the night air on the rooftop I had often heard Sally's soliloquising voice drifting through their open windows, and I must admit to having taken a somewhat unhealthy interest in the noises emanating from their apartment — sounds that ranged from the frankly amorous to others that belied a more explosive relationship. A number of times I had heard shouts, threatening growls, a woman weeping, and had to resist the urge to skim down the stairs and pound on their door, demanding explanations.

James got to his feet and, after rummaging about, produced a half-full bottle of red wine from a cupboard. He poured it into two grubby tumblers and raised his glass before gulping from it.

The combination of the late hour, the alcohol we had consumed and James's apparent ill-humour towards Max — each of which alone might have been an excuse for such indiscretion — encouraged me to mention I had heard Max and Sally quarrelling a number of times.

He licked his lips and put his glass down to light a cigarette. 'Oh, have you?'

I nodded, already feeling queasy at broaching the subject.

'Yes. Theirs is an unusual relationship. Can't say I understand it but, then again, the inner workings of other people's lives are often hard to figure out. They are both desperate to have a baby but so far haven't been able to achieve it. Max organised a weird solstice fertility rite last winter in the Carlton Gardens. God, the things he manages to persuade us to do. I had to pour a jar of cow's blood over both of them and mutter some ancient spell. Then we had to hop about in a circle like rabbits ...'

I recalled what my neighbour Maria had said about seeing them dance in the park like animals.

'The fault is Max's, but he can't bear to admit it,' James went on. He made a pistol of his right hand and depressed the thumb repeatedly in a pantomime of uselessness. 'Our Maxy is shooting blanks. What did I tell you? The Undercheever.'

'How did you find out he's, you know, shooting blanks?'

Another brief pantomime, this time of reluctance to gossip. 'Well. Sally got herself into a spot of bother a few years ago. She and Max have been trying to get pregnant for ages, but only when she has a fling with another man does it happen for her.'

I said nothing, but the expression on my face must have betrayed my incomprehension to James.

He leaned across the table, tumbler in one hand, and said in a stage whisper, '*Abortion*. Pretty women can only ever rely on a man like me. Anyone else has ulterior motives.'

Flushed with embarrassment, I inspected my own deliquescent Paddle Pop, licked a chocolate dribble from my knuckle. 'What do you mean — a man like you?' I asked.

He regarded me for a second before smiling, delighted at my question. 'God, you truly are an innocent, aren't you? Our Sally's not as squeaky clean as you might think. I suggested she keep the child. She could have told Max it was his and no one would have been the wiser. It's not as if it would've been *black* or anything. They could have lived happily ever after. Her having a fling is completely understandable, considering how Max screws around. It's a miracle they don't fight more often.'

I thought back to the night of that first rooftop dinner party or, more precisely, to the blood on Sally's face that prevented her from joining us for a nightcap at El Nidos. Concern at what might have taken place between her and Max behind closed doors had bothered me ever since, but I had not yet been able to bring myself to ask James about it, for fear — I see now — of what the answer could mean for my infatuation with my new friends and the bohemian idyll in which I had found myself. I resolved to bring it up with him, but before I could say anything James staggered from his chair, knocking it to the floor, and vanished to the bedroom, grumbling about Paddle Pop stains on his white shirt. I heard the noise of drawers being opened and slammed shut as he searched for clean clothes.

I finished my ice-cream and smoked a cigarette. I had assumed James would return to the kitchen having changed his shirt but, after ten minutes or so — in which I heard no further sounds — I ventured in to see if he was alright.

His bedroom was as grotty as the rest of the place. Strewn around the room were clothes, cigarette packets, empty Coke cans, liquor bottles, a volume of his beloved Cavafy and a paperback edition of Edgar Rice Burroughs' *A Princess of Mars*. In the middle of this detritus was a mattress upon which James himself was sprawled on his back, shirtless, mouth agape, arms flung to either side like a wayward Christ upon a raft.

He was fast asleep. His body was so thin, the skin of his pale chest almost amphibious in appearance despite the smattering of hair. On his left wrist were two thick, purple scars that looked old, each of them two or three centimetres long. A row of faint dots on either side of the scars marked the placement of stitches. I considered his habit of constantly checking the length of his sleeves and was filled with pity, with tenderness and with shame that I had glimpsed him exposed in a manner that was doubtless embarrassing for him.

122

I covered his sleeping form with a blanket and crossed to the open window. On the windowsill, and along the skirting board, there were at least two dozen cologne bottles, assorted pieces of jewellery, tiny plastic toys and fancy pens arranged in neat configurations. James's kleptomaniac tendencies were well known among his circle of friends, and I was not unduly surprised to notice among the hoard a pen with *Dunley Tigers — Hear them roar!* printed on it that had gone missing from my place.

His room looked out over Smith Street. The display cabinet of the pawn shop opposite was dim, having been emptied for the night of its range of cameras, watches and jewellery. A fluoro light in the drycleaners flickered erratically, illuminating in split-second increments a row of washing machines, grey linoleum floor, a bright blue box of Cold Power.

The first tram of the day ground down the street. In the east, over distant mountains, the sky was lightening. Bulbous clouds were turning deep orange as if, rather than the sun rising beyond, there were instead a magnificent eruption taking place, one so cosmic in scale and so far away that its effects were nigh on indiscernible. In the foreground was an assortment of antennae sprouting from rooftops, the commission towers a block away on Wellington Street, a graffitied wall. This sight might have been dispiriting for some people — bleak, even — but on that morning it inspired in me the most exquisite melancholy. I love beautiful objects, but it is generally those considered less than beautiful (concrete, wire fences, alleyways and broken things) that inspire deep emotion in me and whose desolate charms I find hard to resist.

I closed the window and walked back through Fitzroy to Cairo.

ELEVEN

AS I HAD PROMISED MY PARENTS, ONCE A MONTH I HAD AN excruciating Sunday lunch of half-cooked health food with Uncle Mike and his wife, Jane, at their enormous house in the leafy, middle-class suburb of Malvern.

The pair were keen cyclists and wore lycra around the house on Sunday afternoons after their dawn ride. They had no children but doted on three Siamese cats named after planets. Jane worked as a receptionist at the practice Mike owned. She never said a great deal, but Mike more than compensated for it. His favourite conversational gambit with new acquaintances was to demand they guess his age (usually estimated at around forty-three) just to bask in their gasps of amazement when they learned the truth (fifty-two!). His interest in me was perfunctory, which was a relief because it meant I was rarely placed in the position of having to lie about my attendance (or lack thereof) at university. In fact, the only questions Mike asked about anyone's life were intended as a springboard for him to deliver impromptu lectures on whatever topic (Roman myths, Japanese literature of the nineteenth century) piqued his restless interest that week.

I was lying on the couch in my apartment on a chilly Sunday afternoon recovering from one of these horrible lunches when there was a knock at my door.

I turned down the radio and stayed still on my sofa, thinking it was Eve come to torment me with questions and demands to play with Aunt Helen's jewellery. The obnoxious child had become difficult to avoid; she had begun taking note of my movements and delighted in catching me out if I told her I'd missed a visit because I wasn't home, when she knew for a fact that I was. The child's mother chuckled at these accusations, eager to believe such tactics were indicative of her daughter's brilliance rather than signs of a nascent totalitarian personality.

But the knock came again, louder this time, followed by Max calling out my name.

'Hello there,' he said when I had ushered him inside. 'Not napping, were you?'

'Sorry, Max. I thought you were Eve.'

Max shuddered. For reasons that were unclear, his dislike of Eve was even more pronounced than mine. Taking his cue from Willy Wonka, Max pretended she wasn't there and, if cornered by her on the stairwell or in the garden, would ignore her interrogations ('What is that strange *buzzing noise*?' he'd say) until she went away, preferably close to tears.

He made a face and patted his chest with theatrical delicacy. 'You know her mother still feeds the little palindrome ... from those withered *dugs*? "Special milk", Eve calls it. Truly a disgusting sight, like a scene from one of those medieval end-of-the-world paintings.'

'How on earth do you know that?'

'There's not much that goes on in Cairo that I don't know about. Anyway,' he said, flopping into my armchair, 'I could help keep her away from you.'

'How?'

'Tell the mother you're a child molester.' He made a spooky

twiddle in the air with his fingers. 'They're everywhere these days, you know.'

'Uh, no thanks.'

'But it will keep them both well away.'

'Yes, and everyone else.'

'Not always a bad thing. Helps to get work done, at least. Which reminds me, how's that novel of yours coming along?'

I made a helpless gesture. Perhaps the only thing more foolish than wishing to write novels is making such an ambition public. Pretty much the only fiction I was responsible for at that time were the infrequent phone calls to Dunley when I regaled my mother or father — both of whom were unaware of the change in my educational priorities — with tales of my imaginary classmates and professors, most of whom were based on people I had met at parties or read about in books. I needed to remain on high alert during such conversations lest my mother (with her prodigious memory for names) asked me whether I was still going to the cinema with my new friend Jose Arcadio or if old Mrs Du Maurier was proving to be a more agreeable literature tutor than she was at the start of the academic year.

Washing dishes for a living and going to lots of parties was not always the most fulfilling existence, and when I did become disillusioned at my failure to enrol at university, the idea that I was living the bohemian life and writing a novel became a consolation. Progress, however, had been slow. I had a notebook in which I scribbled things (usually when drunk, late at night), ideas for characters and storylines that on closer and more sober inspection inevitably proved — assuming they were legible — to be nothing short of idiotic.

A visit from Max was rare: I could have counted on the fingers of one hand the number of times he had been into my apartment. He was not himself, nervous even, leaping to his feet every now

127

and then to poke about as if reassuring himself we were alone.

I made a fresh pot of tea and, once we were seated, asked how his own work was progressing.

'Can't say I've done very much lately, but now that the shenanigans of summer are over I'm keen to get back to it. I've been stuck on one or two things that I think I've resolved. I need to hit the ivories, you know. Make some noise.'

He had told me a bit about the nineteenth-century poem on which his work was to be based. It was, I gathered, some sort of proto-surrealist prose poem about the decline of a mad king. He had quoted aloud portions of its fevered text for me ('*Holding a head whose skull I gnawed, I stood like the heron on one foot at the brink of a precipice scored into the mountainside*'), but Max's explanations of his work-in-progress were as garbled as they were enthusiastic, before grinding to a halt with an implication that his interlocutor was unlikely to understand anyway.

I poured tea for us both. Max lit a cigarette, scratched at his chin. He was wearing grey trousers and an unfashionable dark-blue cardigan over a cream shirt. His red tie was askew and hair tumbled across his eyes.

'Look,' he said at last, 'can I talk to you?'

'Sure.'

'We've known each other for a few months now.'

'Yes.'

'I think you are a fine man. Trustworthy.'

I was genuinely flattered. 'Thank you.'

He leaned forwards, elbows on knees, and glanced around before speaking. 'I might as well get to the point. Now, this is serious. We're planning an escapade and I think it's only fair you get a chance to become involved. We all do.'

His tone was comically ominous, and I couldn't suppress a bemused snort, which was met with a reproving glance. I gulped my tea and arranged my features into what I hoped was a more suitable expression.

'You know that Picasso painting at the National Gallery everyone has been going on and on about?' he said.

'*Weeping Woman?*'

'Have you been to see it yet?'

I shook my head. 'Why?'

'We are going to steal it.'

There followed a peculiar lull into which tumbled a torrent of images. Ever since the gallery took possession of the work at the start of the year, the local papers had been full of news and comment on the subject: how the National Gallery of Victoria had paid $1.6 million for it; the folly of spending vast sums on old foreign art instead of funding young Australian artists; correspondence to the editor mocking it as worse than anything produced by the letter-writer's three-year-old niece etc. etc. With minimal effort, I could summon in my mind the portrait's sickly green planes and empurpled lips, the eyes like ravenous sea creatures.

Unsure how else to respond to Max's claim, I laughed.

He scowled. 'I'm glad you think it's funny.'

'Oh, come on. You're not serious, are you?'

'But we are.'

And I did see, with a shock, that he was. 'Who do you mean by *we?*'

'We're all involved in one way or another. Myself. Sally, Gertrude, Edward; another woman called Tamsin and her brother George. Tamsin is a friend of James's. A Bolshevik art student from England. She knows the gallery inside out. These Bolshevik twins will, you know, *take* the painting. They are sort of mad, very political. They smashed that massive front window at the NGV a few years ago as part of some protest. James is being difficult about the whole thing but he'll be included when we divide the proceeds. Basically, he'll do pretty much anything I ask of him.'

I jumped up and put out my hands to stop him talking. 'I can't believe I'm hearing this, Max. What the hell are you talking about? The *proceeds*?'

'Shhh. Calm yourself. I know it sounds crazy.'

'Yes. It does.'

'But it's all perfectly well planned out. We've done it before. Well, not exactly, but we did a similar thing before and no one has ever been the wiser. Now sit down, will you.'

Eventually I did sit down and listened as Max filled me in on their plan that — whether because of my exhaustion or Max's sheer charisma — actually began to sound plausible. These Bolshevik twins had a friend who worked as an attendant at the gallery and knew there was no special security in place for the *Weeping Woman*, irrespective of the painting's value and notoriety. They would hide overnight in a maintenance cupboard in the gallery, come out after closing time and unscrew the painting from its frame with a special tool. In the morning, when the gallery opened for the day, they would mingle with the public and walk out the front door with it.

'Walk out with a million-dollar painting?' I asked.

'Basically, yes. It's not very big when it's taken from its frame. Fifty-five by forty-six centimetres, to be precise. It can be hidden easily under a coat or among some folders. That's one of the things we have to work out. We're not planning to do it until winter. Wait until the fuss over it fades away. We've done a few trial runs already, and no one notices a thing.'

'What kind of trial runs?'

'Well, they've hidden all night in the cupboard three times and taken a stroll through the gallery in the middle of the night. Just last night, in fact. And we'll do it again before the real thing.'

'Aren't there guards patrolling at night?'

'Yes, but they have a pretty fixed schedule. Easy to avoid. For us there's not that much risk. It's not as if they have secret cameras, is it?'

'So you manage to steal a famous painting. Then what?'

Max rubbed his hands together. 'Here's where it gets *really* interesting.'

'Because so far it's been very dull.'

'Yes. No. Anyway. You don't know this, but Gertrude is a brilliant painter, a brilliant technician. She'll make a copy, we'll sell the original to some people who deal in these kinds of things and then give the copy back to the gallery. Stash it where it can be found, leave it at a tram stop or railway station. That way the gallery gets it back and we make a load of money. Everyone is happy.'

'People who deal in these kinds of things? Who might they be?'

'Associates of Anna Donatella's.'

'She's in on it as well?'

'She has the contacts. But not that horrible Queel. He mustn't know a thing about it. He's dangerous.'

'I thought Edward was the painter?' I asked.

'Edward is an awful painter. Sells well but he's basically an amateur. It's what the market wants these days. They want sensation, work that matches the couch and the carpet. Gertrude is the real artist, but no one is interested in the kind of things she does anymore. Too serious, far too skilful, too *profound*. People enjoy things that make them feel equal to the artist, not less than. She was represented by Anna Donatella for a few years, but not anymore. Queel got rid of her. She and Edward make a great team when it comes to this kind of thing, though. He's a crappy artist, but Edward is a genius with colour. He does the mixing of pigments and so on, while she does the actual work. She did that Soutine portrait they've got in their studio as a sort of experiment. Similar era and so on. You know the one?'

131

'Yes. It's a great painting. But I don't think it's as easy to make forgeries as you think. There's the line of ownership, the types of paint used …'

'We don't need provenance for this one. It already *has* provenance. That's why the plan is so brilliant. Besides, we've already passed off a couple of Norman Lindsays.'

This sounded unlikely. 'Which ones?'

Max held up a hand, palm outwards. 'Sorry but I can't tell you. Any knowledge of these things has to stay very, very close. I shouldn't have told you anything about it, as a matter of fact. Look, it's easy if you have the connections. The art market is absolutely *full* of fakes. Dealers and galleries don't want to examine too closely because they don't want to know that a piece they paid millions of dollars for is only worth twenty bucks. We won't get caught.'

I thought back to the night I had overheard him and Edward talking outside my apartment. What was it Edward had said? *This isn't just some old Norman Lindsay painting of ladies with big tits sitting in a river.*

'Why not sell the forgery to these … *associates*?' I asked.

Max hesitated. 'You remember when we were at Edward's place that day of the *Challenger* explosion and some people came around? You stayed in the bedroom with Gertrude?'

The memory of it still rankled. 'You made me go in there.'

'Yes, I know. These … associates don't think a woman can do such a good forgery, so we let them think Edward does it. Gertrude gets in a flap about it but, really, it's neither here nor there. Anyway, there was a man there, Mr Crisp, and he's the chap we'll sell the painting to. Mr Crisp's bodyguard was with him that day.' He grimaced. 'You remember what happened to Buster?'

I didn't answer his question. Poor Buster had remained in plaster for three weeks after the shooting and made a pitiful sight lurching around Edward and Gertrude's warehouse like a grizzled old coot.

Max went on. 'The gallery, on the other hand, will be so pleased to avoid international humiliation that they'll accept almost anything. The police will call off the search, our friends get the real version out of the country, we get our money. Look, Pablo painted it in *one single day*. We reckon we can take a week or so. You haven't seen anything until you've seen Gertrude paint. She's amazing.'

'And you want me to help how?'

'I knew you'd love the idea. I knew you had the guts. Well, we can't very well take the thing out of the city on a tram. It might be raining, for a start. Plus, we need to get away from the area as soon as possible. The painting needs to be thoroughly looked after to maintain its value. It's no good to us if it gets wrecked, is it?' He raised his voice, as if to forestall my inevitable objections. 'We need someone to drive from the gallery to Edward's place, that's all. Anna Donatella can't do it, because she's too well known. You and I will park outside and wait for Tamsin and George. I've talked about it with the others and we all think you're perfect. It's not only about having someone who can drive or who has a car; it's about finding someone who deserves the opportunity. Deserves the money. We want you with us. I had to hold Sally back from asking you straight away, she was so taken with you, but I thought we should wait until we knew you better.'

I thought of two or three conversations among them in the past few weeks that had petered out at my arrival, and another time when I saw Max arguing with James in the Carlton Gardens. Although nothing in their manner towards me had changed, I lived in fear of transgressing the little group's code of conduct in some obscure way that would result in my being excommunicated. I had thrown my lot in with them so comprehensively that such a prospect was unthinkable, unbearable. In this light, the news they had been conspiring to steal a major artwork was, somehow, a relief.

The cups of tea remained untouched. Max stood, fetched a bottle of Aunt Helen's sherry from my sideboard and poured a tumbler for each of us.

'Tom, we stand to make a lot of money out of this. It will set us up for years. Do you want to wash dishes for the rest of your life? Afterwards, we're all moving to France. Me and Sally and James. Edward and Gertrude are going to Berlin, because, well, that's where people like them tend to go. It's much cheaper in Europe. I'll finish *Maldoror*; you can write your novel. Live like Hemingway, like Henry Miller — without the, you know, crabs. It'll be amazing. It will change our lives. Our long exile will be over. This is a chance to make a mark, to do something that people will remember for decades. And all *you* have to do is pick someone up and drive a few kilometres and —'

'Someone who happens to be carrying a stolen Picasso painting.'

Max conceded my clarification. 'Yes. But I'll be in the car with you, if that makes you feel any better. It's — what? — a four-kilometre drive from the gallery to Edward's place? Straight up Swanston Street. No distance at all. The risk is absolutely minimal for us. If Tamsin and her brother don't come out within fifteen minutes of the gallery opening, then we drive away and forget it. There's no crime in sitting in a car outside a public gallery, is there?'

'So,' I asked at last, unable to keep the scepticism from my voice, 'assuming you can pull it off, how much do you sell this million-dollar painting for?'

'Please. Don't be like that, Tom. Mr Crisp will give us — in *cash*, mind — $150,000. All of us have discussed this long and hard and decided that you will get $15,000.'

That was a lot of money, as much as I would make in two years working at the restaurant. I sat back to take it all in. The world beyond my apartment had crumbled away since Max had started outlining the plan. I no longer heard birds, cars or even the trams that were usually so audible as they passed along Nicholson Street. The day, too, had darkened. I hadn't turned on the lamps, and dusk had crept inside.

I listened in a daze as Max filled me in on the extensive research Gertrude had done into Picasso's technique, of the canvases she had painstakingly prepared with historically correct finishes, of a secret manual she owned that was written by a famous Hungarian forger. It was all so unlikely, so mad, so wonderful.

'And the best thing about it,' Max was saying when I tuned in again, 'is that the scheme is similar to the one when the *Mona Lisa* was taken from the Louvre in 1911. Someone waited overnight in a cupboard, took it off the wall and walked out. They didn't even *realise* it was gone for two days! And you know who they brought in for questioning over it? A bowlegged Spaniard called Pablo Picasso. The whole thing is an homage.'

'Or a copy.'

'Precisely! We refer to our *Weeping Woman* only as Dora, after the woman in the painting. Never, *ever* mention it by name from here on. The thing to do now is to sit tight. I'm going to get stuck into *Maldoror*. Nothing will happen for a while, I shouldn't think. All you need to worry about is your part of the plan. It's like a spy cell — everything else is on a need-to-know basis. I'll inform you when it's going to happen.'

Max got up to leave. I walked him to the door, but before I could open it, he pressed one palm to my chest and leaned in so close that, for a second, I thought he intended to kiss me on the mouth. Such a gesture would not have been wholly out of keeping with the clandestine intimacy of the conversation we had just had.

We stood face to face in my tiny entrance hall. I smelled sherry and cigarettes on his breath, the fragrant lotion he applied to his wilful hair. 'Remember,' he said, wagging a finger in front of my face. 'Tell no one of this conversation. Not. A. Soul.' He laughed, but not convincingly. 'Or we might have to kill you.'

When Max left I collapsed onto my sofa and stared at the low ceiling, turning the past few hours over in my mind. The episode had quickly assumed the distorted, aqueous qualities of a tale — written, perhaps, by Poe — in which a mysterious visitor relates his barely plausible adventures to a disbelieving narrator. Fragments of the afternoon floated before my eyes. Over and again I saw the pile of money, Max brushing hair from his eyes, cigarettes heaped in the ashtray, the fronds of the peppercorn tree at my window swaying like the skirts of island women.

TWELVE

THE DAYS SHORTENED AND GREW COLDER. AUTUMN LEAVES rotted in the park, and there gathered about Cairo's ramshackle garden the dispiriting smell of sodden earth and cold concrete. People talked about the football, exchanged statistics and opinion with a degree of seriousness usually reserved for politics or war. I worked long hours at the restaurant and slept until late when I could.

This onset of winter coincided with a hiatus in my social life, in which I didn't see as much of my new friends. James went into hibernation and, although I still heard her spelling out words in her piercing voice, even Eve stopped visiting. This relative quiet was not unwelcome after the heady pleasures of summer and early autumn. By this time I had found my feet in my adopted city; I knew which trams to catch to get around, the best place to buy coffee. Even the fat man at the local milk bar knew my name.

More regularly than before, I heard Max thumping away on his piano, working on *Maldoror*. Every so often, he played portions of it to me, each demonstration accompanied by a convoluted explanation of the particular text that inspired it and a sense of the piece's overall architecture. Much of what he had written was rather jagged, but there was a more spacious section that was very beautiful; a few simple and melancholy notes — barely a melody — that strolled through my inner ear for days afterwards as if lost, but pleasantly so.

Following his example, and inspired after seeing a late-night screening of Jean-Pierre Melville's great gangster film *Le Samouraï* at the Carlton Movie House, I attempted to revive my languishing novel, which had developed into a dirty noir: black streets and blacker-hearted men; a crummy motel, snowy roads. With two fingers I pecked away on a typewriter I had bought for five dollars at a junk shop on Gertrude Street.

Despite the violent nature of the story I was trying to write, it was comforting to be involved so intensely in a make-believe world. Each time I sat down to work, I was reacquainted with people with whom I felt my destiny to be entwined. The writing of novels is often characterised as a solitary enterprise, but I have found the opposite to be true. It's just that the people are not real; or not entirely, anyway.

One person I did see a lot of during that period was, much to my delight, Sally. She fell into the habit of turning up at my door late morning, seeking a cup of milk for her coffee, but after a while these pretexts fell by the wayside and the visits became purely social. She had not been getting as much temp work as usual and Max was so busy with composing that she was bored and lonely.

Sally and I talked of general things and gossiped about people we knew. She revealed details about her childhood that I found delightful; explained complicated games she'd played with her younger brother, Robert, when they were children.

'When I was small,' she told me one day, 'I used to write notes to my parents if I thought I had done the wrong thing. Sorry for breaking a cup, that sort of thing. Sorry I made Robert cry. I was very proper in that way, always trying to be good. I still do it sometimes, send notes to Max if I feel I've hurt him somehow.

They're short, but I always mean what I say in them; they're very sincere. Childish, but there you go. Old habits die hard, I suppose.'

Because Helen's record collection was so dire and mine so rudimentary, Sally began bringing around albums to play while we chatted and sipped our tea or wine. My heart sagged with disappointment on one occasion, when under her arm was the double gatefold edition of the 1970 Miles Davis album *Bitches Brew*. It was more modern than Max's usual listening fare, but its disavowal of any recognisable musical forms appealed to him. Symptomatic of Max's musical obsession were his efforts to unlock a piece of music, as another person might take apart an electronic device to ascertain how it worked. He had played *Bitches Brew* to me repeatedly one afternoon, analysing each burp and squawk and even going so far as to replay sections to demonstrate his points. I liked Miles Davis, but I didn't enjoy that fusion of jazz and progressive rock one bit.

So I was gratified, when Sally dropped the needle onto the vinyl, to hear not *Bitches Brew* at all, but a completely different style of music.

'What is this?' I asked her. 'It's not Miles Davis.'

'God, that album's awful. No one enjoys it, you know. People own it — musicians, especially — because they feel they should.' She gestured to my bookshelf, which was by now overflowing with paperbacks I had been picking up at second-hand bookstores around the neighbourhood. 'It's like novelists with their dog-eared copy of *Ulysses*. No one reads the damn thing, do they?'

I laughed. She was right; I had been trying to read James Joyce's novel on and off for weeks but never got very far before the words and their meanings began to dissolve and slither around the page.

'This is New Order,' Sally said. 'One of my favourite bands. See, I hide it in these other album sleeves. It's a trick I learned when I lived at home. I used to borrow records from school friends and hide them in the covers of acceptable albums, such as versions of the Lord's Prayer sung by Scottish nuns.'

'Is that the *Ulysses* for religious people?'

She smiled. 'My father didn't approve of pop music. Well, he didn't approve of much at all. I also hollowed out the pages of a large Bible so I could fit my Joy Division tapes in there. That took me weeks. I got the idea from a movie where a criminal hid his pistol that way. My father thrashed me with his belt when he found out — desecration and all that. I must say I panicked a bit when Max wanted to play *Bitches Brew* to you a few weeks ago. Had to jump in and swap the albums around.'

'What would he do if he found out?'

She dodged the question and, laughing, asked, 'I take it you've never played Helen's record of *Rockin' and Stompin' with Col Joye*?'

'Um, no.'

'You'll find that's a Smiths album. Your aunt gave me a key to this place, and I used to come over sometimes and listen to records when she was at work or away on one of her holidays. Although I've lost the key now, so you don't need to worry about me prowling through your personal things when you're out. Can I tell you a secret?'

'Yes.'

'You have to promise you won't tell anyone.'

'I won't.'

'And you'll have to tell me one of yours in return.'

I shrugged.

She made an exaggerated face of a girl confessing mischief. 'I'd tell Max I was going to work, and then come here and hang out, drink tea and play records all day. Max was too busy to know and Helen didn't mind. She was great company, when she was around.'

We listened to the music for a while. I slumped in my armchair while she kneeled on the floor near the speakers, hands splayed on her knees, head bowed in appreciation. She was wearing a grey, Russian-style fur hat from which a few strands of blonde hair trailed, lending her the countenance of a ravishing, exiled princess. A smile played along the edges of her red mouth. Like smell, music has the uncanny ability to dislodge an avalanche of memory and connection, and it was clear this record was doing that for Sally. I longed to know what the music conjured for her, but felt it impertinent to enquire. Besides, it would most certainly involve other people. Instead, I contented myself by observing her; her presence was delicious enough, and I didn't want to scare her away with inane chatter.

'Your aunt was wonderful,' she said when the frantic beats of the song *Denial* dissolved into vinyl's distinctive woolly hiccup.

'Yes. She *was* great. I still miss her, even though I didn't see much of her in recent years.'

'I know. She was so depressed about all that. She hated not seeing her family, you most of all.'

'What else did she say about me?'

'Well, nothing much. Only that.' She crawled to the turntable to flip the record over before resuming her position on the rug. The music began again. 'Your turn. What's your secret?'

I answered before I even knew what I was saying, as if I had been waiting my whole life for someone to ask me such a question.

'I think Helen might have been my real mother,' I said, and went on to tell her of my suspicions surrounding my family, how I had never felt at home with them.

My heartbeat thickened. I had never before told these things to anyone, but here, a long way from home, it seemed a natural response. Perhaps I hoped Sally knew Helen's secrets? But then my words, hanging in the air, suddenly sounded like the dream of a foolish child. I wanted to cram them back into my mouth. *Idiot*. A hot blush infused my face. With shaking hands I lit a cigarette and coughed loudly, as if to cover my tracks. *Idiot*.

Sally was startled. She opened her mouth to speak, then thought better of it. Only when the record had finished did she respond.

'She was a bit like a mother to me, as well. The mother I might have chosen for myself, if I had been given that choice. We used to call her Helen of Roy. Of Fitzroy, you know. The face that launched a thousand ships. Families are so complicated, aren't they? Did you ever ask your family about her?'

'I've always been too afraid.'

'Afraid of finding out it's true, or finding out it's not true?'

I didn't answer.

'Well,' she said, 'perhaps you should be brave.'

'Brave like you?'

To this she said nothing. I smoked in a cringing silence. Outside, drizzle hung in the air like dust.

'James told me you ran away from home when you were a teenager,' I said at last.

'Yes,' she said. 'What else did James tell you?'

Having recovered from my embarrassment, I was thrilled to detect a flirtatious undertow in her question, but didn't know how to capitalise on this. 'Do you see your family anymore?'

She lit her cigarette and blew out the match before dropping it into a large glass ashtray. 'Not for a few years. I visit Robert in Sydney from time to time. But not my father.'

'That must be hard.'

'It was at first, mainly because he had told me for so long how evil the world was. He wanted me to be suspicious of outsiders. His sect don't mix at all with people outside their church. But people are generally nice, I think. Besides, I have a new family. Max, Edward, Gertrude, James. A few other people. Now you, too.'

I was flattered to be included on such a list.

'What about you?' she asked. 'What about your family? Or, the people who raised you, I guess I should say. You hardly mention them.'

'There's not much to say. I don't have much of a past.'

'Everyone has a past. Without it they're nothing: they have no real character.'

I sketched a few details about my sisters, my parents, the town of Dunley.

'Do you miss them?'

It was a good question. There was an undeniable thrill in setting out into the world alone, and it accorded with the existential-loner persona I wished to project to the world at large. Even after all these months of living in a new city, I still woke sometimes in the middle of the night wondering where I was. The truth was that I didn't miss any of my family, but it was callous to admit such a thing. I shrugged in lieu of committing to anything.

'It's hard to find a place in the world,' she said, picking a shred of tobacco from her tongue. 'When I first got to Melbourne I was living by myself in a dingy apartment in Richmond. A tiny, noisy place near Bridge Road. I was working as a waitress, not making much money. This was before I moved in here and met Max. One day — don't ask me how — my father found out where I was living. He came to Melbourne and started banging on the door, calling out my name. I hid behind the couch with my hands over my ears, pretending no one was home.'

'What were you frightened of?'

'I don't know, to be honest. By then I was nineteen — old enough to live wherever I wanted, do whatever I wanted. There was nothing he could do to me.'

'And what happened?'

'He went away after a while. I didn't leave the house for two days in case he was waiting for me.' She ground her cigarette out in the ashtray. To judge by the expression on her face, it was a painful memory. 'But a week or so later my little brother wrote to tell me my father had come around because my old dog, Hector, was dying. They thought I should have the chance to say goodbye to him. By the time I found out, it was too late. Poor Hector was dead. And that's the last I heard from my father.'

'Do you wish you'd opened the door that day?'

Sally stared at me. Her eyes were red, her expression wretched. I have never learned the art (for it *is* an art) of comforting a sorrowful woman but then, aged eighteen, I had even less idea. I sat rooted to my armchair, skin prickling, more or less praying for a hole to open and swallow me.

'There is a lot to be said,' she said, 'for knowing where you stand with people. Don't you think?'

'Yes.'

I felt myself blushing under Sally's gaze. In an effort to dispel my discomfort (pleasurable as it was), I stood to go into the kitchen and make us a fresh pot of tea.

Sally had put on another record when there was a loud knock at my front door. Another barrage of knocks, this time followed by Max's voice.

'Open up, will you. I can hear your dreadful music.'

Before I could say a word, Sally gathered up her Mary Janes and her rolling tobacco. 'Don't tell him I'm here. I'll wait in your bedroom.'

Seeing no alternative, I opened the door. Max entered, shouldering me to one side of the narrow entrance hall. 'Goodness. Take your time, why don't you? It's freezing out there today. Our phone's out of action or I would have rung. You haven't seen my Sally, have you?'

'No.'

'Damn. I think she went to the movies with Gertrude. I can't find a clean shirt *anywhere*. Oh well. I'll have to borrow one of yours, if that's alright.'

And before I could stall him, he waltzed into my bedroom. I swore under my breath. How on earth would it look, Sally cowering in there? I prepared for the worst.

But instead of the anticipated fracas, Max wandered back out a few seconds later, holding up a white shirt taken from my wardrobe, still on its hanger. 'Can I borrow this?'

'Um. Sure.'

'I'm going to the opera tonight with Frank Thring. Got to dress up or else he won't take me to supper afterwards. What *is* that bloody awful music you're playing? Sounds like the kind of music Sally might have been into before I set her straight.'

Although I couldn't remember the name of the band, I hazarded a guess, figuring that Max wouldn't know if I were wrong. 'Um. The Smiths.'

He shook his head in mute incomprehension. Then he thanked me and left, slamming the door as was his habit. His visit was a brief tornado.

Sally came out of the bedroom with her tobacco, shoes and fur hat in her hands.

I was angry to have been put in such a potentially difficult situation, but my misgivings dissolved at the sight of her sheepish expression. I couldn't help but laugh. 'What the hell was all that about? I was sure he'd find you in there.'

She smiled and made a face. 'Lucky there's room under your bed.'

'Why are you so afraid of him?'

'Don't be ridiculous. I'm not afraid.'

'Then why all the creeping around?'

She shrugged. 'It's nice to have some time apart, that's all. As you can imagine, living with Max can be intense. This is a man who can't even wash a shirt. There's a joke, you know: a boy says to his

145

mother that he wants to be a musician when he grows up and the mother says, "Well, I'm very sorry, Billy, but you can't do both."'

We laughed.

'I'm sorry I put you in a tight spot,' she went on. 'I don't know why I did that. You're a love.' She stepped over and kissed me on the cheek, before setting about plucking burrs of dust that had accumulated on her sweater and skirt.

'He thinks you're at the movies,' I said when I had recovered sufficiently to speak.

With one hand on my shoulder for balance, Sally slipped on her shoes. 'I'd better go. Thanks for the tea. Perhaps tell Max you borrowed *Bitches Brew*? I'll leave it here for now. Oh, by the way — what's the last film you saw?'

'It was called *Le Samouraï*. French. Why?'

'Can you tell me the plot? If Max asks, I'll tell him that's what I went to see with Gertrude. He'll never know the difference.'

146

THIRTEEN

TWO OR THREE DAYS LATER, JAMES RANG AND DEMANDED TO know what I was doing. He was in a flap. I had no plans, had scarcely seen a soul since Sally's last visit.

'You should come and see a movie with me,' he said.

'What, now?'

'This afternoon. Why not?'

Being unemployed, James often saw movies during the day. In addition to sporadic handouts from his parents, he was on an unspecified government pension for those unfit to work. This was, he intimated, only until he got back on his feet. The nature of his disability was unclear, as was what 'back on his feet' could entail for a man like James; it was impossible to imagine him doing anything more worldly than drinking cask wine in the afternoon or lolling on his mattress, reading *I, Claudius*. I, on the other hand — possibly owing to some vestigial Protestant suspicion of leisure — had always felt uneasy about going to the cinema during the day, and made excuses about having chores to do before my shift at the restaurant that night.

But James would have none of it. 'Meet me at the Valhalla at two o'clock, will you.'

The choice of venue sealed it. The Valhalla was an independent

147

cinema in Richmond that played cult horror movies and various other films with what might be termed 'niche appeal'. Although I hadn't yet been introduced to its charms, I had heard that one could purchase Quaaludes from the box office on Sunday nights when a Chinese girl named Muriel was working, and Edward had talked rapturously of seeing *Koyaanisqatsi* there after gobbling a handful of magic mushrooms. Every student house in Melbourne's inner city had its poster of upcoming attractions taped up somewhere, usually on the back of the toilet door. At more than one party I had scanned the lurid advertisements for all-night Alain Delon marathons, weekend Sexploitation festivals, and the Friday-night screenings of *The Rocky Horror Picture Show* (*Free entry for those dressed as Frank N. Furter*).

By the time I arrived at the Valhalla, James had already purchased our tickets. It was raining and the foyer smelled like wet dogs. Scarily cool people stood about smoking. We saw *Blue Velvet*, a film about a young man who gets involved with a gang of nasty psychopaths. In it, Dennis Hopper plays a character called Frank Booth, who — under the influence of a drug he inhales through a mask — beats up a nightclub singer played by the beautiful, doomed Isabella Rossellini; the violence interspersed with garish suburban landscapes. It was unlike anything I had ever seen, and I adored its blend of the horrific and the surreal.

Afterwards James and I wandered up Victoria Street, known as Little Saigon on account of the Vietnamese migrants who had settled in the area during the 1970s. The streets were crowded with people and with stalls selling exotic fruit and vegetables. The air was fragrant with the smells of wet produce. James propelled me through an innocuous doorway and up some red-carpeted stairs to a crowded Vietnamese restaurant called Thy Thy. The place was noisy with chatter and Asian pop music. We sat at a rickety laminate table and drank jasmine tea from small cups.

Nearby on the tiled floor was a colourful shrine festooned with tiny, flickering lights.

While we ate spring rolls I told James about the afternoon with Sally, how she had hidden in my room at Max's arrival.

James waited until a Vietnamese boy, who couldn't have been much older than eight, had cleared away our soy-smeared plates.

'You know, a friend of mine has a room available in a great share house in Carlton. Benny. I think you were with me when I ran into him a few weeks ago in Lygon Street? Great room, very cool people.'

I shook out a toothpick from the plastic canister. 'I have somewhere to live.'

'I know, I know. I thought you might want to meet some other people in town, that's all. Get out a bit more?'

'But I love living at Cairo.'

'You know who else lives at Benny's place?' he asked in the tone of an adult promising an ice-cream to a child. 'Dancing Susan.'

I had, of course, heard of Dancing Susan, who was regarded as one of the most eligible women in the inner city. Dancing Susan — whose ubiquitous first name made the appellation necessary — studied psychology at Melbourne University and was renowned for her intellect, her red hair and her writhing dance moves. Women were scornful of her, but rumours of her attendance at a party were guaranteed to induce vast numbers of men (single or otherwise) to show up.

'It's for your own good, Tom. You need a girlfriend. A handsome boy like you.'

'You're being dramatic, James.'

'And definitely not Sally Cheever.'

I blushed and muttered something intended to sound suitably dismissive.

James leaned forwards. His eyes were earnest. 'I noticed the way you trembled after dancing with her that day, Tom. I know how tragic it can be to fall in love with the wrong person. The pain that person can inflict on you. You imagine what it would be like to be with them, the ways you could complement each other. The future you might have together.'

Although I would never admit such a thing to James, I knew he was right. Ever since the day when we had danced, Sally had — there was no other word for it — haunted me. It was as if, from some minor but alluring ingredients (the undulations of her waist under my palm, the smell of her neck, her womanly thigh pressed to mine), I hoped to fashion a lover more tangible than that of mere fantasy.

'Why are you going on about this?' I said, having pondered for a few seconds the best tone with which to repel this accusation.

'You heard about the duel, didn't you?' he asked.

I nodded, laughing. I had indeed heard about Max challenging some man to a duel over a perceived flirtation with Sally but I always assumed it was a tall story to be filed alongside Max's claim of having had a camel as a pet when he was a boy.

'It's not funny, Tom. Max was wild over it. If the guy had shown up, Max would have shot him. Assuming he wasn't killed himself, I suppose.'

'He actually had a gun?'

'Well, you can't have a game of Paper, Scissors, Rock over a woman. God knows where he got the pistol from, though. Only a small gun, but still. We waited for an hour at dawn in some park by the river over in Fairfield.'

'You were there?'

James dismissed my incredulous query with a curt wave of his hand. 'It's a long story. I don't want to talk about it. The whole thing was insane.'

'Was this the guy who got Sally pregnant?'

James looked mortified. 'Who told you that?'

'You did. Late one night at your place.'

'Christ. I did? Well, don't tell a soul about it or we'll all be in deep trouble, Sally especially.'

Our bowls of noodle soup arrived and we ate without talking. When he had finished, James rested his chin on his steepled fingers to scrutinise me. 'Speaking of insane things. They told you, didn't they?'

I wiped my mouth. 'Told me what?'

'Don't lie. The' — he dropped his voice to a whisper — 'the *Dora thing*.'

I was relieved the conversation had moved on from Sally Cheever, albeit to the subject of my potential participation in the heist of a painting by the twentieth century's most famous artist.

'He told me you were involved,' I pointed out.

'Only by default, because I introduced them to Tamsin and her brother. Those Bolshevik twins. But you shouldn't get roped into it. Look, the whole thing is crazy. Max is wonderful but, you know, very unpredictable. He has these ideas. He thinks he can pull off these grand schemes. The less you know about, um … Dora, the better.'

I shrugged, endeavouring to make light of James's plea. 'Max said he'd kill me if I breathed a word of the plan to anyone.' I said this in the most jocular tone I could muster, hoping to summon a corroborating dismissal of the threat. But my comment elicited nothing more than an almost imperceptible arching of James's eyebrows, as if I had advised him that Max had purchased an extravagant pair of shoes.

'Look, they're all mad,' he said. 'Tamsin's brother, George, is totally unstable. And Tamsin's great hero is Valerie Solanas, for God's sake. Heroine, I should say, or she'd probably try to shoot *me*. Speaking of which, Edward and Gertrude are both junkies, and they have to do an exact copy of this famous painting. You can't trust junkies to do anything. Except be junkies.'

This revelation was presumably intended to scare me away from Edward and Gertrude but only piqued my interest further. 'They're heroin addicts?'

'The constant shortage of money, the mysterious phone calls, their unique ability to fall asleep *standing up*? Why do you think they both look so sick all the time?'

'Gertrude told me she had a serious illness. She said she's been having tests at the Alfred Hospital ...'

'Ah, yes. The Countess of Groan.'

'In fact, I was going to drive her there last week.'

'And did you?'

'Well, no.'

'Why not?'

I struggled to find an answer to James's question. I had agreed to pick Gertrude up that morning, but when I arrived to drive her to hospital, she had no recollection of our arrangement. When I reminded her she suddenly recalled that the specialist had moved the appointment forwards. She had been there the previous day, she explained, and was now waiting on the test results. At the time I'd found it odd but hardly sinister. Now I was more perplexed.

'Have they asked you for money yet?' James said.

'No.'

'They will. But don't lend them a cent — you'll never get it back. It's not your fault. Plenty have been fooled, doctors included. Gertrude has been on the brink of death for *at least* the past ten years. Maybe longer. We even held a benefit concert for her a few years ago to help with her treatment. All these dreadful punk bands they love like the Wreckery and I Spit on Your Gravy played. But she lives on. She'll outlive us all. Her disease is that one where you think you're sick, but don't have anything wrong with you.

152

Old Sigmund Freud would have a field day at their place, write a book about the pair of them. Her only real problem is heroin, and far too much of it. I'm no saint, but still …'

I recalled that a week or so earlier I had seen Edward sitting on a bench in Murchison Square, a small park a few streets away from Cairo. He'd failed to notice me even though he was looking around anxiously. When I was still a hundred metres away, he leaped up and strode across to a comically beaten-up Holden that had squawked to a halt nearby. Edward got into the car but, instead of it setting off, he and the driver conferred for no longer than a minute before he emerged from the car and stalked off, with his characteristic tilt, in the opposite direction to me. Normally I would have called out, but there was something in his hurried, nervy manner (which I have since come to think of as Edwardian) that made me keep my mouth closed. The car chugged away, trailing blue exhaust smoke, and it was only now, sitting in a Vietnamese restaurant with James, that I realised I had witnessed an actual drug deal.

James called for the bill by squiggling in the air with an imaginary pen. 'It's not too late, Tom.'

I paused, marooned between the present and my memory of what I'd seen at the park, both of which were faintly unreal. 'What?'

'To get out of it. Get away from them. From all of us. You know what the poet Shelley said about Cairo, don't you?'

'No. What?'

He held my gaze, as if desperate to imprint on my memory what he was about to say. '*If there be a place of more beautiful and ruinous charms, then I am yet to hear of it. I shall be fortunate to survive it.*'

FOURTEEN

I DUCKED BENEATH LOW-HANGING BRANCHES INTO CAIRO'S front garden a week or so later, only to be startled by Mr Orlovsky, who lumbered from the soggy undergrowth with a grunt of recognition. Although he affected the manner of one pleasantly surprised by our encounter, it was clear he had been waiting for someone to accost in this manner.

'Ah,' he roared. 'Tom. How-how-how are you?'

'Very well, thanks. And you?'

'Oh, fine, fine. Cleaning out the old magazine collection. Blah-blah-blah blasted day, eh?'

Like a meteorite sailing perilously close to Earth, a morsel of Mr Orlovsky's lunch flew past my face. I stepped back, almost tripped. I had just returned from Sunday lunch with Uncle Mike and Jane, and I was not in the mood for one of Mr Orlovsky's lengthy dissertations on the likelihood of rain.

'Yes,' I agreed. 'Very cold.'

I endeavoured to manoeuvre around him, but the old-timer was alert to my tricks. Under the guise of flailing with his cane towards a flower or plant in the undergrowth that had snared his geriatric interest, he barred my only avenue of escape.

These attempts of mine to truncate our encounters and his sly methods of entrapping me had, over the months, become part of our routine. While he was thus occupied, however, the male half of the New Zealand couple flitted by like a ghost without uttering a word to either of us, and Mr Orlovsky, having missed his chance, gazed after him with dismay before turning his attention back to me.

'Terror-terror-terror terrible about those heroin people, isn't it? To be caught in that way.'

I thought of Edward and Gertrude. 'What?'

'That-that-that that's why you don't want to fight them. Ruthless bunch.'

'I'm sorry, Mr Orlovsky. What do you mean?'

'Your Orientals!'

He was making even less sense than usual. From the far side of the garden I heard the snick of the New Zealander's door closing. I had never seen him talk to anyone. No one in the block — not even little stickybeak Eve — knew his name or that of his wife. To remain invisible to those who would torment you is an enviable talent.

'Go-go-go going to hang them tomorrow, you know.'

'*What?* Hang who?'

'Bar-bar-bar Barlow and whatshisname … Chambers.'

Then I understood. Two Australian men caught in Malaysia for drug trafficking had been on death row for some time, and evidently they were to be executed, despite appeals from the Australian government. The case — with its potent themes of drug running and innocents abroad, combined with a high-minded suspicion of our barbarous neighbours — had gripped the imagination of the nation over recent months.

After several more minutes of baffling conversation I managed to escape Mr Orlovsky's clutches. Upstairs, I was delighted to find Sally waiting outside my apartment. I had been busy the past few days at work and hadn't seen her for over a week. She was cheerful and excited. She smelled clean and scrubbed, as if she had recently stepped from a late-afternoon bath.

'I'm so pleased you're back,' she said, pecking me on the cheek. 'I was about to go home again. Max is staying with a relative of Edward's in the country for the weekend to finish off some part of his score.'

As I opened the door to let us inside, I told her about my lunch with Mike and Jane. But Sally barely registered anything I said, even muttering, 'That sounds nice,' when I told her about the dreadful half-cooked snapper I'd been obliged to eat.

'Tom,' she said, once we had divested ourselves of coats and scarves and hung them in the hallway. 'I'm sorry, but I have an ulterior motive for dropping by this afternoon.'

'Oh?'

'Do you mind if I turn the TV on?'

Max and Sally's television had been broken the whole time I had known them. My own was tiny and so ancient that it required dextrous manipulation of the antenna to receive a decent picture.

I crouched to switch it on. 'What channel?'

'ABC.'

I fiddled with the dials. Before I could ask what she was so interested in watching, I recognised the opening drum riff of *Countdown*, a pop-music program that had been screening on Sunday evenings for so many years that its introductory theme was encoded into the aural DNA of any Australian under the age of forty.

It was six o'clock: tens of thousands of teenagers across the country would be sitting down for their weekly dose of top-ten video hits and garbled interviews with unlikely role models. Max had been asked to perform on *Countdown* during his months of fame, but he disapproved heartily of the show and its inept but loveable host, Ian 'Molly' Meldrum, whom he referred to as The Cretin.

To the accompaniment of the screaming teenage girls that made up *Countdown*'s studio audience, I went to the kitchen to make tea. While waiting for the kettle to boil, I observed Sally from the doorway.

As so often, she had arranged herself on my green sofa with her legs tucked up beneath her, chin resting in one cupped palm. She brushed hair from her forehead and reached down to scratch her calf, before turning to me with a smile so delightful I could barely stand it.

'I remember you,' she said.

'Pardon?' I said, startled to have been caught out so flagrantly admiring her.

'During summer, right before we first met. I saw you in Rhumbarella's that morning. You were watching me, like now. This handsome boy I'd never seen before. I was flattered. Look at you, you're *blushing*.'

'I don't remember.'

Sally reached for her tobacco and set about rolling herself a cigarette. 'You're not like most of the people around here. Not trying to be someone else. You should be proud of that. Try to stay that way.'

How little she knew of me. She turned her attention to her cigarette, and in that instant I understood love as a symptom for which the only cure was love itself, a riddle from which there was no escape.

The *Countdown* voiceover guy had by this time announced the line-up for the next hour: Madonna, Wa Wa Nee and Pseudo Echo, among others. The hormonally charged audience screamed and whistled. The kettle boiled, and when I re-emerged with a pot of fresh tea, the opening act was underway.

Sally clapped with delight and pointed at the television. 'Oh. Look.'

On the screen, a female singer danced jerkily amid plumes of dry ice and flickering lights; a synthesiser player with a sculptural hairdo pressed his keys and pouted. The camera zoomed and weaved. My television screen was so small that the band members resembled a family of robots fighting their way out of a burning box.

'It's the Smiling Assassins,' Sally said. 'I was their singer once. In fact, I worked on an early version of this song. *Silent Dreams*.'

I recalled Max recounting how he had saved Sally from this fate. Although I was not au fait with current trends in pop music, the Smiling Assassins didn't seem to have much to distinguish them from any other pop group doing the rounds — theatrical gestures, androgyny, lightweight choruses sung with joyless insouciance. (The band, incidentally, was misnamed: there were few smiles or ruthless tendencies in evidence.)

Sally was excited to see her former band on national television, and when the song had finished she asked for my opinion of them. Caught on the hop, I told her the Smiling Assassins were great.

'Oh, you're so sweet. They're not that good, but thanks for saying so.'

'They're no worse than, well, any of the other stuff on *Countdown*.'

'I do have a soft spot for Madonna, but don't ever tell Max I said that. I'd be excommunicated. Max loathes the Smiling Assassins. I can't believe they got a record out after all these years. And they're doing a national tour! Nick would be so rapt. I had a lot of fun with those guys.' She sipped her tea, put the cup back on the saucer with a grimace. 'You don't have champagne, by any chance?'

'No, but I might have some wine.'

She waved away my offer and stood. 'We need champagne. We

159

should toast the Smiling Assassins. I owe it to them: they were good to me. We've got some at our place. I'll go and get it.'

Before I could say anything she dashed out, and returned with a bottle wedged under her arm. It had begun to rain. Her hair was damp and her cheeks glowed as if burnished by the cold night air. It was hard not to be swept up in her excitement as she wrenched off the cork and filled two glasses.

'To the Smiling Assassins,' she said, tapping her glass against mine.

I laughed. 'Long may they reign.'

We raised our glasses and drank. Bubbles tickled my nose. With her palm hot at the back of my neck, Sally drew me towards her and kissed me, this time on my mouth.

Spending a night with the woman you have for some time desired is a frightening experience. Although not a virgin (a fierce and rather large girl called Marlene had seen to that one night behind the clubhouse at Dunley Oval), I was woefully unschooled when it came to the opposite sex.

Sally was patient with me, kind, unguarded. She made love with wordless ferocity. She had a thumb-sized birthmark on her hip in the shape of a fish. At times she sighed with what sounded like surprise.

Many hours later, she rose in the dawn light as birds chirruped outside my window. There is a sharp, joyful sadness in watching a woman with whom one has spent such intimate hours get dressed; her shrugging into sweaters, running a hand through tousled hair, the way she swivels her skirt around her hips. It is when the fire is reduced to handfuls of private ash, perhaps more than any other time, that a lover is most blatantly revealed.

She told me we could never do this again, that no one must ever know. We had done a most unwise and dangerous thing. She forbade me from coming around for at least a week and said

160

she wouldn't return to my apartment. I agreed, of course. Yes, anything. 'Nobody can know,' she said again. 'Max will kill us, I'm serious.' I listened to her tender footfall, the squeak of the loose floorboard in my hall, the click of my front door closing.

And then I listened some more, imagined her (shoes in hand) creeping along the walkway to her apartment, a glance over her shoulder, the key in the lock, gone.

But I kept listening, in case she should change her mind and return.

Despite her warnings we managed to steal a few more times together in the next week or so. The pattern was the same each time. There would come a knock at my door at obscure times — ten in the morning, four in the afternoon — and I would open it to find Sally there, eyes shining. 'Max will be out for a few hours,' she would say as she slipped inside, taking off her coat.

It was on one of these visits that I made the mistake of asking her what we were going to do. We were lounging in my bed, naked, awash in the peculiar melancholy of those whose desire has been sated. The day was nearly over, and the light was fading. Soon it would be dark, and I would have to leave for work, and Sally would go back to her apartment and tell Max whatever it was she told him of her day, of where she had been.

Without bothering to cover herself, Sally walked over to the armchair where she had slung her jacket. She scrabbled around in a pocket for her tobacco.

I waited for her to answer and then, thinking she hadn't heard me, I opened my mouth to ask her again.

She coughed as if to forestall my query. 'Don't ask me again. Not now.'

I sat up, filled with the dread that arises from asking a question

161

to which one is unwilling to know the answer. But I couldn't help myself. 'Then when?'

She sat in the armchair, legs crossed, luxuriating in her nakedness, and I understood I would never again witness anything so wonderful as long as I lived. Her cigarette smoke trailed upwards, and her watch glinted in the pale afternoon light. She observed me for a long time. For a minute it seemed she was preparing to reveal something serious — a secret, perhaps — but instead she said, 'You're nice, you know that? I read somewhere that writers are liable to become corrupt.'

I didn't know what to say.

'Don't become like them. *Us*. Don't become like us.'

There was an uncomfortable silence — charged with sorrow, desire's inevitable twin.

She rolled her cigarette, raising her eyes to mine as she licked the gummed edge of the paper. 'I know that we're not supposed to talk about it, but I'm glad you're helping with … you know. It makes me feel safer, somehow. And it'll be so great in France. Imagine it. All of us there, eating baguettes. The house looks amazing, doesn't it?'

Aside from the chat with James after seeing *Blue Velvet*, none of us ever talked in any explicit fashion about the proposed theft of the *Weeping Woman*. In some ways it was as if the conversation had never happened; in other ways, that afternoon was on a continuous loop in my mind. Certain phrases returned to me, especially when I was attempting to sleep at night; they floated up like phantasms through the darkness.

Now and again, we did, however, discuss our proposed life in Europe, details of which had begun to come into focus. While Edward and Gertrude went to live in Berlin, James, Max, Sally and I would live in a house owned by Max's Uncle Carl. His father's older brother had bought the fourteenth-century farmhouse five years earlier but had only lived there for six months before deciding a life in the French countryside was not for him, whereupon he decamped to New York. The place was empty, and we were welcome to live there if we took on the responsibility of undertaking minor repairs and tidying up the grounds.

Max had once produced from his wallet a crumpled photograph of the farmhouse (ramshackle flower garden, shuttered windows, woman in a white dress standing at frame's edge shading her eyes), and I at once understood the dream into which I had been co-opted. The place was shimmeringly beautiful and the tantalising lack of detail — not only in the photo but also in anyone's specific knowledge of the property — encouraged us to embellish the fantasy with our own elements. In those blank spaces we built an artists' studio in the large barn on the property; dreamed up a grapevine arbour under which a table groaned with plates of food and bottles of red wine; conjured a nearby creek in which we might swim; and whiled away summer afternoons, trembling with creativity.

Over the months, the farmhouse assumed a place in the halls of my imagination more akin to a memory than a wish. The rational part of me didn't believe the plan to take the *Weeping Woman* would ever be enacted, but this vague but persistent assumption was overwhelmed by my constant brooding over our exotic life in Europe until my participation in the heist became a fait accompli. It was as if I had agreed to it behind my own back.

'I have to go,' Sally said, squashing her cigarette out in an ashtray and bending to collect her clothes. 'We can't do this again, Tom.'

'That's what you said last time. And the time before that.'

'This time I'm serious,' she said, and I understood that she was.

Unable to speak, I nodded and watched her dress. Sally Cheever: I loved her from the time I first saw her, and for the rest of my life, but I loved her most intensely on that afternoon. And, perhaps

163

more naively, on that day — despite what she said — I believed she loved me back.

The visits from Sally stopped, as she said they must. It was no great surprise, but I was wounded and terribly sad. The first flush of love is like a nostalgia for the present; we know, on some molecular level, that it cannot be repeated. The tragedy is that one can never calculate such instances until one knows there will be no more of them.

FIFTEEN

A FEW DAYS LATER I RAN INTO JAMES AT THE CORNER OF Gertrude and Nicholson streets. I had been to see a movie in the city and decided to walk home and get some air rather than catching a tram. James was heading in the opposite direction, towards Carlton Gardens. It was a grim evening, the clouds low and threatening. He looked embarrassed to see me. We chatted briefly, each of us huddled under our respective umbrellas. I told him that I had been to see *The Hitcher*.

'What's that?'

'A movie.'

'What about?'

He listened without interest as I recounted the plot of the film, which concerned a sociopathic hitchhiker who frames an innocent man. It has always been a childish weakness of mine, this tedious relating of films my listener has not yet seen.

'Right,' interrupted James. 'I see. That sounds pretty ... *violent*.'

'Well, it's about a serial killer.'

A tram lumbered around the bend, like a thick-set man angling through a tight spot. Its windows were fogged with the breath of those inside. Gloomy faces stared out. I imagined what they saw — a wet and dismal street corner, two men cowering under umbrellas, the jaundiced glow of a streetlight.

'Max tells me you've been down in the dumps these past few weeks?' James said.

I started. 'What? But I've hardly seen him.'

He eyed me warily from beneath his soggy fringe. 'Drifting around the place. He thinks it's over a woman. Then again, he thinks everything is about women. I hope you're not doing anything dumb?'

I thought it judicious to refrain from offering any response, and instead muttered about getting out of the rain.

'Why don't you come with me?' he said. 'There's a good chance of finding an eligible lady where I'm heading.'

I prevaricated but, as usual, James talked me into walking with him. I figured the company would do me good. Besides, it delayed my return to Cairo, where I would have nothing to do other than brood over the nights Sally and I had spent together. I feared my untreated feelings for her were festering into emotions altogether less pleasant; I listened when I thought she might have been walking past and lay awake at night wondering if she were lying awake thinking of me. I didn't want an *eligible lady*, as James had so crudely put it; I wanted Sally.

'Where are we going?' I asked when we had crossed Nicholson Street.

He stopped. 'Can you keep a secret?'

'You know I can.'

'To an AA meeting,' James whispered, although there was not a soul (certainly none who cared) in earshot.

'What's that?'

He chuckled and set off walking. 'Ah, yes. A nice country boy like you wouldn't know about these things. Alcoholics Anonymous.'

I stopped in my tracks. 'What? I thought we were going to a bar or a party.'

James grabbed my elbow and eased me onwards. 'God, no. Listen, AA meetings are absolutely full of lonely women. Lots of failed marriages and so on. And most of the men who go along to these places are complete Neanderthals. Jailbirds and the like. I was at a meeting once, years ago now, and saw that fat grub who used to host that game show, the one with the ponytail. What's his name? Edward used to watch it all the time, claimed it was rigged, which it probably was. Had a spinning wheel, a woman in evening wear, even though it was screened in the middle of the afternoon ...'

'Wheel of Fortune.'

'God help us. So you're already streets ahead if you don't have some sort of sexually transmitted disease or a tattoo of barbed wire around your neck. In the kingdom of the blind, the one-eyed man is king, right? Half those people only go to, you know, pick up.'

'Are you serious?'

'If there is one thing women love even more than a troubled man, it's a troubled man who is trying to improve himself.'

'I don't know about this, James. I might go home. I'm pretty exhausted.'

'And let's face it, they're complete *soaks*, so their judgement isn't spot on, either.'

'Thanks for the vote of confidence. Besides, I'm not an alcoholic.'

With one hand, James pinched his worn velvet jacket tighter around his torso. He scowled when a bitter wind buffeted us as we walked alongside the Carlton Gardens, bringing with it the scent of rotting leaves and chlorine from the fountain.

'That doesn't matter,' he yelled above an ambulance careering out of nearby St Vincent's Hospital with its siren whooping. 'No one will know. It's not as if they give you a breath test before letting you in. Half of them aren't even true alcoholics; they're stupid, boring people who got drunk three weekends in a row and love the idea of having a distinguishing problem. It's a badge of identity. Everyone wants to be a victim these days. It's part of the culture. People don't want to be better than the next person; they want to be *worse*. Honestly, Tom. Come on. It'll be fun.'

'How long have you been doing this?'

'Oh, years, I guess.' He hesitated. 'My psychiatrist recommended meetings as a way of coming to terms with myself. After I, you know, tried to do away with myself. And it was useful for a while. Made me see there were people far worse off than me. Sometimes it helps to talk. Dispels the loneliness. That's good, isn't it?'

James, who was so forthcoming about the personal lives of other people, was notoriously secretive about his own, and I was taken aback by his unexpected candour.

'But aren't you supposed to stop drinking there?' I asked.

'Well, I've never been drunk *at* a meeting,' he said, scandalised that I should think him capable of such blasphemy.

I stopped walking. 'James, I'm serious. I'm going home. I'll see you later.'

But he was reluctant for us to part company. He grabbed my arm. 'Alright, then. Let's go and get a coffee.'

I relented and we walked back through the drizzle to Cafe Rhumbarella. The waiters milled around the bar, preening and gossiping. We took a table at the rear and ordered drinks. The cafe was only half full, but snug. The coffee machine hissed; plates clattered. From our position, I could see through the large front window to the rain-streaked street outside, where trams and cars passed by like undersea machines prowling an aquarium floor.

We didn't speak until we had sipped from our coffee and lit cigarettes. Only when these two rituals had been enacted, it seemed, had we truly settled in. James nibbled at a fingernail. A bead of rainwater trembled at his jaw.

'I'm sorry,' he said after several minutes, 'I shouldn't have even mentioned that to you. It was stupid of me. Very inappropriate. But please, don't tell anyone I still go there. Max and Edward would laugh me out of town. I couldn't stand it. I …'

'What?'

'I'm scared.'

'Scared of what?'

He rubbed a hand over his face, chewed on his lower lip. He looked tormented, but explained no further. 'Nothing. It's nothing.'

Although perturbed by his behaviour, I didn't press him further. I went to the bathroom. On the wall above the toilet was scrawled a crude joke — *Why did they have coke on board challenger?? Because they couldn't get 7-up* — under which was written, in a different hand: *it was a CIA Plot.*

When I rejoined him, James was lost in thought, almost unaware of my presence. He stared forlornly over my shoulder, and I realised it was from this table that I had admired Sally all those months ago as she sat reading and smoking. It occurred to me, quite unbidden, that James was in love with her and had perhaps been so afflicted for many years. This thought prompted in me a poisonous jolt of jealousy. I recalled the afternoon Sally and I had danced together, when he had been so sullen. Was that why he had been so eager to warn me away from her?

'Never mind,' he said after a few minutes, as if in response to my unspoken thoughts. 'Shall we get a bottle of wine?'

'Are you sure?'

'Oh, I'm sure.'

James was an excellent drinking companion, and I reeled home two or three hours later, giggling to myself all the way at how the night had developed. As usual since the time Sally and I had spent together, my heart thudded with anticipation at the

169

thought that, somehow, she had changed her mind and found her way into my apartment to wait for me.

It took numerous attempts to fit my key into the lock and get inside, and when I did, I was startled to find Max sitting in my armchair.

'Where the hell have you been?' he demanded. 'I've been waiting for hours.'

My keys fell from my hand and clattered to the wooden floor. 'Max, I —'

'Hush!' He looked crazed, unkempt; the very picture of a cuckold.

I had no idea how he'd got inside. As he rose and dashed over to me, I stepped backwards, steeled myself for a blow. None came. Perhaps he had a knife?

Max closed my front door and gripped me tight above my elbow. 'We're doing it tomorrow. Early.'

All I could think of was the story of the ridiculous duel — the misty Yarra River at dawn, a brace of pistols, death. I could barely speak. 'What?'

'We're liberating Dora. In the morning.' He mimed loosening a screw right next to my head. 'Tamsin and George are there *as we speak*.'

It began to sink in. The theft. Tomorrow. I laughed with relief, with fear and with astonishment.

SIXTEEN

THE NATIONAL GALLERY OF VICTORIA IS A RECTANGULAR, Stalinist bunker covering three or four blocks on St Kilda Road, one of Melbourne's widest and leafiest thoroughfares south of the Yarra River. On the opposite side of the road, several hundred metres from the vast arched entrance, is the Queen Victoria Gardens' floral clock — which is right next to where Max and I were parked on that Sunday morning in August, ten minutes after opening time.

Inside the gallery, figures were moving behind the large water wall, which attracted children as a magnet did iron filings. The two large, shallow pools of water in front of the building threw their shimmering aquatic designs onto the exterior's grey stone walls. I was dreadfully hungover. My mouth was gummed up. I was about to participate in the heist of a major twentieth-century artwork. What the hell was I thinking?

Max, however, was composed. He cleaned his fingernails with the teeth of a key, looking up every now and then to scan the clumps of people milling about on the gallery forecourt. He hummed to himself. At my apartment the night before he had reiterated how calm we needed to be at all times. 'Two people going out for a drive somewhere. Nothing to be nervous about. Tamsin and George are taking all the risk. As soon as I give the word, start the car and we'll wheel around to the front of the gallery. Then the twins will hop in the back seat and we'll be off to Edward's place. Remember to drive very carefully. We don't want to draw attention to ourselves.'

My skin felt tender, goose-bumped, horribly alive. I was sweating, despite the cold. Surely, I thought, everyone passing by — any jogger, dog-walker, morning stroller — must realise what we were up to? Two men sitting in a car at twelve minutes past ten on a Sunday morning?

In the rear-vision mirror I spotted a young man with a trim moustache loitering two cars behind, *just standing there* with his hands in his trouser pockets. A policeman, it must be. I cursed my stupidity, my blind faith, my greed. I had spent most of the previous night awake, wondering whether I shouldn't sneak away before dawn, never to return to Cairo again. I had rehearsed countless variations of disaster in my imagination: the car wouldn't start; Tamsin and George would be detained as they tried to get in; the police would pull us over before we'd even crossed the bridge. Stealing a Picasso painting from a major gallery to sell it off to a bunch of international criminals, one of whom was named Mr Crisp. The kind of people who shot dogs. *What the hell was I thinking?*

The answer to that question was that I had been thinking about Sally. Or, rather, she was the persistent soundtrack to which every action of mine had become an accompaniment. If my participation in the ridiculous plan was ever in doubt, her pleasure at my involvement had convinced me. Although we had hardly spoken since our few (all too few) times together, she had stood in the garden of Cairo to see us on our way earlier that morning. I detected no change whatsoever in her demeanour until Max (who, thankfully, showed no sign of suspecting anything) charged off to the car, and she and I were alone. I felt terrified — of her, of what I had become involved in. Then she grasped my hand, reached up to kiss me on the mouth, murmured 'Good luck' and ran back up the stairs. A glance, a few words. On lesser ephemera have men been emboldened to commit more foolish acts.

I remembered a question I had been meaning to ask Max for some time. 'You know those guys you told me about who stole the *Mona Lisa*?'

'Hmm?'

'Did they get away with it?'

'Sort of.'

'What does that mean?'

'They had it for a couple of years, then tried to sell it to an Italian gallery.'

'And got caught?'

'Only because they were very stupid.'

'Did they go to jail?'

A pause. 'Yes.'

Before I could digest the implications of this, Max whacked my thigh with the back of his hand. 'There they are. Quick! Start the car.'

I fiddled with the ignition but accidentally turned on the windscreen wipers. Due to the prohibitions of his much-vaunted 'need-to-know basis', Max had not described Tamsin to me in great detail, but he had told me enough ('Short, surly, feels she's letting the sisterhood down because she's not a lesbian') because I spotted her instantly on the footpath across the road. The very image of a Bolshevik art student, she was wearing Doc Marten boots and a man's grey overcoat. A chap I assumed was her brother hovered behind her, dressed similarly.

Trembling all over, I started the car, pulled out into the light traffic and completed a stately circuit of the large block. Like a dog on the scent, Max sat forwards in his seat, both hands perched on the dashboard in front of him.

'Easy does it,' he was saying. 'I think she's spotted us. Yes. Alright. Park behind that white truck. But keep the engine running.'

It all went remarkably smoothly. I pulled over in front of Tamsin and George, behind the ice-cream van Max had indicated. He opened the back door and the siblings slid into the car. I waited for a break in the traffic, then drove off. The steering wheel was slippery under my sweating grip. No one said a word until we crossed Princes Bridge, on the south side of the city centre. I was amazed any of us managed to breathe.

Without turning around, Max asked how it went. For the first time, his voice betrayed a hint of nervousness.

In the rear-vision mirror I saw Tamsin smirk at her brother. She had short, black hair and grubby eyes.

'That was a piece of cake,' she said in a slight English accent. 'Those fat old windbags won't know what hit them. I need a bloody cigarette. You got one?'

James, who knew the twins reasonably well, later told me that Tamsin was herself a struggling painter who lived in a draughty, dilapidated house in North Fitzroy with her brother and two other artists. George was a conceptual artist who had worked briefly at Channel Ten in some junior administrative capacity before being fired for smoking a joint in the bathroom. The pair were forever railing against the powers that denied them funding and obliged them to live a pauper's existence or — worse — work a straight job to make ends meet.

We approached the inevitable snarl of traffic around Flinders Street Station. A busker in a wheelchair played the bagpipes amid the crowds on the famous corner outside the main entrance. A large group of punks, complete with mohawks and leather jackets festooned with studs and badges, gathered on the steps beneath the timetable clocks.

With difficulty, Tamsin eased the painting out from beneath her large overcoat. I felt a surge of fear at the sight — glimpsed in the mirror — of the plain paper in which she had wrapped it. I knew the painting was not large, but it was much smaller than I had envisaged, hardly bigger than a tea towel.

I kept checking the rear-vision mirror for police cars and flashing lights, expecting at any second the windscreen to be stove in or an undercover cop to dive — *Starsky and Hutch*-style — across the Mercedes' dirty bonnet. Nothing.

We cruised unmolested up Swanston Street, past Chat 'n' Chew (the seedy cafe where, over a plate of ancient chips and a couple of steamed dim sims, Max had further expounded to me his theory of benign dictatorship), past the town hall. No one in the car spoke. Tamsin slouched in the back seat and smoked. George stared through the window, to all appearances unperturbed.

At a red light at the corner of Lonsdale Street, they hopped out leaving the painting lying flat on the back seat in its paper wrapping. This must have been part of the arrangement all along because Max evinced no surprise at their departure.

'OK, guys,' Tamsin muttered before slamming the door. 'Over to you now.'

'Ta-ta,' said George, and he gave a curt wave.

We drove on to Edward and Gertrude's warehouse. As soon as we had parked in the empty lot out the back, Max put his hand on mine to prevent me undoing my seatbelt. 'You drive home. I'll take it upstairs. And don't breathe a word.'

'I want to see it.'

'That's not part of the plan.'

'I should be able to see it after taking all that risk. Please.'

I was shocked by the uncharacteristic steel in my voice,

and Max hesitated, taken aback by my tone. He glared up at the shuttered warehouse windows, at which, as usual, there was no sign of life. 'Alright,' he said. 'But only for a minute.'

We placed the painting under a bright lamp on Edward and Gertrude's studio workbench, where Max, Edward, Gertrude and I crowded around it in deferential silence. Even Max was lost for words. As soon as it had been unwrapped from its brown paper, Gertrude had examined the canvas edges with white-gloved fingers and pressed her eye almost to the surface. A smell rose from it — of dry paint, of thinner, of something smoky — and it was difficult not to imagine the great man himself (face ascowl, Gitane wedged between meaty fingers) inspecting his handiwork from this very same distance and angle. That dizzying sensation, for me, was almost reward enough for all my anxiety over the theft.

I had seen numerous reproductions of the *Weeping Woman*, but nothing prepared me for the vibrancy of the original when viewed at such close range. The image fairly hummed. Despite the energy of the work, the means of its creation were evident. There was a blob of brown paint under her right eye, a splodge of green on her neck. The lower portion of her green and black hair covered what might have been an angular collar.

During our brief acquaintance Edward had sometimes exasperated me with his hair-splitting ruminations on colour (not to mention the lengthy explanations on their origins and manufacture) but, upon seeing the *Weeping Woman*, I understood at once the need for subtle and precise gradations of hue and tone. Ordinary terms were hopelessly inadequate. Here I saw the difference between cadmium green, olive green, sap green, leaf green, sea green. The urge to touch the painting was almost

176

irresistible — to finger the canvas where once Picasso himself had — but we had all been warned in advance not to do so. Only Gertrude would handle the work as part of the forgery process.

Gertrude turned the canvas over. The work looked in remarkably good condition, perhaps owing to its having been stored in galleries since its creation, rather than sitting around in attics or the like. On the bottom rung of the frame was a faded purple stamp that read 10F. There was a smudge of pale-green paint on the top left, in addition to a number of tiny holes where screws must have been used to fix the work to a variety of frames. Gertrude was delighted because none of these marks was difficult to replicate; the painting wasn't even signed. Like a pair of improbable generals poring over a garish map in preparation for an assault, she and Edward began to mutter and point out other details of the painting that caught their eye.

'Interesting, that mark there,' Gertrude said. 'And the splodgy way the paint has been applied next to her hair.'

'Hmm. It looks to me as if the window was originally larger. And look at the line of her nose.'

Now all business, Gertrude didn't respond. She picked up a comically large magnifying glass and hunched over the painting. She was more alert than I had ever seen her, as if galvanised by the challenge of replicating this work.

Since learning they were heroin addicts, I had become adept at discerning Gertrude's and Edward's moods — whether listless and impatient or good-humoured and focused — and how they could be determined by the amount of time that had lapsed since their latest hit. Today they were rather chipper and, sure enough, I glimpsed a smear of blood in the scabby crook of Gertrude's left elbow when she reached out for an exercise book, which was so battered it was held together with sticky tape.

Oblivious to my and Max's presence, she and Edward flicked

177

through this book, a handwritten manual full of sketches, notes and chemical formulae.

I returned home, leaving Max at the warehouse. It was still only midday. Too fearful to leave my apartment but unable to think of how else to spend my time, I passed the afternoon in an agitated state, prowling the confines of my tiny rooms, listening to the radio for news of the theft. There was no mention of it on any bulletin. The day dragged on. The sound of anyone entering the grounds of Cairo invoked in me a paralysing terror in which I saw (in lurid technicolour) my arrest, the trial, jail, my mother's tears. At least I could write a novel about it. My life story? The thinly veiled autobiographical novel had always been to me a pathetic specimen, but tales have been built on flimsier foundations.

There was nothing about it on the six o'clock television news. It was impossible the gallery didn't know the *Weeping Woman* — their costly new acquisition — was gone. I had no appetite but managed instead to gulp a large glass of whisky that only made me nauseated. I tried to read but words on a page slithered about like worms. I played Sally's Smiths album but Morrissey's plaintive wailing got on my nerves. Eventually, I showered and went to bed early. Gripped alternately by panic and exhilaration, I lay awake all night, smoking in the gloom. Hysterical imaginings. Any voices outside were those of the police, the slam of any door that of the fraud-squad van. Wind hissed through the leaves of the peppercorn tree. What sleep I stole was thin as gruel.

The following day, Monday, was a blur. At two o'clock I hovered by the radio to hear the news bulletin. The police had a lead in the ongoing case of the Moonee Ponds killer, an old lady had won a fortune in TattsLotto, an update about the Chernobyl disaster a few months earlier. But nothing about the theft. I realised that somehow, unbelievably, we had gotten away with it.

Of course, the gallery did discover the *Weeping Woman* had been taken, and all hell broke loose. On Monday evening, the gallery's director, Patrick McCaughey, sporting his customary bow tie, was assailed by a ferocious media demanding answers.

It turned out that Tamsin and George had placed a card where the painting usually hung. The gallery attendants assumed the card was an official notification of the painting's removal for curatorial purposes, which is why the alarm wasn't raised for a whole day.

The card bore the initials ACT, an acronym for the (previously unheard of) Australian Cultural Terrorists. Tamsin had also posted a letter to one of the TV stations, in which the ACT demanded a prize be established to fund new Australian work; the theft was still primarily a political act for Tamsin and George. Max was furious at this development: he reasoned (correctly, as it turned out) that if the police suspected artists were behind it — as opposed to ordinary art thieves — there was a good chance they would knock on the door of every artist's studio in town.

There was, however, nothing we could do about that. Mr Crisp was now aware we had the painting and would be expecting it within a week or so. Work on the forgery got underway.

SEVENTEEN

FOR THE NEXT FEW DAYS AND NIGHTS, IN BETWEEN DISHWASHING shifts at the restaurant, I became a mixture of guard and errand boy for Edward and Gertrude, a role I was happy to adopt in exchange for permission to observe them as they worked. I should have been more circumspect about being present during the commission of a crime, but Edward and Gertrude's warehouse exerted an irresistible attraction.

In addition, hanging around the warehouse kept me away from Cairo, where I obsessively listened for Sally's voice, for her footfall, the knock upon my door that never sounded.

No one unconnected with the heist was permitted into the warehouse. James never visited and Max only rarely. Edward had a new exhibition scheduled for the following month, so the rush to finish some paintings was a convenient pretext both for his unavailability and for his paint-stained fingers. Perpetually on the brink of chaos, he and Gertrude scrounged for money and drugs during the day and then painted right through the night.

I fetched takeaway souvlaki and pizza from Lygon Street or cigarettes from the newsagent. I took Buster — who had recovered from his injury — for short walks. Once or twice I was despatched to prise Edward away from the computer game Galaga at Johnny's

Green Room, where he could become entranced for hours while taking a break from mixing pigments.

The theft of the *Weeping Woman* featured daily in the news. Gallery director Patrick McCaughey was bailed up by the press at every opportunity, and I must admit to feeling rather sorry for him. There was much hand-wringing over the flimsy security and the fact the guards, when patrolling after hours, didn't even turn on the lights but merely shone their torches through the cavernous rooms. When McCaughey removed the attendants' chairs to smarten them up, they went on strike. People demanded his resignation. A prominent religious leader wrote to the newspaper, saying it was a relief such an abominable painting was gone. All planes and ships leaving the country were searched, and the minister had the art school turned upside down.

Rather than distracting Edward and Gertrude from the task at hand, the mood of the studio — its freezing air barely ameliorated by an old radiator, the constant threat of arrest, the paltry diet of bread and cigarettes — focused their energy, perhaps in the same way these elements had focused Picasso's. Despite the difficult conditions, the studio was often serene.

As Edward and Gertrude bickered over how best to proceed with this or that element of the forgery, I leafed through their monographs and biographies about Pablo Picasso and regaled them with interesting titbits from Picasso's life: how he'd met Dora Maar in a cafe in 1936, as Hitler was preparing for war; how, although he was by then one of the world's most famous living artists, he was yet to rise to the heights that saw him become the wealthiest artist in history. That year, Picasso was on the verge of great things; idiotically, I believed we were as well. He had remarked that painting wasn't an aesthetic operation but a form of magic designed to mediate between the hostile world and ourselves. Here then, in front of me, was a tangible part of that magic.

Usually dithery and vague, Gertrude adopted the upper hand in her role as the actual forger, with Edward as her grumbling assistant sidelined to mixing pigments, fetching tools and cleaning brushes. While working, Edward developed a set of superstitions he believed assured the success of the enterprise — he despised bananas, for instance, and would not allow one into the warehouse under any circumstances; he had to have a candle lit at all times while work was underway; he would only mix ingredients in a clockwise direction. Gertrude, however, was visibly relaxed and even appeared for the period less encumbered by her various life-threatening ailments.

A paint-spattered radio–cassette player in their studio was almost always on, tuned to local community radio station 3RRR or playing mixed tapes of weird music that was either infuriating or relaxing. It was there that I discovered the dubious delights of bands such as Throbbing Gristle, Foetus, Swans, Einstürzende Neubauten, Sonic Youth and the Birthday Party. In my mind's eye I can still see Edward in his overcoat dabbing at a paint concoction, analysing it from every angle while *I Love Her All the Time* drones on and on in the background.

The flimsy notebook Gertrude and Edward had consulted when we first brought the *Weeping Woman* back to the studio was, in fact, a manual put together by an infamous postwar art forger called Elmyr de Hory, whom Gertrude had befriended when she was a girl.

In the coming days and nights, Gertrude told me more about this de Hory; indeed, what she told me of his life is worthy of its own book and (as I learned later), de Hory was the subject of a biography by Clifford Irving that, in turn, inspired *F for Fake*, a rambling, stream-of-consciousness documentary by Orson Welles.

'I met Elmyr in 1964,' she told me as she worked on the forgery. 'I was only a kid. He was hiding out in Sydney when Interpol became suspicious that certain paintings being passed off in Europe as modernist originals were actually his.

'Anyway, my father met him somehow when he came to Australia and started inviting him around for barbecues, although my mother never liked him. My dad thought of himself as a cultured businessman, you see. He was disappointed when Elmyr left after only a year.'

With his European accent, cravat and monocle, de Hory must have been exceedingly exotic at that time, a migratory bird blown way off-course. The charismatic foreigner befriended the eight-year-old Gertrude and — perhaps recognising in her a talent and ambition commensurate with his own, perhaps merely offloading evidence that could land him in jail — he gave her the notebook, along with a ratty cardboard suitcase stuffed with tools of his trade.

'It's an absolute goldmine of techniques,' Gertrude said one night, as I flipped through the notebook's hundred-odd pages covered with dense scrawl and illustrations. 'Some of it's hard to read but I can understand more than enough to get this done. Recipes for pigments, preparing surfaces, tips for applying paints and ageing canvases. It's incredible information.'

'How come it's in English?'

She shrugged. 'A boyfriend of his wrote it up, I think. Knowing Elmyr, he hoped to make some money out of it one day.'

Deciphering a number of passages, I learned that ink can be made to look aged by mixing it with the same quantity of water and leaving it to evaporate to its original strength; that borate can be used to dry oil grounds; that to make so-called 'fox-marks' (indicative of great age), scrape rust from an old nail onto damp fabric, press it to paper, and seal it in a plastic bag for a week.

'And the best thing of all,' Gertrude went on, 'is that because de Hory was painting in the same era as Picasso, many of the materials he gave me were what Picasso would have used himself.'

In the suitcase was a jumble of horsehair brushes, palette knives encrusted with paint, vials of powdered pigment, jars of spirits, bottles of linseed oil, extra pages of notes, ink-pads, rubber stamps and all manner of art paraphernalia. There were clumps of charcoal, nubs of chalk, tiny pots of mordant or thinner. When it was flung open in front of me, the smell released was earthy and potent and rich. At once I laughed with appreciation of forgery's fabulous allure; it was the wish to pit oneself against the acknowledged artistic genius of the century. All artists enter into ghostly discussion with those who have gone before. No artist has his complete meaning alone, as T.S. Eliot has noted. The challenge to reproduce a Picasso was akin to entering the ring to fight Ali, writing theatre that Shakespeare might watch from the wings, playing for Beethoven. *I am as good as he is,* the aspirant fumes. *Why is he rich and famous while I toil in obscurity?* This was all the more trenchant for Gertrude, who as a woman had struggled for credibility in a world that had so eagerly nurtured the cult of the solitary, anguished male painter: Rothko, Pollock, Caravaggio, van Gogh. Like most forgers, Gertrude's ambitions were not about money; they were about getting even.

'My very own father discouraged me from being an artist,' Gertrude told me another night. 'He mixed with bohemians, but just because you like dogs, it doesn't mean you want your daughter to walk on all fours and bark. He thought it was, I don't know, déclassé. I had to elope with Edward, and we were married at the registry office here in Melbourne. My father was embarrassed when I went to art school, then pleased when I had some success. That all ended, of course. I fell out of fashion a few years ago. That bastard Queel talked Anna into dropping me from her gallery with his French postmodern piffle. My work is too old-fashioned these days. Real painting is pretty much dead now. Edward sometimes does well selling his work, but people have mostly moved on to other things.'

This was at around three a.m., late in the first week we had the painting in our possession. The original *Weeping Woman* was fixed to an easel. Beside it, on its own easel, was the other canvas on which the forgery was being painted. On the workbench were other squares of canvas for daubed experiments in colour and line. In addition, there were books filled with reproductions of Picasso sketchbooks, from which Gertrude hoped to understand the underlying armature, as it were, of the paintings. All were lit by bright lamps.

The forgery was taking shape, but not as fast as we had hoped. Gertrude had promised to complete it within a week, but she had been delayed. Inexplicably, the version on the easel in front of me looked less developed than it had on the previous afternoon. When I mentioned this, Gertrude told me in no uncertain terms not to be ridiculous and to leave matters of such expertise to her.

Although I said no more about it, there were a lot of blank spaces on the canvas and they, along with Edward and Gertrude's lack of urgency, started to irk me. Edward had already spent three hours earlier that night finding heroin (there was some sort of 'drought' on) and, once they had injected it, he and Gertrude wasted more time arguing over who produced Iggy and the Stooges' first album. Edward fossicked through the hundreds of records stacked in green milk crates but was unable to find the record in question to settle the dispute, partly because he kept getting distracted and putting on other albums. 'Oh,' he would say, holding up a cardboard sleeve, 'I haven't heard *Trout Mask Replica* for ages ...'

I was too timid to remind them that the sooner they completed their forgery, the quicker we could offload it, after which they could buy endless supplies of heroin and argue about the personnel of obscure rock albums as much as they wished. I remembered James warning me about them, and I wondered what on earth we would do if the forgery wasn't good enough, or if Anna Donatella's associates didn't come through for some reason. It didn't bear thinking about.

'Art forgery has an illustrious history of its own,' Gertrude went on. 'Who was that guy during the war, Edward? Who did the Vermeers?'

Edward gazed up from the square lid of an ice-cream container he was using as a palette. His mouth was unhinged, his pupils like hawks hovering in the pale sky of his irises. 'Van Meegeren,' he croaked. '*Christ at Emmaus.*'

Gertrude wound a wayward strand of red hair behind her ear. 'That's right. And there's lots more. There's meant to be a few *Mona Lisas* floating around after that was stolen. The art market is full of fakes, you know. I have it on very good authority there's a van Gogh portrait in the gallery right here in Melbourne that's fake. Warhol gets his assistants to run off a few screen prints so he doesn't get his hands dirty. Rodin had a whole army of assistants. Dalí signed *thousands* of blank sheets of paper before anything was even drawn on them. The name on the work is not always the person who made the thing, but it doesn't usually bother people in the least.'

'What happened to this van Meegeren?' I asked.

Gertrude coughed into her fist and muttered.

'What?'

'He was arrested for peddling art to the Nazis, got addicted to morphine, died.'

'Oh. And what about Elmyr de Hory?'

There was an uncomfortable silence. Edward busied himself with his vials of pigment.

'Ah, poor Elmyr. He sort of, ah, died in the 1970s. Of a pill overdose. Suicide, they think.'

Addiction, collaboration with Nazis, suicide. This was not encouraging.

'What are you *doing*, Edward?' Gertrude said. 'I need some purple for her lips. And a bit thinner this time, please.'

'It's violet, actually. And I'm looking for it. Give me a minute. I think I need a bit more of this …'

'Well,' Gertrude said with a droll chuckle, 'don't look; find.'

Edward tested his colour on a scrap of canvas before proffering her the paste he'd concocted. They analysed it under the light, then Gertrude, satisfied, dabbed her brush in the blob and gazed at the two canvases — the original and its half-formed twin — before darting in and making a few quick brushstrokes.

This was her method: much inspection and comparison, combined with sudden bursts of action. She'd told me how difficult it was to generate the slapdash effect that characterised the *Weeping Woman*, how she needed to make her strokes with speed. This increased the danger of making an error of line or colour. She lessened this risk with careful consideration before she struck.

Although this way of working was painstaking, I had to admit it was effective; her own *Weeping Woman* was (very) slowly but surely taking shape on the canvas, a jagged green monster rising to the surface of a milky bath.

She stepped back, grunted with approval. 'Forgery is a much purer way of making beautiful and interesting things.'

Edward groaned. 'Oh dear, here we go. I'm off to make some coffee.'

'You want to write novels?' Gertrude asked me after Edward had ambled away.

I nodded, reluctant, as ever, to articulate this so boldly.

'Why?'

This was an excellent question. Writing novels sounded like an interesting thing to do, but I hadn't interrogated my ambition too deeply. If I were brutally honest with myself, there were cravings for fame and recognition in there somewhere, but it felt dishonourable and creatively dubious to admit this. I longed to be in the weekend newspapers, to have my work pored over by experts, to be praised for my creation in a field of endeavour I regarded with awe.

I prepared a more principled answer — about having meaningful things to say, about wishing to contribute to the corpus of literature — but my confusion must have confirmed Gertrude's point, which she now pressed home with the relish of one despatching a floundering opponent.

'Do you think anyone would bother making a painting or writing a novel if they couldn't attach their name to it? Artists talk about the joy of making work, but I wonder if they'd get so much of this so-called joy if they had no chance of being known for it. Would you write a novel if it was published anonymously? Because the forger doesn't sign her name to a work, there is no ego involved. The pleasure is in the creation, in putting beautiful work into the world. It is, as I said before, quite pure.'

'You're still engaged in deception,' I said, reluctant to yield to her argument, which would only cast my motives in a suspect light, 'passing off an artwork as authentic when it isn't.'

Gertrude jabbed me with the gnawed end of her brush. 'We,' she pointed out, 'are engaged in deception. Don't forget that. Secondly, authenticity is mostly about the person making the work, not the work. Why should we care about the artist? Thirdly, why does it matter, if the work gives people pleasure? Does it matter they're admiring a canvas painted by Gertrude Degraves in a Carlton warehouse in 1986 and not by Pablo Picasso in Paris in 1937? If people see meaning in it, take pleasure or solace in it? That Vermeer forgery was acclaimed as being a work of genius until they realised it was by someone else. If the differences between an original and a copy are so small as to be indistinguishable, then clearly they are as good as each other. And this *Weeping Woman* will be every bit as good as the original. Think of those Ern Malley poems. Everyone thought they were great — and some of them *are* great — until they were exposed as a con.

'Our appreciation of a work of art often has nothing to do with the aesthetic virtues of the work alone,' Gertrude went on, warming to her theme. 'It's the aura that surrounds it. The artist, the time in which it was made, and so on and so on. The brand, essentially. It's ridiculous. You see people in the gallery walking straight past a painting because they don't think much of it. Then they realise it's by a famous painter, someone who's supposed to be great, so they stop to coo over it. Bang! Like that, their opinion is turned right around.'

Edward reappeared with a cup of steaming coffee. 'Is the lecture finished?'

Gertrude ignored him and lunged once more at the canvas. 'Trouble is that the skills involved in making modern art have so deteriorated that there's no challenge in trying to copy any of it. They don't even *do* drawing at art school anymore. Only a bunch of theory. Look at that Keith Haring mural down the road in Collingwood. Anyone could do that. Nothing skilful about it. A bunch of green cartoon characters riding on the back of a giant slug. Pfft. Could have been painted by a gang of retarded teenagers on a community outing.'

Edward guffawed, snorted his coffee down the wrong way and lapsed into a coughing fit. When he had recovered, he and Gertrude continued to work in peace for a while.

On the wall above the workbench hung a dozen or so of Gertrude's original paintings, part of her series of gargoyles. Each no larger than a postcard, they were frightening portraits of spectral creatures peering out as if from the murder holes of a medieval castle. Some of the figures were cowled, others grasped the sill of their canvas with bony fingers as if preparing to leap into the corporeal world. From their unlit windows, they resembled a monstrous jury of goblins casting their tumid, bloodshot eyes over the studio with horrified glee, as if it might be cadavers, rather than art, being assembled in front of them — an impression only enhanced by the candle burning on the bench and the air of criminality that hovered over the room.

Gertrude sat back to smoke a cigarette and assess her handiwork on the *Weeping Woman*. She seemed to fall asleep for a second, as heroin addicts are accustomed to do, before jerking awake in time to tap her sagging caterpillar of ash into a coffee cup.

'What happened about Tamsin?' she asked.

Her query was presumably in reference to a second letter that Tamsin had sent to the media about the painting's fate. In it, she had threatened to burn the painting if the so-called Australian Cultural Terrorists' demands (which included the establishment of an art prize called the Picasso Ransom) were not met. Max was again furious at what he saw as her increasing the likelihood of putting the police onto us.

'Max thought it best if James talked to her. He knows her better than anyone.'

'Quite so. No point sending Max. We don't want to aggravate her further. Who knows what she's capable of.'

'I don't know if James is the right person to speak to her,' Edward said.

'James is tougher than he looks,' Gertrude countered. 'Besides, he'll do anything Max asks.'

This was true. James and Max had a lopsided friendship, based at least in part on James's readiness to endure any humiliations Max dished up.

'Why is that?' I asked. 'Why does James put up with Max bossing him around so much?'

As if in sympathy, Gertrude pursed her lips and leaned in to make an alteration to her *Weeping Woman*'s mouth. 'Because James is hopelessly in love with Max, that's why. And when you have a situation where one person loves another more, there's often exploitation. Max is not a kind man. He uses these things to his advantage.'

Although I tried to appear unmoved by this information (a goodly portion of being cool, after all, lies in being unshockable), I was taken aback. To my knowledge I had never met a real-life homosexual before, let alone been friends with one. I considered the numerous times I had been alone with James — the way he rested his hand on my shoulder; the nights we'd staggered home from bars, propping each other up, when we'd both drunk too much. There had even been an instance, some months earlier, when he had insisted I sleep in his bed rather than walk home so late at night and so drunk.

'Oh, I wouldn't worry too much about our James,' Edward said. 'He does alright for himself. He goes to that gay bathhouse in Peel Street every so often.'

Peel Street intersected Smith Street several blocks from James's house. I had, in fact, picked James up from that very corner late one night when I happened to drive past on my way home from a party in Collingwood and spotted him walking. I mentioned this, adding that James had been rather pleased with himself for reasons he had refused to disclose at the time.

Edward threw his head back and hooted with laughter. A gold tooth at the back of his mouth glinted, a treasure among the ruins of his other blackened teeth. 'That's because he'd just had his cock sucked by some brute dressed like a member of the Village People.'

Gertrude smacked Edward with her paintbrush. 'Oh, Edward.

Please. I cannot work with language like that around. Get to work. Can you make up some more of that violet colour? I need it *very* pale, for the bottom of her handkerchief. See that? The same.'

Still chuckling, Edward scratched his neck and scrutinised for some time the portion of the original painting to which she referred. 'Hmmm. Very thin, isn't it?'

At dawn I bought newspapers at a Lygon Street newsagent and trudged through Carlton Gardens back towards Cairo. A beautiful morning. The wide paths were strewn with leaves the colour of tobacco. There were a few people walking their dogs or jogging. *Jogging!*

I sat on a dewy wooden bench to smoke a cigarette and read the papers. *The National Times* had a two-page feature on the theft, accompanied by a large photo of gallery director Patrick McCaughey looking haggard, despite sporting his floppy bow tie. Speaking from New York, art critic Robert Hughes described us as 'burlap terrorists', while the chairman of twentieth-century art at the Met suggested the theft was not committed by a group of artists but 'one screwball'. *The Weekend Herald* had a reproduction of the second typed ransom letter on its front page, in which Tamsin and George had referred to the arts minister as a 'tiresome old bag of swamp gas'. An accompanying analysis from a handwriting expert (improbably named Mr Humphrey Humphrey-Reeve), who had studied the scrawl on the envelope, determined the writer to be a homosexual loner with an artistic disposition.

Despite the huffing of the gallery director, the police and the minister, it was clear no one had any idea how the theft had been committed or who was responsible. A woman had even come forwards claiming to have seen four men and a woman acting suspiciously in the gallery on the Sunday morning (around the time Max and I were waiting in the car), but the sketches drawn up from her evidence bore no resemblance to anyone involved.

Water dripped from the elm trees around me. Exhaustion and elation pulsed through me. I felt I was seeing the world anew after years in darkness; the colours were brighter, the details so much more piquant. A light plane flew low overhead, birds warbled. For a while I watched two attractive women with ponytails play tennis on the nearby courts. One of them lunged for a wide shot, squealed, almost fell over.

It was Sunday morning. Around me the city was gradually waking. I imagined a suburban father preparing his two children for their weekly football match; elsewhere a girl fed her ash-grey cat; while in another part of town an old man squinted through his frayed curtain to see what kind of weather the day promised. All those paltry, quotidian lives running down like toys. What was it Max had told me? *Their laws don't apply to us.*

It was cold but sunny, the sky a magnificent ultramarine. I sensed other things in the city around me — dozens of police investigators heading into work and preparing to search for the *Weeping Woman*. I had to laugh. I knew where she was, how close to police headquarters she was. Secrets conferred power; and the larger the secret, the more potent its power.

Even an encounter with Mr Orlovsky ('How about that pay-pay-pay painting, eh?') in the garden on the way up to my apartment that morning couldn't quell my burst of optimism. Despite Gertrude's erratic progress, and Tamsin's rather wild ransom letters and general unpredictability, the plan — improbable as it was — was going ridiculously well. Until a few nights later, that is, when a series of unsavoury events changed things forever.

EIGHTEEN

I WAS AT HOME WATCHING TELEVISION, TRYING TO KEEP WARM.
My aunt's radiator was woefully inadequate; I could see the mist of
my exhalations. I was thinking about Sally, brooding over losing
the memory of her body (the small of her back, her calf) as an
artist might fret over an inability to get a line just so.

The *Weeping Woman* had been in our possession for more
than a week, several days longer than had been intended. Max
was growing anxious about it, and Mr Crisp had contacted Anna
Donatella with concerns about our progress. Although the forgery
was nearing completion, it would still take a couple more days,
assuming there were no further hiccups. There were fears of the
deal falling through — despite assurances from Gertrude that
everything was moving ahead swimmingly.

The phone's ring startled me. It was Edward. He groaned as if
in pain. After a minimum of chit-chat, he asked to borrow some
money.

'How much?'

'Two hundred?'

'*Dollars?*'

He sneezed. 'Can you? Please? We can't … We won't be able to
finish the … Dora without it. We're so sick. And then we'll all be

screwed. I don't think you realise how scary Mr Crisp is.'

This inspired in me a sudden terror, as if, like a pack of wild dogs, the fear I had held in abeyance for so long was let loose. 'What do you mean?'

Edward grunted. 'Do you honestly want to know? He threatened to cut off my fingers with a pair of secateurs once.'

'Jesus.' I reached for my cigarettes with one shaking hand. With the other I gripped the phone receiver, inhaled its homely smell of plastic and electrical wiring. What had I thought would happen if we were caught, if the forgery were not good enough?

'We'll pay you back as soon as we've done this thing,' Edward went on. 'When we've been, you know' — another sneeze — 'paid.'

'I'd have to go to an ATM,' I said at last.

'That's OK. Great. Thanks. Oh, and Tom? Can I ask one more favour, please?'

I hesitated. 'Sure,' I said, even though I wasn't sure at all.

Which is how I found myself in the unlikely position of chauffeuring Edward around on a freezing Thursday night looking for drugs. He told me the police had launched a crackdown that had put their regular dealers out of business. Gertrude was too ill to accompany us — she could hardly raise her head from the bed to greet me at the warehouse — but I drove Edward to half-a-dozen different places around the city. It was raining, and the car heater was broken.

Usually affable, Edward's demeanour was unsettling; he resembled a famished ghost, sneezing, sniffling and trembling in the passenger seat beside me. His breath stank of rotting fruit from the cough syrup he was swigging from a bottle ('For the codeine, you know'). He groaned and shuddered in his seat, as if the discomfort were unbearable. The windscreen wipers squawked horribly at each pass.

Following his directions, I pulled up outside a double-storey terrace house in nearby George Street. He vanished inside for ten minutes while I sat in the car. After re-emerging he directed me to another house in Napier Street. Again nothing, but he had been given a scrap of information and was confident he was on the scent; it seemed there was a clandestine network throughout the city that he was tapping into.

We drove south of the Yarra to the seedy beachside suburb of St Kilda. Knife-eyed hookers loitered along Grey Street, clutching collars to their chins. I sat in the car in a side street while Edward scuttled into Mandalay apartments, which overlooked the bay. There was a woman in one of the apartments who knew someone who still had some heroin to sell. A black hairball of Goths — like offcuts from The Cure — stalked past. I fiddled with the radio dial and smoked.

I didn't have long to wait. Soon the car door opened and Edward folded himself like a collapsible ruler into the passenger seat. A woman he introduced as Skye got into the back seat. They conferred and Edward directed me along Canterbury Road back towards South Melbourne.

'Where are we going now?' I asked Edward.

'The Orphanage,' he said. 'We're going to see Spider.'

The Orphanage was a huge squat on Clarendon Street. It was indeed established as an orphanage in the 1850s but had been abandoned twenty years earlier. More recently, it had been taken over by a disparate tribe of subcultures who had set up camp in its derelict buildings.

I parked off the main road, next to one of the property's high walls. Against the low cloud I could make out the silhouette of a crooked spire, the sharp angle of a slate roof. Amid assurances of a hasty return, my two passengers alighted from the car, Skye leaving a scent of fresh sweat and stale patchouli in her wake. I watched them trot away and turn the corner into Clarendon Street.

Half an hour went by, then an hour. No sign of them, no sign of anything. I got out of the car and wandered down the street. After some indecision, I went through the unhinged gate at the Clarendon Street entrance.

The buildings were ruined, unlit. Here and there on the ground were sodden piles of rubbish, bits of plaster, lengths of wood. The air stank of burning rubber. The place possessed a distinctly malevolent atmosphere, and I was not reassured by my first glimpse of some of its tenants — a pair of lanky, army-booted skinheads warming their hands over a fire, reminiscing, perhaps, about Kristallnacht. I hesitated to ponder the best course of action, but advertised my presence by stepping on some broken glass.

The two skinheads, mouths agape like a pair of laughing clowns, turned to look in my direction. Neither of them spoke. My instinct was to turn and scurry back the way I had come, but by that stage my instincts were easily ignored, rather as a parent learns to fob off the squalling demands of children. Instead, I took a step towards the skinheads and told them I was looking for Spider. It was then I noticed another skinhead — a girl — sitting on a chair behind the first pair, swigging from a bottle of Green Ginger Wine.

All three considered me for what felt like an age. At last, the girl explained how to get to Spider's place: through the courtyard, along a passageway, turn left up a flight of stairs.

'Look out for a sign that says *Asylum*,' she said. 'But watch out for the hippies. They're fucking crazy tonight. They've all taken some psychiatric drug.'

As if to underscore her warning, there came from somewhere in the darkness a distant crash, followed by a shriek of delight. The skinheads grinned at one another.

I thanked them and set off in the direction she had indicated. I spent a surreal and distressing half-hour wandering through unlit corridors, stepping over piles of rubbish and feeling my way through abandoned rooms. Occasionally, around me in the monstrous building, I detected music, the reverberations of a party. It was an immense effort to maintain my nerve, and the single thing that kept me going was the fear of never finding my way out alone.

The only person I came across was a teenage girl in a corridor who ignored me and, chewing on a strand of her hair like a crazed Ariadne, stared at some point on the crumbling ceiling. All this was terrifying enough, but the room that unnerved me most was an orphans' washroom: a row of dusty little sinks set low to the ground, cracked mirrors, dozens of broken children's shoes heaped in a corner.

By some miracle, I stumbled upon Spider's abode. As the skinhead had advised, there was a metal sign outside his room that read *Orphan Asylum* — the name of the original establishment, prised free of the main gate — but with the A in the second word enclosed in a crude texta'd circle. First skinheads, now anarchists. Great.

If I had hoped to enter an exotic opium den of luxurious decadence (rugs on the floor; slippered eunuchs stuffing pipes for prone, hollow-cheeked raconteurs) then I was sorely mistaken. Spider's room was cold and dingy, illuminated only by a medical-looking lamp on the floor. No one displayed any surprise at my unannounced arrival.

It was clear they were all very stoned. Edward and Skye were sitting on a sagging couch, intent on a game of cards laid out on the torn upholstery between them. Another fellow — presumably Spider, our host — crouched on the floor, doubtless engaged in some nefarious pursuit. He was the thinnest, most evil-looking person I had ever seen, a sub-species of human being I had never before encountered: scabby cheeks, eyes like bullet holes, hands patterned with tattooed swastikas of various shapes and sizes.

Unschooled in the etiquette expected in a drug dealer's lair, I sidled over to Edward and suggested we get back to Gertrude, who must be worried about us. Spider snickered and tore a square of paper from a page of a *Penthouse* magazine. With a razor blade, he was apportioning quantities of white powder into tiny handmade sachets. A flicker of glossy breast and mouth was manipulated by his ragged fingers and added to a small pile. He hummed as he worked.

Edward was too preoccupied to respond to my suggestion, but Skye glanced up and smiled. 'I'm doing a reading, honey. We won't be very long.'

I realised the cards arranged on the couch between them were Tarot cards.

Skye turned her attention back to them. 'Uh-oh,' she said, unable to keep a note of dismay from her voice, 'the Nine of Swords. Hmmm.'

Edward sat up. 'What?'

Skye cupped her chin and pondered the array of garish cards, which included, by my layman's reckoning, a whole bunch of unfavourable things — a skeleton on a pale horse not least among them.

'What is it?' Edward asked again, pointing to the skeleton on horseback, around whom people were falling in states of distress. 'Is that one Death?'

Skye grimaced and bobbed her head, reluctant to make so bold a prediction. 'Not necessarily death. Change, more like it. And change can be really, really good, you know.'

'What sort of change?'

'Who knows. You got anything planned?'

'Well, yeah, I'm planning to give up dope pretty soon and go and live in Berlin.'

'Good for you. Might be that.'

'But it could also be Death?'

'Well. Could be.'

Edward pressed a hand to his forehead and uttered a throaty gurgle of despair.

'But not necessarily yours,' Skye added.

She then pointed to the Nine of Swords, which featured an image of a woman sitting up in bed with her hands pressed to her face. On the black wall beside her was the arrangement of nine swords.

'This one here represents your current position,' she said brightly, perhaps hoping to move on from the dismal prospect of foretelling anyone's demise. 'See the swords hanging over the woman? That's usually about anxiety, despair. It can be about deception, too … But placed where it is in the overall spread, it might not be so bad. Let me see. What else do we have here?'

Spider stalked across and bent over with hands on knees to inspect the cards. He breathed stertorously, as if he had run a marathon rather than walked three metres.

'You reckon you can do Janie's cards after?' he croaked. 'You know, like with the baby's fortune and stuff?'

Skye gazed up at him with her kohl-rimmed eyes. 'OK, Spidey. How you doing over there, Janie?'

There came a stirring from the furthest corner of the room, and a face materialised in the gloom like a pale moon rising in the night sky. A girl stepped forwards with a shy smile. 'OK, I guess. You know how it is.'

Skye tutted sympathetically. 'Yeah. Not long now, though.'

The girl called Janie nodded, approached and allowed herself to be enfolded into Spider's clumsy embrace. With horror, I realised she was heavily pregnant.

In the dim light, with their heads bent over the spread of cards, the four of them resembled a Goya-esque coven. Junkies — in my limited experience — tended to be a cynical lot, and I was surprised at their esteem for this mumbo jumbo. In later years, however, I came to see how aligned were heroin addiction and the occult. There was the obsessive secrecy, a fetishism for specific objects related to its practice (special spoons for mixing up, a favoured belt as a tourniquet), a love of cryptic language (smack, horse, dope), delight in the sinister and — above all — a belief in one's enlightenment in relation to those unfortunate mortals yet to sample the divine. Both the heroin addict and the occultist are in love with death, or at least their own flavour of it.

For a minute I seemed to be the only person awake in the room. Then, as if activated by a signal discernible to them alone, they stirred. Skye flicked a dreadlock from her eye. Spider led Janie off into the darkness from where I heard the squeak of a mattress, murmured endearments.

And Edward, as if addressing my unspoken misgivings about the ritual being enacted in front of me, scratched his nose and said, 'Skye's grandmother was a psychic, you know.'

I felt beholden to express interest in this snippet of family history. Besides, any conversation would cover the creepy sounds emanating from the other side of the room. 'Oh, is that right?'

'Yes, she was,' Skye said. 'In the nineteen-twenties. She was in a travelling sideshow with her older brother. It's a gift that's handed down through all the women in our family. My brother can't read the cards. He can't read a comic book. I've read tons of people's cards. Loads of musicians. That guy from Shower Scene from

Psycho. Even did Nick Cave's when he toured last year.'

I stifled a chuckle and checked Edward's response to this claim. He had often mocked the tendency of Melbourne's heroin addicts to claim kinship with the underground rock hero on the flimsiest of pretexts. 'If you believed Melbourne's junkies,' he had told me only a day or two earlier, 'then everyone in town's shared a syringe with old Nick.'

Edward, however, had nodded off again.

'Yeah,' Skye went on, 'he had a weird reading. Anyway, let's get back to you, Eduardo. Nine of Swords. Deception. And the woman sitting on the bed is crying.'

Edward jerked to life, wiped his mouth of drool. 'Crying?'

'Yes. That's a pretty bad card to get. Beware the weeping woman. She's always going to be trouble.'

It was after two a.m. by the time we stumbled from the Orphanage. I dropped Skye at her flat in St Kilda and drove through wet and deserted streets back to Carlton. I trudged up the warehouse stairs for a glass of wine. Instead of going home straight afterwards as intended, however, I fell into a deep sleep on Edward and Gertrude's couch.

By the time I woke, it was late morning. There was no sign of Edward or Gertrude. Someone had thrown a blanket over me in the night, but I was still cold. I heard the sound of a door banging in the wind. Repetitive, insistent, annoying.

Once they awoke, and with their drug supplies replenished, Edward and Gertrude were back in fine fettle. The whole day leaked away. Fearful of seeing Sally, although fearful of not seeing her, I procrastinated over returning home. The weather outside was foul; windy and wet. The three of us spent the afternoon in the studio, the cosiest place in the warehouse. In the late afternoon,

Edward and Gertrude retreated to their room to inject some more heroin and, after more dithering, settled down to work. Rain pattered on the tin roof, almost drowning out the music playing on the cassette deck.

After observing Edward and Gertrude for more than a week, I had learned that painting was an alchemical enterprise as much as an artistic one. Edward spent some time flipping through Elmyr de Hory's handwritten manual and other books on technique, mixing his pigments and various other substances to match colours precisely and attain the proper consistencies. He had a wealth of recondite facts about the history of colour and paint: Prussian blue was discovered in 1704 or thereabouts; carmine red is made from insect blood; violet was discovered accidentally by a young chemist hoping to create synthetic quinine in the nineteenth century.

A variety of sickly greens, however, were the colours most used in Picasso's *Weeping Woman*.

'And surprisingly,' Edward said as he used a spatula to smear a mixture about on his plastic palette, 'green might be the most natural of colours but has been one of the hardest to create in paint. Yellow mixed with blue. Cennino used malachite. You get it from corrosion of metal. Oxidation on copper, that sort of thing …'

From the main body of the warehouse came the sound of the doorbell jangling on its rope. Gertrude, who had no doubt heard all of Edward's little art lectures, slipped away to answer it.

'Some bloke did make a magnificent green in the eighteenth century using arsenic. Scheele's green, it was called. Became very popular and was used in wallpaper and everything, even though it was highly poisonous. Probably contributed to Napoleon's death, in fact …'

There came the murmur of anxious chatter. Edward halted midsentence, perturbed. Even Buster, who had been dozing on a chair, looked up.

The voices drew nearer. It was Max, raving, his tone high-pitched and frantic. 'A disaster,' he was saying. 'An absolute disaster.'

Then he was in the doorway, dishevelled, a red woollen scarf askew at his throat. His hair and the shoulders of his gaberdine coat were soaked with rain.

'He knows,' he announced.

Edward gestured with his spatula, a sort of referred shrug. 'What are you talking about, Max?'

'Queel. He knows the *Weeping Woman* is here. He knows what we're up to.'

There was a stunned pause as the news sank in. I noticed Sally bobbing around behind Max. Her hair, too, was wet. A thick strand of it clung to her jaw. She avoided my eye. I had hoped, by not seeing a great deal of her, that my desire might be suppressed, but at that instant my heart beat against my ribs, a fish caught in the shallows.

'We're screwed,' said Edward.

'But how,' said Gertrude. 'You still haven't told me.'

Max flopped into a chair. He looked as if he hadn't slept for many nights, and he smelled of sodden wool.

'Anna Donatella rang me. Said Queel had rung her earlier this afternoon. Very excited, he was. He told her he'd called around here this morning on the pretext of checking on the progress of Edward's show. Claimed he'd had a funny feeling about the whole thing. Suspected we had Dora all along, he reckons. Anyway, the bottom door was open when he arrived and he walked right in ...'

I recalled the banging door that had woken me.

'How many times did I tell you to be careful?' Max said. 'Tom here was fast asleep on the couch' — he glared at me, as if such deep slumber were itself a crime — 'and you two were completely comatose.'

'We had a late night,' Edward said.

'Yes,' said Gertrude. 'A very late night.'

Max sighed. 'Be that as it may, somebody left the studio key on the kitchen table and he let himself in. He saw *both paintings*.'

'Well, that's preposterous,' said Edward.

Gertrude pressed a tiny, paint-spattered hand to her mouth in distress. She looked tearful. 'Oh no. We were sick last night, Max. I must have left the keys out. I'm so sorry.'

'And who left the bottom door open?' Max asked.

I raised one hand in a sheepish admission of guilt. 'That must have been me. I was last inside and I was only planning a quick visit. Sorry, but I was so tired.'

Max shook his head with seething disappointment. I felt a pang of childish shame and sensed a blush crawl up my neck as far as my ears.

'What do you think he's going to do?' Edward asked.

'What does Queel always want? He's a bloody art dealer. He wants a cut.'

'How do you know?'

'Because I rang him. What else could I do?' he said over our outraged exclamations.

Gertrude, who had been hovering in the doorway with Sally, scooped up Buster and came into the studio. She indicated the paintings. 'But we're so close to finishing. Another two days, at the most. Can't you hold him off? We're *nearly* there.'

The two paintings were side by side on their respective easels. I realised I had ceased noticing how much the forgery had come to resemble the original. At a glance, they were difficult to tell apart. All that was required was to age the surface some more and touch up the brown portions at the bottom of the canvas. As Max had promised, Gertrude had performed an extraordinary feat; the marvel of it almost outstripped Picasso's original achievement.

'Nearly isn't good enough, Gertrude. It's safer if Queel's on our side, rather than risk him going to the police or jeopardising everything. Need I remind you that we are already over schedule? *Way* over schedule. You said it would only take a week, but it's been nearly two. Mr Crisp is getting anxious. He wants his painting. His buyers won't wait forever, you know.'

Gertrude waved her hands about like a flummoxed schoolgirl. 'I know. I'm sorry. We've had some trouble with ... supplies and so on. I'm sorry, Max.'

Max looked mollified, albeit reluctantly. 'We need to shut Queel up for now. We can't have him going to the police for the reward. If he breathes a single word of this to *anyone* then we all end up in jail.'

Jail. Although I had read in the newspaper that prison was a possible consequence of being caught for the theft, none of us had mentioned the actual word before. We had for so long been living in our private ecosystem that it had been easy — far too easy — to forget we were all implicated in a major crime and, if discovered, could be imprisoned for some years. *Jail.*

The cassette playing Mark Stewart and the Maffia strained at the end of its tape and clacked to a stop.

Max grunted with satisfaction. 'Thank God that's finished, at least.'

Edward put down his palette on the bench already strewn with paint materials, shards of paper and canvas. 'How much does he want?' he asked. 'The reward for information is $50,000.'

Max dug out a packet of cigarettes from a pocket and lit one before answering. 'I don't know. I'm going to see him tonight. It's all arranged.' He jabbed his glowing cigarette end at me. 'And I need you to drive me over to his apartment.'

'Max,' Gertrude said, 'you can't trust Queel.'

'I do know that, my dear. There's a party at that big house in Drummond Street tonight. I think you all should go along.

Gertrude, can you ring James and tell him what's happened? Tom and I will meet you all there in a few hours.'

Gertrude bent down and placed Buster on the floor. 'Max? What are you going to do?'

'Talk, you know. Talk to him.'

We lapsed into a brooding silence.

NINETEEN

ROUNDING A BEND OR CRESTING A HILL IN THE FAMILY CAR when I was a boy, long before I knew my left from right, I was always convinced that the approaching cars wouldn't know which side of the road we were driving on and we would all be killed in a head-on smash. All my life I have, on occasion, been possessed by a presentiment of doom while driving, the seeds of which I could trace back to that childhood fear. It is a sensation that has never left me, and has never been more acute than the wintry night I drove Max to see Queel. Cars swished past on the wet roads and at every turn I expected to see — too late! — a truck bearing down on us with a spray of water sluicing up from its enormous front wheels, a trucker's startled face in the headlights, a yelp of fear. Smash.

We were driving to South Yarra, an upmarket part of the city with leafy streets and discreet mansions tucked behind hedges and high brick walls. Although he spoke very little, I could tell that Max was excited, as if he were lit from within. We stopped at a red light at the top of the Punt Road hill. A car packed with teenagers pulled up beside us; I could hear thudding rock music, the excited squeal of their voices. One of them, a chubby blond guy, glanced over and raised his can of Victoria Bitter in salute. They were probably driving to St Kilda to see a band or go to a nightclub, and for a second I envied the simplicity of their night: beer, girls and loud music.

'I should have seen it,' Max was saying. 'I do see things sometimes. They're visions, I suppose. Remember that *Challenger* disaster? I had a feeling it was going to explode in that way. I knew it. You remember I said it would never work? On the morning it lifted off? And another thing. You know what the smoke was like, the bits that separated?'

I was anxious, impatient with this discussion. 'No. What did it look like?'

He placed a raised index finger to either side of his head. 'The devil. Next time they show that footage on the news, you take notice of it. There, in the blue sky, you'll see the face of the devil. Hiding in plain sight. Horns and everything.'

The light turned from red to green, and I was absolved from responding to this outlandish claim. The neighbouring carload of teenagers sped off, fishtailed, righted itself and vanished down the other side of the hill. We followed at a more sedate pace.

'Left at Toorak Road,' Max said at the bottom of the hill. 'Left again up here. That's it. Turn off the headlights and pull over near that building.'

We were in a dark and dripping side street. Water rippled in the gutters. A jogger pounded past.

Max punched the car lighter and waited. When his cigarette was lit, he turned to face me. 'You're not very close to your family, are you?'

I was taken by surprise. 'What?'

His expression was sincere. 'I don't mean to pry, but none of them has visited since you moved here. In — what? — eight months. Your mother? Your father? No one. And you haven't visited them, either. And you *never* talk about them.' He paused before going on, as if choosing his words ever more carefully. 'I think perhaps you are not well loved at your home.'

I was too stunned to speak. Although I had not thought a great deal about it, it was true that no member of my family had visited me, or even offered to do so, and phone calls were infrequent. In March my sister Rosemary had mailed me a postcard (beachside kangaroo in a red bikini) from a Queensland resort where she had holidayed with her family but, generally, weeks passed without contact from any of them. I was not much bothered by this, but the notion this state of affairs might be indicative of a lack of affection for me was thrilling. As a white, middle-class boy I had lacked the requisite background for authentic artistic angst; if nothing else, this would furnish me with one such reason.

'It's hard, isn't it?' Max went on. He waved his cigarette about as if, like air, the answer were all around us and only needed pointing out. 'It's hard when you don't have anyone to show you how to be in the world. We all need someone to admire. Even I had my parents, while they were still alive. My father was always wise.'

He was right. And because my parents (if indeed they *were* my parents) were hardly role models, I had become wary of adults — real adults, that is, with real lives and real jobs — and it was clear to me how much I flailed around in the quicksand of my life.

'What would he have done in this instance?' I asked.

Max stared through the windscreen with smoke trailing from his nostrils. 'That's a good question,' he said. 'I can no longer see what he might have advised — my memory of him is fading. Most likely he wouldn't have been so dumb in the first place. There are things I have never learned, things I'll never learn now. I make it up as I go. There are no shoes for me to fill. That's what's hard, isn't it? And you have an orphan's heart, too. It's one of the reasons I like you, I think. You're lucky you met us. We'll be your family now. I am so looking forward to taking you to France: you'll love it. You'll write novels there, I know it. I see the future better than I see the past, and that is definitely one of the things I can see — all of us in the garden wearing straw hats. I'll finish *Maldoror*; I'm almost there. You'll be Uncle Tom to our children, you know. James tapping away at his typewriter, you unwrapping the very first copy of your debut novel. Wine in the afternoons. Cheese. Imagine it. We can go to Berlin to visit Edward and Gertrude. They can get off those awful drugs.' He shook his head. 'It would be dreadful if things fell apart now, if Queel somehow wrecked it all. We've planned our escape for so long.'

I was unaccountably moved by Max's speech — by his sensitivity to my familial situation — and had to fight down a lump in my throat. No one had ever been so generous towards me. And it *would* be terrible if things fell apart now. The very idea that our plan of getting to France could be disrupted at this late stage was intolerable.

'*To complete a stage of a journey in a single breath is not easy, and the wings become very weary during a high flight without hope and without remorse.*'

Bemused, I could only stare at him.

'From *Maldoror*,' he said by way of explanation. 'One of my favourite bits.'

For several minutes we sat smoking, before Max ground out his cigarette in the overflowing ashtray and pulled his coat tight around himself.

'OK,' he said. 'Let's go and chat to our friend Queel.'

We stepped from the car into the cold winter air. Did I know what was going to happen that night? For many years I told myself: no, I didn't. But, really, I probably did.

Queel lived on the top floor of an apartment block built in the late sixties; stylish rather than fancy, cut like a good suit. Although there was a lift, we took the inside back stairs. We saw no one else, heard nothing from any of the floors as we ascended. Once upstairs, we shuffled our feet on the thick, blue carpet outside Queel's door. Max put his ear to the door to listen.

'Alright,' he said, and pressed the brass doorbell set into the wall.

A grinning Queel opened the door at once, as if he had been hovering inside awaiting us.

''Allo, gentlemen,' he said, with a shallow bow, ushering Max and me inside. He was, as usual, inordinately pleased with himself.

The apartment was enormous, lamplit, fragrant with tobacco, liquor and cologne. The floors were strewn with Persian carpets, and the walls were covered with dozens of paintings and drawings. Line-drawn nudes, expressionist portraits, at least one Roy Lichtenstein print. In addition, there were piles of art and fashion magazines on sideboards amid sculptures and esoteric trinkets, African masks and the like: a wooden bowl glittering with jewellery; a painted Egyptian bust. The place was like nothing I had seen before, outside the pages of a magazine or the reels of a James Bond film. I was dumbfounded.

Max, too, looked uncharacteristically unsure of himself. He clasped one hand in the other; his knuckles strained white against the thin sheet of his skin. Like a hungry waif he looked around and licked his lips.

Queel gestured for us to follow him into the open-plan lounge room. He glided soundlessly towards a sideboard on which bottles of liquor and glasses were arranged like a miniature city of crystal. He brandished a bottle of Scotch. 'Drink?'

We nodded. As soon as he had turned his back to mix our drinks, Max hissed at me, 'Keep an eye on him.'

Max left my side. 'I might use the bathroom,' he announced.

Queel shrugged and handed me a tumbler of Scotch and ice. 'As you wish. Why don't you sit down? Tim, isn't it?'

I watched Max creep up the hall, out of sight. I stepped forwards and took the glass of liquor. 'It's Tom.'

'Tom?'

'Yes,' I said. 'We've met a few times at openings. I'm friends with Edward and Gertrude.'

Queel ran a finger delicately across his mouth and lowered himself with a greasy creak into a paunchy, black-leather couch. He crossed his legs, revealing a hairless shin above the line of one grey sock. A red handkerchief peeked from the breast pocket of his pinstriped jacket. He inspected me, nodding and smiling to himself as if what he were seeing accorded with a rather unfavourable conclusion he had already formed. 'A friend?'

'Yeah.'

'*Yeah*,' he mimicked. 'In French we have a different word for this: *arriviste*.'

Although I didn't understand this expression, the tone in which it was uttered left no doubt as to its implied scorn.

'How did they do it?' Queel asked.

'Do what?'

'I mean the painting is only small but ...' He sipped his drink and then slapped his knee, as if what he had imbibed sparked inspiration within him. 'Perhaps you're the thief, eh? The newspaper said someone was maybe hiding in the cupboard. Was that you? Amazing. What I do not understand, though, is why there were three versions of this *Weeping Woman* painting at the studio.'

I looked around for Max. From a far corner of the apartment I heard a tap running, the slam of a cupboard door. What the hell was he doing?

Queel contemplated me, wiped his mouth again. 'Let me give you some advice. You should be more careful who you associate with. They are — what? — fun, interesting?' He gave a theatrical shiver. 'They are glamorous; all this is glamorous. You want to be like them, don't you? But that is not the same as being their friend. I saw you with them at some openings. They let you come along with them, like a leetle, um … *pet*. That's all. I can see maybe what you get out of it, but what do they get from you? Who knows, eh?'

My determined refusal to answer only goaded him. 'And that girl, what's her name? Sally? *Leetle*, innocent Sally. Very attractive, no? She would pretend anything to get what she wanted. Let's say you would not be the first to fall for her. In fact I myself —'

'Shut up, will you!' I said, furious — not because I thought he was wrong, but because I feared he was right. Embarrassed at my outburst, I scrutinised the ice melting in my glass.

He raised one hand palm outwards in surrender and recrossed his legs. 'I have a sense for this sort of thing. Besides, I saw you and her together. At that Roar Gallery in Fitzroy, out the back one time.'

I knew the night he was referring to. It was a month or so ago, at the opening of an exhibition of drawings by a friend of Edward's. We were all there: Gertrude, Edward, Max and Sally, even James. The crowded room was thick with the fragrance of hair gel and pencil shavings. It was not long after Sally and I had spent our first night together, and I was sick about her. I had drunk too much cheap white wine, and when I happened upon her alone in the dim back stairway, I couldn't resist clasping her around the waist in a clumsy attempt to steal a kiss. It happened quickly, but the memory of it was still vivid: her warm body pressed to my own, her hand at my hip, the winey flavour of her lips. My actions were stupid, dangerous, but I was confident that nobody had seen us.

I said nothing, but Queel — relishing the raw nerve he had touched — smirked. 'You're lucky it was me who found out,' he said. 'Lucky it wasn't someone else.'

I didn't know if he was referring to the theft or to the incident with Sally, but at that instant Max materialised in the lounge room.

He was pale and war-eyed, like a desperado from one of Egon Schiele's drawings come to life. My first thought was that he had done something terrible.

Queel sprang from the couch to fix Max a drink. 'There you are, Max. Now join us and let's have a good talk. We were chatting about your wife.'

I couldn't stifle a low groan. Surely he wouldn't say anything about Sally and me? My body felt heavy, almost too much for my legs to support.

Although I have — most reluctantly — relived the next few seconds over and over in my mind, what happened is forever unclear. The memory footage is grainy and scratched.

Max strode across the room as Queel turned (wet smile on his fishy lips, tumbler in hand) to face him. An expression of puzzled alarm.

'What do you have there, Max? No!'

Then a crack. Queel grimaced and doubled over. The glass slipped from his hand as he collapsed to the floor. The twitch of his leg, ice glistening on the plush carpet. I had never seen a man shot before, but I was familiar with the choreography of murder from a thousand such cinematic snapshots and realised at once what had happened.

For the following twenty minutes we might have been underwater. Noises dark and muffled, gliding down the back stairs and onto the street. Not a word about what had happened. The drag of a wet, black night. Driving up Punt Road, tail-lights of cars ahead fragmenting beyond the glass, the digital clock on the abandoned silos displaying — between juddering swipes of windscreen wipers — *11:12*. A city soundless and full of sound. *11:13. 12°.*

'*Merde,*' Max said as we passed beneath the Richmond station bridge. 'We did it, Tom. We did it. What a thing to do. It's not like I thought it would be. I have a weird taste in my mouth. Like metal. I never heard of that. Have you got that, too?'

I shook my head, watched the traffic straight ahead. But I felt his searching gaze upon me. Those glittering eyes, that beatific smile, the exultation eerily reminiscent of the minutes after the *Challenger* disaster. We drove on. Our breathing loud and close in the car interior. And seconds passing like hours.

TWENTY

THE PARTY WAS BEING THROWN IN A LARGE TWO-STOREY, Victorian-era share house in Carlton. Max and I arrived around eleven-thirty and parked on the opposite side of the wide street. I clenched the sticky steering wheel to keep my hands from shaking.

Proceedings were in full swing; snatches of a Prince song and ragged outbreaks of laughter drifted over the road to where we sat smoking in my car. I saw a long-haired woman writhing in the hall. The famous Dancing Susan. People spilled from the front door onto the porch. Despite the wet weather, others gathered on the upstairs balcony. For some reason I was sickened by the sight; they reminded me of maggots thronging a carcass.

'Do we have to go inside?' I asked. 'I don't feel very well.'

'People need to see us here. You understand that, don't you?'

I nodded.

Max gripped my shoulder. 'It will be alright. I promise I'll look after you. We need to keep ourselves together for another week and then we'll be out of here. Just think of it — we're almost in France.'

My throat felt sour and swollen, as if a lump of vomit had congealed there. I nodded again; it was all I was capable of.

Ebullient, he opened his car door and stepped onto the pavement. 'Alright,' he said, 'let's get shickered.'

We encountered James in the busy entrance hall. He was more anxious than usual, tugging at his sleeves and rubbing his neck. It was clear he was drunk. His mouth glistened with red wine, and there was ash scattered on the lapels of his black velvet jacket like flakes of grubby snow.

'Well?' he asked. 'What happened?'

'Don't you worry your pretty little head,' said Max, looking around with his hands jammed into his trouser pockets. He nodded a greeting at a woman descending the stairs.

But James was not so easily deterred. 'What do you mean? Tell me what happened.'

Max waved him away. 'Don't worry about it.'

'Your idiotic plan,' James hissed. 'As if you would *ever* get away with this.'

Max grabbed James by the sleeve, but James shrugged him off. Max took hold of him again, more firmly this time. 'Look,' he said in a low voice. 'Pull yourself together, for God's sake. We're almost there. Don't wreck it for everyone now, James. It's all been sorted out. Trust me.'

James gulped wine from his plastic cup. He shook his head and tightened his mouth; he was on the verge of tears.

Realising his aggressive approach was not working, Max put an arm over James's shoulder and pulled him close. Until then I had not noticed the disparity in their respective heights; Max was several centimetres taller. He nuzzled his mouth into James's silvery hair. He kissed him there.

'It will all be fine,' he whispered. 'It will soon be over and we can get away from this place. Alright, baby?'

People brushed past us in the hall. I felt distinctly uncomfortable, but James smiled, reassured.

'I know,' he said. 'I'm sorry, Max. It's …' He drank the last of his wine and made a face. 'I think I'm a bit drunk.'

Max released him. 'A drink. Yes. Excellent idea. I'll fetch us each a glass of wine, eh? Are you alright now?'

'Yes.'

'You're sure?'

James nodded and straightened his jacket.

'Make sure he doesn't do anything crazy,' Max whispered to me as he brushed past and waded into the throng.

James cast aside his empty plastic cup and wiped his nose with a handkerchief. After some fumbled attempts, he extracted a crooked cigarette from a packet and lit it. 'Tell me, Tom. What happened tonight? What did Max do? What did you both do?'

I didn't know what to say. There were some acts too monstrous for the paltry words that might describe them. I gazed around. Most of the people at the party were a few years older than me. I recognised a junkie friend of Edward's who was wearing earrings that glowed different colours. A woman who had modelled her look after Madonna (torn fishnets, bright red lipstick, layers of necklaces) slouched against a doorjamb, smoking. I wondered if she had witnessed the incongruous tableau between Max and James and, for a few seconds, my embarrassment at being associated with them overcame my nausea at the events of the evening.

Just then, a pair of very drunk guys crashed into a bike that had been resting along the wall and sent it toppling to the floor, where it lay with one wheel spinning lazily. James and I watched them lurch off into the melee with arms around each other's shoulders. I didn't answer James's question, and he didn't press me further. Either he sensed already what had happened or he didn't want to know. He smoked his cigarette and staggered out the front door without another word.

The next few hours were a weird and busy nightmare. Edward and Gertrude had, I was told, been at the party, but no one had seen them for an hour or so. Sally had not attended at all.

Although I liked the idea of parties and was always grateful to be invited, I was never sure whether I enjoyed them. My woeful self-consciousness made it difficult to talk with strangers or dance. Instead, I hovered on the sidelines smoking and drinking, uncertain what to do — how to convey the impression I was enjoying myself with the least outward suggestion of doing so. All this was intensified to an almost unbearable degree that night.

In the bathroom I discovered a bathtub filled with melting ice and bottles of beer. When I lifted a bottle from it, the ice cubes rattled like cheap jewellery. When that bottle of beer was finished, I gulped some horrible red wine from a plastic cup. I was cornered by a tall Englishman named Rod, who related his saucy seaside adventures in Byron Bay earlier that month. I caught glimpses of Max throughout the remainder of the night: arguing about Cole Porter with a moon-faced boy with braces on his teeth; warming his hands over a fire in a rubbish bin out the back; sitting on the stairs with his hand on the knee of a freckly, redheaded girl.

At some point a grinning hippy handed me a joint as I waited in line to use the outside toilet. I was not a fan of marijuana, but I sucked on the joint gratefully. When the outhouse was free, I sat on the cold toilet lid for as long as I dared without incurring the wrath of those still queuing in the garden. From a hook dangled a string of Tibetan prayer flags on which were printed, supposedly, invocations to the goddess Tara in the Dzongkha language but might have been recipes for yak-butter tea or directions to Lhasa by road for all anyone knew. Every time I managed to forget what had happened earlier, the memory of it cuffed me like a furious lion freed from its shackles. I put my head in my hands. I might have wept; anything was possible. Anything.

Some time later I found myself in the kitchen, talking to a girl with black eyes. We had exchanged greetings before at parties, and Naomi had always seemed to me one of those people rather enamoured of their burgeoning intellect. She wore a tight red sweater and smelled of fruity perfume and — rather more exotically — of five-spice powder. She was, I guessed, the type of person I would have studied alongside at university, had I bothered to enrol. This thought reminded me of the drive back from the animal hospital with Max and Gertrude after Buster had been shot, and the groups of students we had seen. Although only eight months earlier, it felt a lifetime ago, on the distant shore of my Rubicon. *Alea iacta est*, as Caesar himself is reported to have said as he crossed that river. The die is cast.

I was stoned, senses sharp and prickling, mouth uncomfortably dry. Every so often the physical world looked to be on the verge of melting or assuming a more gelatinous state; the chipped cupboards, the glinting sink, the fridge, all trembling at their edges. The black-and-white linoleum floor tilted and pitched.

In an effort to maintain a veneer of sanity, I forced myself to concentrate on Naomi. She was majoring in cultural studies at Melbourne University. I was acutely aware of the heat of her hip against my own. I feigned interest in her subjects, nodding and sipping my ghastly wine as she expounded on Roland Barthes and semiotics but, really, all I wanted was to retreat somewhere secluded with her. I had never found her that attractive before, but I longed for the type of solace that only another human can provide. If I could only lose myself for a short while.

'It's very interesting,' she was saying. 'You do a close semiotic analysis of, say, *Sale of the Century*, and you'll find that the project is nothing more than … Oh no. Is that that arsehole Max Cheever?'

I followed her gaze. Sure enough, Max had lurched into the adjacent lounge room and was instructing the redhead in the intricacies of the foxtrot. They were both drunk, and the room was far too crowded to attempt such a step. When they almost knocked over a man, frowns of disapproval rippled from face to face. Someone called out, 'Watch it, man!'

'Do you know him?' Naomi asked me.

I was reluctant to admit my acquaintance with Max lest it jeopardise my chances of spending the night with Naomi, but figured it impossible to get away with a lie on the matter. Fortunately, she required no confirmation from me to elaborate on her antipathy.

'He slept with a good friend of mine, Danielle, over summer. She was so keen on him and he promised her all sorts of things. Led her on. Turns out he's married to some mousey blonde. Ugh. Can you believe that? Bloody creep. I'd love to give him a piece of my mind. Dani was devastated. Lucky she's not here tonight …'

I remembered the letter addressed to Max that I had found in my apartment when I first moved into Cairo. *Dearest Max, Thank you so much for last night.* So that was who the mysterious 'D' was.

'He got into a fight with Michael Hutchence at a party in Brunswick last year,' Naomi continued. 'When he was here to make that movie *Dogs in Space*? Hutchence got a bit sleazy with the wife and Max tried to punch him. I don't know. That's only what I heard. And anyway, someone said he hits his wife.'

I lost sight of Max and the redhead. It was late. Every table or window ledge was covered with ashtrays and empty bottles. A thick slab of smoke hovered above the heads of the remaining dancers in the lounge room. Hand in hand, Naomi and I wound our way through the crowd and cosied up at the top of the stairs. She was so warm, so soft. Her lips were sweet and fizzy, like cider.

'Tom! There you are. I've been looking everywhere for you.'

Naomi and I turned to the voice. It was Max, standing a few steps below us and waving a bottle of beer around. His stance was precarious. The redhead was nowhere to be seen.

'You know this guy?' Naomi asked me.

Max looked affronted. 'Of course he knows me. This man here is pretty much my best friend. Come on, Tom. Let's go. I'm tired.'

Naomi pulled back from me, as if scorched. 'You lied.'

'Naomi, I —'

'Natalie! My name is *Natalie*. Ugh, you're all the same.' She stood up, steadied herself against the wall and stomped down the stairs, pushing past Max, and disappeared.

Max wiped hair from his eyes. 'Well, she's a' — he stopped talking to belch — 'cute little firecracker, isn't she?'

It was only when we attempted to cross the road that I realised how drunk Max was. He could hardly walk. When at last I guided him to the car and shoved him in the back seat, my endeavour was rewarded with boozy cheers from revellers watching from the balcony.

Although the effects of the joint had worn off, I was still drunk and in no condition to drive. I did not, however, relish the prospect of getting Max home on foot across the park and figured I'd take my chances. Besides, it was almost five a.m. and there were few cars on the roads.

Unwilling or unable to sit up properly, Max collapsed along the length of the back seat, where he lay muttering and moaning to himself. I set off as carefully as I could, talking myself through each manoeuvre, as if in so doing I might assume the precision of an automaton. 'OK. Indicate right. Turning here into Johnston Street. Easy does it. Car coming, that's it. Slow and steady …'

Waiting at a red light at the corner of Nicholson Street, Max loomed up from the back seat like Michael Myers in *Halloween*. I jumped in my seat. The car jerked and stalled.

'Jesus, Max! You scared the hell out of me.'

His breath was hot on my neck as he leaned between the front seats. 'Natalie, eh? She was a very pretty thing.'

Unimpressed, I restarted the Mercedes but waited until we had

225

turned safely into Nicholson Street before responding. 'She said she knew you.'

'Did she?'

'Yes. You had a fling with a friend of hers called Danielle?'

He was unfazed by my knowledge of his affair. 'Danielle! Oh yes. Now she was a real beauty. Absolutely in*credible* thighs.'

This was more than I could bear. 'Max, why on earth would you chase other women when you're already married to Sally? She's …' I chose my words deliberately, barely able to stifle my outrage. 'I mean, she's so great.'

Max harrumphed. 'Oh, Tom. You're a sweet boy, but you're so …'

'What? So *what*?'

'You know. So bloody old-fashioned. So, I don't know, *boring*.'

I bristled. This was among the worst possible insults in Max's lexicon, one he invested with a moral dimension; rather than being a mere social inconvenience, banality was a spiritual failing. In his world it was preferable to be nasty, unlikeable, ugly, crazy — almost anything but dull.

'You can't let yourself get all tied up with such nineteenth-century claptrap,' he went on. 'It doesn't do anyone any good. And I bloody adore Sally. I miss her when she takes a bath. I miss her body, the smell of her, when she's not there. I would do anything for her and she would do anything for me. Anything at all.' Max stopped talking and sat back, doubtless feasting on memories of Danielle's thighs.

When I pulled up in Hanover Street, however, I realised he had passed out. I was tempted to leave him to sleep in the car, but relented.

There followed a long and frustrating rigmarole of coaxing him from the Mercedes and half dragging, half carrying him through the gate and up the outside stairs. Cursing drunkenly to myself, it occurred to me that lugging him was perhaps akin to transporting a corpse and, at such a hateful thought, I dropped him to the concrete, where he landed with a fishy slap.

'Ouch,' he grumbled. 'Cold. So cold.'

Dawn was breaking, and the clouds above us were swollen with pearly light. Birds chirped and flitted from branch to branch in the trees; it was hard not to interpret their chatter as anything but mocking. Despite the cold, I was damp with perspiration. I wondered whether I should leave him there.

Then Sally was with us, barefoot, clutching a white fur coat about herself. She was wan, dishevelled, shockingly beautiful. I was troubled by her unexpected appearance. She, however, seemed wholly unsurprised to see us in such a state.

'Darling,' she murmured, crouching beside Max. 'Darling, come on.'

Max groaned.

Again Sally attempted to get him upright. She rubbed his shoulders, ran her fingers through his black hair.

Max got to his hands and knees. 'I've done a terrible thing,' he muttered.

I stepped forwards, panicked. That precise moment, on a public walkway outside a neighbour's apartment, was neither the time nor the place for a confession. 'Max,' I hissed.

Max gazed blearily at Sally, then at me. His lips were flecked with spittle. 'I've done a *lot* of terrible things. *Beaucoup de choses* …'

'I know,' Sally said. 'We all have, my love. But it doesn't matter to me.'

He grabbed her by the arm. 'It was amazing, Sally.' He looked at me as if seeking confirmation. 'Wasn't it, Tom?'

I was too petrified to speak. Eve's piercing voice drifted from the apartment across the garden, saying something about a protester, her voice muffled by glass.

Max smiled to himself and stumbled to his feet. Sally and I each took hold of an arm and managed to propel him into their apartment, along the hall and into the bedroom. He toppled facedown onto the bed and into a deep and oafish slumber. He was still wearing his rumpled gaberdine raincoat.

'You need to keep an eye on him,' I told her as she walked me back towards the door. We stopped in the hallway.

'Thank you,' she said.

'It's nothing.'

She kissed me on the mouth. 'No,' she said, 'it's a lot and you know it.'

I wondered what she suspected. I felt that meaningful words needed to be said but, alone in her presence, I was overcome by shyness. She considered me with an expression resembling love, but not quite. Pity, perhaps. A long pause. Those divine fingers tucking loose hair behind her ear, a stabbing glimpse of her sloping breast in the fall of her coat, a waft of her sleep.

'It's OK,' she said with a shake of her head, as if eager to dispel any sentiment threatening to cloud the situation. 'We're almost there. It will be over soon.'

It was a small consolation. 'And then what?'

She took something from her pocket and handed me a plastic bottle of Serepax. 'Here. Why don't you take one or two of these? You look like you need some sleep.'

I took hold of her wrist. 'Please answer me. What will happen afterwards? To us?'

She brushed me off. 'Please don't.'

'Do you know what happened last night?'

There was a shout from the rear of the apartment, followed by a thump. I backed away from Sally as Max appeared, more disorderly than ever.

'Ah,' he said, spying me and staggering down the short hall.

'Leave us,' he whispered to Sally before turning to me.

'Max, I think —' Sally began.

He loomed over her. He raised a hand as if to strike her — indeed, she flinched ever so slightly — but he smoothed his hair instead. 'Sally, please. I said: *leave* us alone for a second. I need to speak to Tom. It's private.'

Sally turned on her heel and stalked back towards the bedroom.

'You shouldn't talk to her like that,' I said in a quavering voice.

Max gave me a withering look. 'What did you say?'

I opened my mouth to speak but faltered before uttering another word.

'Don't you worry unduly about my wife,' he warned, peering after her up the dim hallway. Then, satisfied we were alone, he fumbled in his coat pocket. 'Here, put this back under the floorboards, will you. I forgot about it.'

I looked at what he held out in his hand. It was the pistol. Horrified, I shrank back.

Perhaps mistaking my disgust for mere reluctance to accept something that didn't belong to me, he pressed the pistol on me again. 'No, no. It's yours. It's your aunt's.'

'Max. I don't want that thing in my apartment.'

He grabbed and screwed up my shirtfront with unexpected violence. 'Listen,' he said in a voice low and fierce. 'What happened has happened. I did it for all of us, you included. And you're involved, whether you like it or not. You were there, my boy.'

The pistol was jammed into my ribs. I was too frightened to speak. When at last I could, I whispered, 'Are you going to shoot me now?'

He scrutinised my face as if he'd forgotten who I was. Then he released his grip on my clothes. 'Don't be ridiculous. I unloaded it before we left Queel's place, remember?'

I recalled nothing of the sort but shrugged nevertheless with agreement or, at the very least, compliance.

'It goes in a shoebox under a floorboard in the entrance hall. Beneath the rug. Wedge the board up with a butter knife and toss it in. Perfectly secure. Your aunt kept it for her own safety. Had it for years.'

I took the pistol. It was cold and solid. I stared at it there in my palm. 'How did you even get into my place?'

'I have a key.'

I recalled the night before the heist when I had returned home to find him in my apartment.

'Your aunt wanted Sally and me to have one in case she fell over in the shower. You know how old people are. Now, put that thing in your pocket, for God's sake. Mr Orlovsky likes to be up early. Don't let anyone see it.' Max pushed past me towards the front door.

The idea of going back to my apartment alone was intolerable, and I grabbed his arm — idiotically, like a *Titanic* survivor expecting succour from an iceberg. 'What happens now?'

'Nothing. Say nothing to anyone. Stick the pistol in your pocket, take it home and put it back where it belongs.'

'Shouldn't we throw it away? Chuck it in the river?'

'Pull yourself together. The worst thing you can do now is panic.'

He yanked himself free of my grip and watched me pocket the gun before opening the door and stepping aside to let me pass.

'One more thing,' he whispered through the crack in the door before he shut it completely. 'Wipe it clean. Your fingerprints are all over it now.'

There was indeed a shabby shoebox beneath the loose floorboard in the hall. It was, of course, the board that always creaked when stepped upon.

I wiped the gun with a tea towel, wrapped it in the same tea towel and put it into the shoebox before replacing the board and arranging the Persian rug over the top. I pressed my weight on it. Sure enough, it squeaked as if in pain. I re-checked to ensure it was not noticeable, walking over the spot a number of times and crouching on hands and knees in search of telltale lumps or inconsistencies.

In the bathroom I washed my hands and splashed water on my face. Then I sat on my sofa and tried to rest. Everything was alien, as if my furniture had been switched with replicas during the night; good replicas, but off kilter enough to snag my attention. Did my coffee table always have that chip in the corner? Was the sideboard always that height?

I stood up and paced about before sitting, this time in an armchair. After a few minutes I removed the gun and wiped it again with a wet dishcloth before returning it and reconfiguring the hiding place — the board, the rug — once again. Standing in the kitchen, I threw down a large slug of whisky. The linoleum was cold, even through the soles of my shoes, as if I were standing on an Arctic cliff. I held a shaking hand out in front of my face for a long time. I don't know why. I wondered, as I have wondered ever since, how I should feel about what had happened last night. I couldn't say I felt bad about Queel's death, or certainly no more than a formal regret, but I was aghast at my unwitting involvement.

I had a very long, very hot shower, just stood there with the water pouring onto my head and shoulders. Afterwards, I inspected myself in the cabinet mirror. My face vanished beneath the film of steam, only to be revealed again when I wiped the glass clear with my palm. Over and again I performed this task — hoping, perhaps, to surprise myself and catch a glimpse of the man I was becoming, rather than the boy I had been for eighteen years.

What did people see now? When they published photographs in the newspapers, rapists always looked like rapists, serial killers like serial killers — almost as if their physiognomy had determined their actions, rather than the other way around. Could one tell, by looking at me, that I was implicated in murder, in theft and forgery? For obscure reasons I have always assumed the worst of myself; on that morning I had the feeling that, rather than having done something totally unexpected, I had uncovered an aspect of my character hitherto well concealed. Years later, with a chill of recognition that is perhaps the only real measure of artistic truth, I encountered the passage in Freud where he speculates: *In many criminals, especially youthful ones, it is possible to detect a very powerful sense of guilt which existed before the crime, and is therefore not its result but its motive.*

The phone rang, startling me. I didn't move and let it ring out, but it rang again and didn't stop.

I picked up the receiver and held it to my ear. I was still naked and damp from the shower. Water dripped onto the floorboards. All I heard was an electronic crackling noise, as if sparks were festering at the other end.

Then the voice of an English-sounding woman. 'Hello? Hello?'

'Yes, hello?'

'Oh, at last. I'm looking for Helen.'

'She's not here.'

'Pardon?'

'I said she's not here.'

'Oh. I've been ringing for ages. There's been no answer for weeks. Is she away?'

I was unsure what to say.

'Hello?' the woman said again. 'Can you hear me? It's rather a bad line.'

'Who is this?'

'Could you please tell me where Helen is? I'm a very old friend of hers.'

'Helen is … Helen died. Late last year.'

The connection fizzled some more, then dropped out. I hung up. A minute or so later the phone rang again, but instead of answering it, I ripped the plug from the wall in a sudden fury.

I put on a bathrobe, swallowed two Serepax, and lay on the couch. It was still early Saturday morning. My skin felt thick and uncomfortable, more like an ill-fitting coat than part of my body. Under the door, the wind moaned like a goblin. I heard birds, the equine *cloppity clop* of two women wearing high heels walking in the street below. Then nothing, or nearly nothing, just oblivion's dark roar.

TWENTY-ONE

I DIDN'T LEAVE MY APARTMENT ALL WEEKEND. I WAS SUPPOSED to work Saturday night at the restaurant but couldn't face it; I didn't even phone in sick.

The discovery of Queel's body was on the television news on Sunday evening. Police said there were no leads yet, although he was known to have made enemies during his years working as an art dealer. There was footage taken outside his apartment block, and a shot of Anna Donatella's gallery space in Richmond. A female neighbour said he was a quiet man, who sometimes threw small parties. No one had heard anything out of the ordinary on Friday night, which was a relief.

Despite this, it seemed impossible that we would not be caught. I waited — with fear, yes, but also with resignation — for the police to pound on my door, and it was during these interminable few days that I understood that vertiginous longing of the criminal to be apprehended; it would, at least, bring the whole episode to an end.

But nothing happened. I endured myself utterly alone. Every few hours I would wake, whereupon I'd shuffle about my apartment before taking more sleeping pills. I wasted an entire morning perched on the edge of my bed. I contemplated the walls and chewed my fingernails until they bled. When hunger occurred to me — as an obligation rather than a physical need — I chewed dry bread and slurped souring milk from the carton, spilling it down my chest and onto the kitchen floor.

I might have gone to the police to explain my role in the crimes in which I was implicated and to make a bid for some sort of clemency. Although present, my participation was incidental to what had happened. I drove the getaway car, as it were, but didn't take the painting, nor did I paint the forgery. I was there when Queel was murdered, but I had no idea what Max had planned and I didn't pull the trigger myself. Justifications, certainly, but the truth nonetheless.

But — and this is also true — it never occurred to me to go to the police. Not once. I wanted to live in France with Sally and Max and James and have the life they promised me; I wanted to catch the train to visit Edward and Gertrude in Berlin, to wander by the Seine, write books. Already I knew my future to be entwined with theirs, and there was no way that future was going to take place in this faraway land in which we were unlucky enough to be born. I had found my people; I loved them and would have done anything for them. Even the risk of jail was preferable to losing them. And I wanted, most of all, to be with Sally.

Very early on Tuesday morning there came a rapping on my front door. I was in the kitchen washing the dishes, only two metres from whoever was knocking. I froze, and listened with a soggy scourer in one hand. The tap dripped. Finally, a voice whispered my name. It was Max. I opened the door, glad to see a familiar face.

'I thought you might have been the police,' I said.

Max scowled and gestured for me to be quiet. He came inside, checking that we were alone. 'I've been ringing you.'

He picked up the telephone receiver and jiggled the cradle. 'It's disconnected.'

I was puzzled for a second before remembering. 'Oh, yes. I, er, unplugged it. To try to get some sleep.'

He bent down. When he stood again, he held up the plug ripped from the wall socket. It was no more than a broken rectangle of plastic and a spray of torn wires.

I shrugged.

He replaced the receiver and regarded me through his fringe of black hair. 'You look dreadful.'

'Thanks. I've been having trouble —'

'And it smells in here. Like an old dog.'

'Again. Thanks.'

'We need you at the warehouse.'

'Why?'

'The forgery is ready. We're getting rid of it today. That National Gallery director was knocking on studio doors all over the city at the weekend. He even published a letter of appeal in the paper. They're convinced that local artists are responsible. It's only a matter of time before they come to Edward and Gertrude's place. Anyway, you have to drive us to Spencer Street Station, and George and Tamsin are going to leave the forgery in a locker.'

'In a *locker*?'

'Yes. Then we'll ring the gallery and tell them where it is.'

'What?'

'We need to get rid of the bloody painting, get rid of both of them. Wash our hands of the whole thing, get out of this country.'

'I can't drive you.'

'Why the hell not?'

'I can't. You said all I had to do was drive you from the NGV to Edward and Gertrude's place. That was the deal.'

He came towards me, and not in a friendly manner. 'Look,

I know this hasn't gone the way we intended but we're almost there, I promise.'

I stepped back, almost tripping over a pile of books stacked along a wall. To buy myself some time, I lit a cigarette. Without warning, rain drummed on the roof and spattered from the gutter onto the walkway outside my apartment. Then the squall passed, and everything again fell quiet.

'We need your help, Tom. You've been great. So helpful. You're one of the few we can trust. Please.'

'I'm scared.'

'I know you are, but there's no need to be. We're nearly there. No one saw a thing the other night.'

'How do you know?'

'Trust me. I know what I'm doing. Look, if there was any chance of us getting caught it would have happened by now. There is nothing to worry about, I promise.'

This didn't make much sense, but I was assuaged by his paltry reassurances — because, I suppose, I so desperately wanted to be.

Max indicated the rug in the hallway. 'Did you put the you-know-what back where I told you?'

I nodded.

He went over and smoothed out a stubborn ridge of the Persian rug with the toe of his shoe. Then he glanced up at me and smiled. 'Shall we go then?'

There was no point in arguing but, in a pathetic display of autonomy, I made a show of hesitating before agreeing to accompany him.

It is perhaps a testament to my inherent narcissism to assume that great alterations within my soul must be reflected in the physical world, although I doubt I am alone in this. After all, who has not — after enduring the death of a parent, say, or surviving severe illness — felt an urge to impress upon others an aspect of one's newest self, even if it is only telling a passing stranger of what has happened?

And so it was for me on leaving the grounds of Cairo for the first time in days. I was perplexed and disappointed to notice that everything looked exactly as it had the week before, indeed much the same (change in season notwithstanding) as when I first arrived eight months ago: trees, roads, tennis courts, traffic. People went about their business. A dog chased a ball in the park across the road. Two mothers pushing prams laughed at a joke as they ambled beneath the trees. Did they not know, I thought, whom they had passed in the street?

Everyone was at the warehouse when Max and I arrived there on that cold Tuesday morning: Edward and Gertrude, James, Sally, George, Tamsin, and the fearsome Anna Donatella. Tamsin, who would be doing the drop-off, was wearing a skirt and high heels to blend in with the city business types as much as possible. George was also dressed more smartly than when we had met previously.

Our greetings were muted. Nobody mentioned Queel; however, I detected from the gathering a sort of exaggerated respect, which is, after all, a variation of fear. No one said very much as we crowded into the studio to inspect the canvas, which was lying face-up on the workbench. To my eyes the forgery was perfect, and although I admired the painting, it gave me little pleasure. The thing was done.

After soaking up our praise, Gertrude started wrapping the canvas in soft curatorial paper.

'Wait,' said Tamsin, producing an envelope from her pocket. 'Tuck this in there.'

'Look here,' said Max. 'Your damn notes almost led the police right to our door.'

'But they didn't, did they? Come on, Max. Don't be such a wanker.'

'What does it say?'

Tamsin handed it to him. Max read it, then gave it to Gertrude. 'Alright, then. The usual claptrap. Put it in.'

Gertrude used brown paper for the package's outer layers, tied it up with string and handed it to Tamsin. 'Be very careful with it. Those ten-cent lockers on the concourse at Spencer Street Station are the perfect size. Should be a piece of cake. Drop it into one of those and away we go.'

'Walk in confidently,' said Max, 'and no one will suspect a thing.'

Tamsin grinned. It was clear she was enjoying herself.

Whether I was still dozy from all the Serepax or my benumbed state was a psychological response to the events of the past few days, I'll never know, but I more or less sleepwalked through the following hours. Max and I dropped Tamsin and George off at Spencer Street Station, the rectangular parcel tucked under Tamsin's arm. To me the Bolshevik twins were incredibly suspicious, but no one else gave them a second glance. We parked in nearby Bourke Street and sat smoking in the car.

Fifteen minutes later, George knocked on the window, told us it was done and walked away with his sister. 'We'll see you at the warehouse later,' he said over his shoulder.

It was not much after ten a.m. Dropping off the forgery was, as Gertrude had predicted, a piece of cake.

Max and I returned to the warehouse. Once inside, Anna Donatella told us she had spoken to Mr Crisp on the telephone. It was arranged that she and Edward would meet him that afternoon at an airfield out of town.

Edward was thrown into panic at this development, and I recalled him telling me how scary Mr Crisp was.

'But this wasn't the plan,' he wailed. 'Why me? Only Anna needs to go. She arranged everything. I've never had to go along before.'

Anna crossed her arms. 'He wanted you there. He was adamant about it. You and me.'

'But why?'

'I don't know, Edward. Perhaps he wants the actual forger there. What the hell's the matter with you?'

Edward appealed to Max. 'But you promised you would handle this part of the operation.'

'I'm not sure what I can do. Mr Crisp wants both you and Anna.'

Gertrude interceded. She rested a hand on Edward's forearm. 'It will be fine. I promise you.'

He contemplated her. His forehead shone with perspiration. 'Do you?'

It was an unexpected gesture, freighted with a significance I would not understand until days later.

'Yes,' Gertrude said at last.

'But how are we getting to this airfield?'

Everyone stared at me.

I shook my head. Edward's dread of the expedition had infected me. 'Why not take your car? Drive there yourself?'

Anna stepped forwards. 'Because people know my car. I mustn't be seen driving around today. Besides, you're in no position to argue, young man.'

'What's that supposed to mean?'

'You know very well what it means.'

And I did know what she meant: I had ventured so far into the cave that the only way out would be through the other side.

In that clumsy fashion the matter was settled. It was cold but sunny, a pleasant day for a drive. Although I hadn't slept much the night before, I was calm as we arranged a stolen, million-dollar modernist masterpiece beneath heavy blankets in the boot of my old Mercedes.

241

TWENTY-TWO

SUNBURY AIRFIELD IS AROUND FIFTY KILOMETRES NORTH-WEST of Melbourne, set among flat, wind-sheared plains. Driving at a steady pace, we took an hour to get there. The city gave way to suburbia, which in turn gave way to pastoral vistas of fields and horses.

The journey was tense. Everything hinged on the next hour or two. Edward sat in the passenger seat and smoked cigarette after cigarette, drummed his fingers on his knee. I had noticed before that, during conversational lulls, there often passed across his face the expressions of one engaged in wordless argument (mouth pursing, head shaking) and during that drive his features were especially animated.

Anna Donatella sat imperiously in the back seat, hands clasped in her lap, as if she were a queen being escorted to her country seat. Every so often she clucked her tongue with disgust at the sprawling housing estates scattered around past the main airport, and I recalled her boasting at an art opening that she had not left the inner city since 1979. Clearly, the mere sight of suburbia disturbed her.

Edward, too, was baffled. 'What do people *do* out here,' he would mutter every so often. 'Milk their cows, I suppose. Make things out of, I don't know, wood or rocks. What is that horse thinking, do you reckon? *Watching* us like that? Ugh. Creepy animals.'

Anna directed me off the main road and across a railway line. The airfield was small and forlorn. In addition to a hangar that housed a blue, twin-engine plane, there was a tin shed that obviously served as an office. A weathered church pew stood outside the office. Three other light planes were moored nearby. A pair of shrubs shivered in the wind. No one spoke as we all peered through the car's windscreen, searching for signs of life.

Edward grew even more agitated. In addition to drumming his fingers, he had started jiggling his knee and wiping his palms repeatedly on his trousers. I felt his anxiety was misplaced: surely this final stage of the operation — swapping the painting for the money — was a mere formality.

'There,' Anna said, tapping a fingernail on the glass as a thin, bearded man wearing dirty overalls stepped from the office and waved us over. Edward groaned, swore under his breath.

Anna squeezed Edward's shoulder. 'Steady, Edward. Steady.'

Following the man's directions, I pulled up on the grass outside the office. Anna wound down her window, and the man leaned in. He was sucking energetically on a sweet, and his caramel-scented breath filled the car interior.

'G'day,' the man said, nodding to Anna and Edward.

'Hello, Oliver,' Anna said. 'How delightful to see you.'

'Who's this, then?' the man asked, pointing at me.

'This is Tom,' Anna replied. 'Our driver.'

I turned in my seat and stuck out my hand to shake his, but he ignored me and stepped back to open the rear door. 'Come on then. Crisp is in the office. He's already pissed off you kept him waiting so long. Don't let's make it longer, eh.'

We got out of the car, removed the swaddled painting from the boot and crowded into the tiny office to find Mr Crisp inside.

There was a round of greetings but — strangely, considering the fuss over who was to attend the handover — no one paid the slightest attention to me.

Hanging on the wall was an out-of-date calendar featuring photographs of light aircraft, alongside a crumpled centrefold of a blonde Playboy Playmate lounging on a picnic rug. There was a glass-fronted fridge containing cans of soft drink, and a shelf of screws and various machine parts.

'About time,' Mr Crisp said. 'I was despairing of you, Edward. Truly despairing. My buyer is getting most anxious. What's taken you so long?'

'Sorry,' Edward said. 'We had some unexpected trouble.'

'What kind of trouble?'

'Nothing to worry about.'

'That is where you are so very, very wrong, Edward. It's my job to worry. Now, let me ask you again: what kind of trouble?'

Edward brushed his hair back and glanced at Anna. 'Well, er …'

Mr Crisp smiled a Dickensian smile — avid, spittle-lipped — and I understood at once why Edward was so afraid of him.

'We had some trouble scoring smack and got held up, that's all. There's a bit of a drought on.'

Mr Crisp — who was by this time sitting on the edge of the desk, as if settling in to wait as long as necessary for Edward's response — rubbed the knuckles of one hand under his chin. He pondered this for a few seconds before standing, satisfied. 'Alright then. Let's see what we have here, shall we. Careful, Oliver, careful.'

Oliver took the package, laid it on the bench and unwrapped it as Mr Crisp hovered at his shoulder issuing instructions with an air of jovial menace. He breathed through his mouth and spoke in abrupt barks, as if language were a bad taste of which he was eager to rid himself.

'Not the knife! You wanna wreck the thing? Fuck, Oliver. Untie

245

it. Get that bit there. Watch that bit of sticky tape. There you go. Jesus, look at that, will ya.'

At the sight of the painting, I was startled anew by its energy, by its spiky eroticism. No one spoke. Mr Crisp gestured impatiently for Oliver to hand him a cigarette. Oliver complied. They both lit up and ogled the *Weeping Woman* without talking (mouths puckered, wincing, cocking their heads), like a pair of gobsmacked pirates trying to decipher an unexpectedly complex treasure map.

'What a fucking piece of shit,' Mr Crisp said. 'I wouldn't give you more than a coupla dollars for that thing, but there's no accounting for taste, eh. No accounting for it. A million bucks for *that*. I seen photos of it in the paper but ...' Words up to the task of articulating his outrage failed him.

Eventually, Edward clapped his hands together and jerked his thumb towards the closed door. 'OK. So that's that. The *Weeping Woman*, as you can see. Perhaps we should just get the, uh, money and be on our way?'

Oliver and Mr Crisp looked at him in disbelief. The door behind us opened, ushering in a blast of cold air.

Mr Crisp beamed. 'Eric! There you are. Thought you must have fallen in. You are a brave soul. I hate taking a dump in public toilets at the best of times, but the one out here is very unpleasant. I'd have hung on meself.'

Mr Crisp's commiseration for Eric's plight sounded genuine, but Eric glanced at him with undisguised contempt before approaching the painting.

'Why is he here?' Edward asked.

'Well, if you're willing to fool the state gallery, who's to say you're not gonna try and fool us? Gotta be sure you're giving us the right one, eh? I don't wanna hand over money for nothing. You wouldn't want to doublecross me now, would you?'

With one hand he mimed using a pair of shears to cut the

fingers off the other. The action alone was intimidating enough, but it was accompanied by a horrid wet sound in his throat; a remarkable simulation of cracking bone.

At this, Oliver giggled, and I realised he was the man I had seen from Gertrude's bedroom window all those months earlier: the man who had shot poor Buster. If I were not already disenchanted to discover that those involved in the world of art theft were not cigar-smoking, skivvy-wearing, Lear Jet-flying aesthetes but merely grubby, foul-mouthed gangsters, then this exchange nailed shut the coffin on my naive expectations.

Eric was evidently an art authenticator, and he slipped on a pair of white gloves before manoeuvring a desk lamp over the painting and applying himself to his task, his face only millimetres above the canvas. He produced various items from a Gladstone bag: cotton buds, a magnifying glass, vials of liquid, a Picasso monograph.

He checked the painting against a handful of notes. He held the canvas up to the light, pressed here and there with his thumb, considered it from all angles. He turned the painting over and inspected the wooden stretcher, humming as he worked, grunting every so often with approval or recognition.

As if he were facing a firing squad, Edward stood staring ahead at some point on the opposite wall. His hands were clenched into tight balls and, reflexively, mine did the same. Anna, who seemed to have missed the implications of Mr Crisp's little pantomime, had installed herself in the only other chair in the office and was busy poking at the heel of one of her shoes.

Eric, meanwhile, dipped a cotton bud into a bottle of liquid and rolled the bud across the painting's upper right corner. Then he examined the bud, presumably seeking telltale signs of fresh paint or a finish that would reveal the work's true age. Mr Crisp's eyebrows arched in anticipation. Anna looked up attentively. Even

Oliver broke off his slack-jawed consideration of Miss June 1984. Finally, Eric placed the cotton bud to one side, took up the painting at arm's length and gazed at it. This, I sensed, was the final test.

But Mr Crisp was impatient. 'What the hell you doing now?'

'Waiting for the feeling.'

'The *feeling*?'

'You've heard of those, I imagine? The feeling that this is the real one. Instinct.'

'What kind of feeling?'

'Hard to describe but you know when you get it, that's all. It's like love, I suppose. You know when it's real. You have to divine the intent of the artwork.'

'Wait a sec. You're telling me that you're going to advise me to drop a buncha cash on the basis of a *feeling*?'

'It's called connoisseurship. It's what you're paying me for, as a matter of fact. I'm afraid it's the best thing to go on.'

Mr Crisp was appeased for all of thirty seconds. 'Time's up, mate. You got a good fucking feeling or what?'

Eric nodded. 'Yes. It's the real thing.'

Edward made a gasp of relief in his throat.

'Well, of course,' Anna Donatella snapped. 'What did you expect?'

The warehouse erupted into jubilant cheers upon our return. With chopsticks raised aloft, Max and Sally formed a guard of honour. Gertrude made tickertape from shredded newspaper. The money was fondled and admired before it was stashed beneath the kitchen sink for safekeeping. Anna bought bottles of wine and Scotch from Chalky's. Edward vanished — no doubt to score heroin — and on his return, he and Gertrude danced over and again to the David Bowie song *Heroes*, which had become an anthem for them on account of its references to Berlin and its infamous wall. For once relinquishing his disdain for modern music, even Max clapped along and performed a jig. I managed to dance with Sally and tried (in vain) to glean from her movements any sign of her feelings for me. She was restrained, even a little cold, but I was determined to ignore it.

We toasted Gertrude and Edward for their skill, George and Tamsin for their audacity. We toasted our brilliant selves. We all hooted and stamped our feet in appreciation. Anna Donatella stalked about the warehouse, saying every now and again, 'I knew we could pull it off …'

Even James, usually so bashful, stood on a chair (drink in one hand, cigarillo in the other) to recite some poetry he claimed was especially fitting.

> Now I find that once more I have shrunk
> To an interloper, robber of dead men's dream,
> I had read in books that art is not easy
> But no one warned that the mind repeats
> In its ignorance the vision of others. I am still
> the black swan of trespass on alien waters.

There was a stunned pause afterwards, as if he had articulated an uncomfortable truth. At last Max spoke. He raised his glass to propose another toast — 'Well, here's to those bloody black swans' — and, obediently, we threw back our drinks.

Shortly before eight p.m. Max and George walked to the phone box on Lygon Street to ring *The Age* and tell them where to find Gertrude's version of the *Weeping Woman*. They returned after ten minutes or so, all smiles. The call had gone off without a hitch. It was intoxicating to be part of history, to know the news before anyone else.

The party continued for hours. We kept the television on, waiting for a news update. A late bulletin came on, in which the lead report was about the arrest of a vagrant in connection with the case of the Moonee Ponds killer. There was crime-scene tape, a mangy-looking house, a thin woman being bundled into the back of a police car. The return of the *Weeping Woman* was the next item. There was footage of the forgery being removed earlier that night from locker 227 by a forensic scientist. A shot of a beaming Patrick McCaughey announcing that, without doubt, it was the real painting, unharmed, back safely where it belonged.

'It appears to have been returned exactly intact,' he said.

The party broke up very early on Wednesday morning. There was a long discussion over the division of the money and it was decided that, in light of our drunken state, we would return the following afternoon to settle. Any concerns I had about leaving cash with a pair of desperadoes such as Edward and Gertrude were mitigated by Max's trust in them.

Outside, it was almost dawn. A chill wind rummaged about the vacant lot where the Mercedes was parked, tossing wrappers, empty cans and clumps of dried grass about as if seeking something. On my way home that morning, the city resembled a beautiful and patient machine, preparing to rumble into life.

As I drove, snatches of James's poem echoed in my inner ear, and the verse acquired an accusatory meaning I hadn't initially registered. I puzzled over its final striking image; indeed, that black swan (so foreign yet so familiar, like visiting a city one has long dreamed of) haunted me for years to come, until — with a surge of bitter disappointment at discovering the poem to be not one of James's — I encountered the original Ern Malley poem ('Dürer: Innsbruck, 1495') from which he had quoted.

As usual, I parked in Hanover Street. I stepped from the Mercedes and walked through the gate into Cairo's soggy grounds.

Everything felt surreal, but at least it was done with. Not only that but also, somehow, we had gotten away with it. As I mounted the stairs, I mused about how later that day I would fill in the paperwork for my passport and then, later that week, we would all go to a travel agent and organise flights to Europe. I remember the smell of wet foliage and of eggs frying. I remember the oyster-coloured clouds overhead. But what I remember most — with an acuity that has not dimmed over time, and the mere thought of which never fails to send through me a tremor of pure, blood-sizzling panic — is what happened on the landing.

I detected a hubbub of conversation, a familiar voice, others not so familiar. Across the concrete, a wedge of light spilled from my open front door. I vacillated — tense, doubtful — on the walkway. A bulky man carrying a clipboard stepped from my apartment. He wore an ill-fitting grey suit jacket and black trousers.

At first this stranger didn't notice me. A sparrow landed on a nearby branch, dislodging a cascade of rainwater. A door slammed somewhere below. Then the man considered me. He had a bushy moustache, ruddy cheeks. Although I registered that something was awry, this confetti of discrete impressions refused to coalesce into anything coherent. He smiled, glanced down at his sheaf of notes. He nodded in response to the familiar voice emanating from my apartment. Then he turned to me again, brow knitted, and I noticed the holstered pistol at his hip.

'Ah,' he said, flashing a shiny badge at me. 'Hello there. I'm Detective Sergeant Bird from Melbourne CID. We've been looking everywhere for you.'

The jig, it seemed, was already up.

TWENTY-THREE

DETECTIVE BIRD CHECKED HIS NOTES AGAIN.

'You *are* Tom Button, aren't you?'

I hesitated. The moment fell apart like an overstuffed file, in which I glimpsed the crumpled documents and items bearing witness to my fate; saw handcuffs, my trial, my mother weeping, the bars of a prison cell, a mugshot, scandal.

He motioned for me to approach, and when I was close enough he grasped my upper arm and presented me to a crowd of people hovering in the hallway of my apartment.

I was unsure whom or what I expected to see (a judge in his wig? the hangman?), but was astonished to see my father, as well as Uncle Mike and Jane. In addition, there was a middle-aged man I didn't recognise standing in the lounge room with his arms crossed.

'Here he is,' the detective announced.

To my immense confusion everyone cheered. Jane even clapped, as if I had won a prize. My father jostled past Uncle Mike to give me a bear hug that almost knocked me over. His tears were cold on my neck. There was general confusion, expressions of amazement.

With his hands on my shoulders, my father stepped back to inspect me. 'Are you alright?'

Unable to speak (at a loss as to what I could possibly say), I nodded.

He looked me up and down. 'Where the hell have you been? We've been calling you. No one's heard from you for weeks. We thought something terrible had happened. In fact, you look sick.'

'No,' I managed to say. 'I'm tired. I've been at a party.'

'At a party?' he repeated, as if this were the most wonderful news he had heard in his life.

Uncle Mike edged forwards. 'Your mum rang us last night. Said you hadn't shown up for work last weekend. Your boss at the restaurant rang her. And you were supposed to come for lunch on Sunday, remember? When we couldn't get hold of anyone, we called the police and came over. Got in with your dad's key.'

My father, who had never thought much of my mother's brother, gestured for Uncle Mike to back off.

Detective Bird cleared his throat and shouldered his way through the throng, asking me to follow him into the lounge room. 'Shall we clear this up?' he said. He pointed to the other man. 'This is Senior Detective Powell. We're both from Taskforce Bolt. Mind if we sit down, Tom?'

I indicated the couch. Detective Bird sat with his clipboard balanced on one meaty knee. I was puzzled at their geniality. I stared around; in the fantasies of my arrest, the scene was much more chaotic than this, with flashbulbs and hordes of people, probably a smack around the head, arms twisted behind my back.

I slumped onto the couch and lit a cigarette with trembling hands. Might as well get it over with. I wondered if they had already raided the warehouse, how much they knew. The question of loyalty was a tricky one. After all, who has not considered how long they might hold out to protect their friends when their own safety or freedom was in jeopardy? We all imagine ourselves a part of the Resistance rather than Vichy but, until it comes to the crunch, who can ever know?

Detective Bird leafed through his papers while whistling a jaunty tune through his lower teeth. Most inappropriate, I thought, considering the gravity of my situation. The other detective perched on the arm of my lounge chair, looking rather bored. Perhaps it was some sort of good-cop, bad-cop routine. My palms were sweaty.

Detective Bird found what he was searching for. 'OK. Now. Looks like the confusion started when you didn't show up for work on Saturday night. Let's see, the chef at your work called here and said there was no answer. You were meant to work Sunday night, as well. The chef rang your mum. She rang here, rang your uncle and aunt the next afternoon, who said you'd missed your Sunday lunch. They dropped over here yesterday but none of your neighbours had seen you for a couple of days. That's when they called your dad.'

My father chimed in. 'The phone has been ripped from the socket. That's why we thought the worst.'

'I've been at a friend's place for the past few days,' I said.

'Girlfriend?'

'No. Just a friend.'

Detective Bird scratched his moustache. 'Uh-huh. And your mum called the university yesterday and they had no record of you. Which is odd because your mum was pretty sure — and your dad here, for that matter — that you were studying up there. Even had a few names of lecturers and so on you had talked about. Other students. A literature tutor called — let me see — a Mrs du Maurier? And your dad told us you had become friends with a boy called Jim Joyce, said you'd even been to his family's holiday house at Point Lonsdale. For Easter?'

Detective Powell smirked.

'Now,' Detective Bird continued, 'none of that is police business but ...'

Indeed, I wondered what on earth all this had to do with the theft of the *Weeping Woman*, not to mention Queel's murder. I assumed he was setting the trap — Detective Columbo-style — from which it would be impossible for me to extract myself.

'... as it happens, there weren't any records of the lecturers you had mentioned. Or the students, for that matter.'

Detective Bird contemplated me with concern. There was a fleck of food (egg yolk, perhaps) in his moustache, and this grooming oversight, more than anything, made him seem a safe and kind man. He would understand if I told him everything. I imagined him nodding sagely, saying *It's OK, son*. Everyone was looking at me. My body was burning with terror and shame and guilt. I wanted to dissolve into the fabric of the couch. I ground out my cigarette in an ashtray.

My father, who I had noticed becoming impatient with these preliminaries, interjected. 'And when we couldn't get hold of you, we feared the worst. That some horrible psychopathic freak ...'

'I heard he chopped off men's you-know-whats,' Jane said primly.

'... so we called the police.'

'And did all sorts of other things to them.'

'You've been sacked from your job anyway.'

Detective Powell held up a palm for everyone to be quiet. 'The thing is, Tom. I take it you've heard about the case of this so-called Moonee Ponds killer?'

'Yes.'

'OK. Well, yesterday we picked up a lady in connection with those crimes, and it turned out she had in her possession a couple of documents belonging to you. University enrolment papers and so on.'

No one spoke as Detective Bird produced from his sheaf of notes my enrolment papers. Each page was in a clear plastic divider marked with police stickers, but I could see they were filthy, crumpled, stained here and there with what might have been blood. The sight of them creeped me out, but I was still confused as to what all this had to do with the painting, or Queel, or anything I had been involved with in the past couple of weeks.

Detective Powell stood and smoothed the creases from his trousers. 'And when your dad called the police to tell us about you going missing, and then we found these enrolment papers in our suspect's possession, well, we thought the worst might have happened. The woman we've got in custody said you had given them to her at a laundromat but we didn't think that was very likely, and considering she is under suspicion for involvement in these brutal killings, well ...'

The detective continued talking, interrupted now and then by my uncle or father, but my attention slipped its mooring and drifted elsewhere. It was all too bewildering. The front door was still wide open, and I stared vaguely at the tree beyond the walkway, at the light reflecting from the opposite window. I heard Eve shrieking in the distance. 'Wild protester!' she seemed to be saying again. What *was* that?

Meanwhile, Detective Powell was fending off salacious questions about the Moonee Ponds killer.

'I read in the *Herald* that it was a Satanic thing,' my father was saying.

Jane offered to make tea and went into the kitchen, where I heard the click and slap of her opening and closing cupboards. I wondered if I'd run out of tea. With all these people standing around, my apartment felt low-ceilinged and cramped.

'No,' Uncle Mike was saying to Detective Powell when I tuned in again to the conversation around me. 'Seriously. How old do you think I am?'

The detective gave him the once-over. 'Forty-five?'

Mike glanced about for his wife, who was still in the kitchen, washing the dishes by the sound of it. He shook his head and leaned in to reveal the answer, as if it might be a mystery Detective Powell had been sweating over for some time. 'Fifty-two.'

'Oh?'

'It's all in the diet. Plus the kays every morning on the bike.'

I tried to focus. Gradually it dawned on me. 'So you're only here because my parents thought I was missing?'

Detective Bird didn't even bother to look up from the report he was writing. 'That's right. There was a bit of confusion over where you've been for the past few days. Remember in future to let your parents know what you're up to.'

My relief was sudden and intense, as if I had surfaced after being held underwater for several minutes. I inhaled deeply; colour rushed back into the room. I felt the nip on my thigh of a spring that was poking through the couch's ragged green upholstery.

'Tom? Tom?' Detective Bird was saying, and I realised he had asked me a question.

'What?' I said.

'You were at a party all night, did you say?'

'A party. Last night? Yes.'

He rested his elbows on his knees, clicked his pen in and out. 'And how do you think our suspect got hold of your enrolment papers?'

Click-click. Click-click.

'I gave them to her.'

'You did?'

'Yes. In that laundromat in Brunswick Street. Months ago.'

He and Detective Powell looked at each other. 'But why would you do that?'

What could I tell them? That I had decided to forgo a bland formal tertiary education in favour of lessons in art and history and friendship and love? That I had sacrificed my ordinary life for one so filled with excitement and danger that it was almost unbearable? I looked at them. I wanted to laugh in their faces. They would never understand, not if they lived to be a thousand years old. All I could do was shrug in response.

Predictably, my father was outraged. 'Why in hell did you do that?'

As Jane glided from the kitchen with a tray of steaming mugs, Detective Bird tucked his papers under his arm, and stood. 'Well,' he said, 'it doesn't look like there's any need for us here.'

The detectives declined tea, bade farewell and made their way to the front door, accompanied by my father (not before he had promised to deal with me later).

Jane smiled and handed me a cup of tea. 'We're just glad you're OK.'

I had never liked her a great deal, but Jane's gesture of making tea felt like the kindest thing anyone had ever done for me and I was filled with gratitude. My eyes clogged with tears.

After a whispered conference in the hallway, the detectives departed. I sipped my scalding tea, comforted by the menial task at hand.

'What the hell?'

It was my father, who was looking quizzically at the floor underneath his shoes, eyes narrowed. He pressed down with one foot. With renewed despair, I realised he was standing on the squeaky floorboard — beneath which rested the shoebox containing Aunt Helen's pistol. Again he rested his weight on the floorboard and grunted with satisfaction at the resultant squeak.

Like many Australian men, my father fancied himself a home handyman (saw it, in fact, as intrinsic to his masculinity), and it was with no small degree of horror that I recognised the expression on his face: it was that of a man discovering a construction fault he might be able to repair himself.

With the intention of manoeuvring him away from such a dangerous spot, I jumped up and strode towards him. Before I could distract him, however, he had crouched on one knee and peeled back a corner of the Persian carpet to expose the offending floorboard.

'This needs fixing,' he muttered. 'Probably needs something to wedge it. Do you have a bit of wood, by any chance?'

'What?' I said.

'Wood. Are you deaf as well as stupid? A bit of *wood*. As a matter of fact, it looks like you might be able to …'

I became aware of a high-pitched voice nearby. A few seconds later, Eve was standing in my front doorway. She was gasping for breath, as if she had run some distance to get there.

Still on one knee, my father swivelled around and said good morning to her.

'Eve,' I blurted out, grateful for once to see her, for the distraction she would provide. Grateful, that is, until she opened her mouth.

'There's that child protester!' she announced, and I detected her piquant revenge for all the times I had avoided her. She was nodding so energetically that her pigtails flopped about behind her.

Then I heard the voice of Detective Bird, who was still on the walkway outside. 'What did you say, little lady?'

My father looked back at me, eyebrows raised. I felt I was sinking into a dreadful zugzwang in which I might be compelled to implicate myself in one awful crime to absolve myself of a worse one.

'He's a child protester.'

Caroline, the horrible girl's mother, loomed up behind her, also short of breath. 'It's *molester*, honey. Mo-les-ter.'

Detective Bird peeked around the doorjamb at me. Then, addressing Eve: 'What makes you say that? Did he hurt you?'

Eve, usually so eager to be the centre of attention, was struck mute. Confused, she glanced back and forth between me, her mother and the detective, who had lowered himself onto his knee to meet her eye.

'No, no,' she said at last.

Caroline, ever astounded by her child, chuckled.

My father was by then standing again, hands on hips, mouth agape.

'Then what makes you say that, honey?' Detective Bird persisted.

The child hopped from foot to foot. 'Um, um.' She gazed around, unable to contain herself, then pointed to the middle of the apartment block. 'Max told me!'

I recalled Max joking that he would use this to keep the girl from bothering me, but I never considered he would do it.

Submitting to the childish belief that I might render myself invisible if unable to see my persecutors, I closed my eyes.

TWENTY-FOUR

FORTUNATELY, THIS MOST HEINOUS OF ALLEGATIONS WAS SOON cleared up. With Detective Powell left to watch over me, Detective Bird trooped over to Max and Sally's apartment with Caroline and Eve. Although nobody answered the door, on the way the detective managed to ascertain from Eve and her mother that I had not touched her at all and that her allegation was based on the throwaway comment of an eccentric (and often drunk) neighbour. Finally, most of my unwelcome visitors left.

My trials were not, however, finished for the day. Hungover and exhausted, I endured a gruelling lunch with my father at bustling Tiamo in Lygon Street. We made small talk: Barbara had damaged her Achilles tendon playing tennis; their real estate business was going well; the Dunley football club was raising money to build a new locker room. To my ears it was news from a distant land for which I cared not a jot. I hadn't been alone with my father in many months, and I knew I was being sullen and uncooperative.

My father stared at me, a steaming forkful of spaghetti marinara suspended between his mouth and plate.

After a while, he put it down. 'You were such a sweet boy when you were small,' he said, taking up a paper napkin and wiping his mouth. 'I remember once, when you were about eight years old, you tried to run away. You had a bag of stuff, some sandwiches and an apple, things like that. Meredith and Rosemary caught you sneaking along the side of the house. You had some idea you were adopted. I don't know where you thought you were going. To find your real family, I suppose. I'm not sure if you remember that.'

I did remember the day — the whine of cicadas, the rough drag of pampas grass trailing through my fingers as I crept past the house.

My father laughed to himself and began shovelling spaghetti into his mouth.

I thought of what Sally had told me once about being brave in the face of one's family.

'Well,' I asked, 'am I?'

My father chewed his pasta. 'Are you what?'

'Adopted.'

'You serious?'

My heart was beating hard. I nodded.

My father licked his glistening lips and arranged his cutlery on his plate. 'Why would you even think that?'

'Rosemary and Meredith always said I was.'

'Oh, I see. Since when did you listen to them?'

I was surprised to feel hot tears forming behind my eyes. A young waitress dropped a wine glass near our table, prompting a round of cheers from a group of tipsy students.

By the time the shattered glass had been cleared away, I was able to speak. 'I thought Aunt Helen was … that she might have been my mother.'

My father looked as if he were about to laugh, but managed to control himself. 'Helen? Why Helen, of all people?'

I shrugged.

My father sighed and held his face in his hands. 'God,' he said when he resurfaced. 'OK, OK. Let me tell you a few things about Helen.'

He observed another waitress, the prettiest one, bearing aloft plates of spaghetti as she navigated between tables. He cleared his throat. 'Your aunt wasn't your mother, Tom. Your mother is your mother and I'm your father.'

'Then what was that big fight about, the one you had with Helen?'

'Oh, that. Is that what this is all about?' He lowered his voice. 'Listen. It would be a miracle if Helen was your real mum. Your aunt, well, your aunt liked, uh, *women*. The fight was when her … *girlfriend*, I guess you'd call it, moved in with her. An Englishwoman she'd met on a bloody cruise down the Rhine. And she wanted to bring her to Christmas dinner. And we wouldn't allow it. Not in front of you kids.'

'Why not?'

My father looked at me aghast but declined to respond, no doubt considering the answer to be self-evident. 'She didn't last long, at any rate. Pat moved back to England a few years ago.'

'An Englishwoman?'

'Yeah, that was the, you know, girlfriend's name.'

I remembered the mysterious phone call, the postcards. 'I think she rang me. Last week.'

'Yes, she rang me, too. She and Helen were still friendly — even still wrote to each other — but Pat didn't know your aunt had died. She said she'd rung Helen's old place. That someone had told her. You, I presume.'

I felt betrayed and sad that my relationship with my aunt had been severed over this.

'Look,' my father continued, 'it was right before your mum and I divorced. It was a bad few years for everyone. And once it happened it was hard to go back. Some pretty nasty things were said.'

This revelation should, by rights, have provided me with some relief, but its effect was indeterminate; I had for so long assumed I was not of my family that it was confronting to be told otherwise.

My father looked genuinely dismayed. 'I'm sorry your mother and I split up. I think perhaps you didn't handle it very well, but you mustn't blame yourself. We both adored you children. It was just that, I don't know, sometimes things run their course, that's all. And you can't always predict how it will go. You always think it will be forever. That's the best thing about relationships when they're new and the worst when they're over, because it always feels like such a failure.'

This was about the only reference to an emotional life my father had ever expressed, and I was confused by its unexpected articulation. I doubt I'm alone in finding it difficult to see my relatives as complete human beings with their own interior lives; I usually deflected any such exploratory overtures, preferring them to remain frozen in the role I had designated for them.

In any case, my father appeared to regret his uncharacteristic outburst almost immediately. He pushed his plate of pasta away and ordered coffee ('A cup of chino, please').

Fiddling with his shirt cuffs, he told me that — in light of the fact I wasn't even studying at university but was just 'bumming around' — he had decided to sell his late sister's apartment at Cairo. Rosemary was having yet another child, and he wanted to help her out with some money.

'Besides,' he went on, 'you were meant to paint the place, remember? That was part of the deal. As far as I can see, you haven't done a single thing.'

I attempted to disguise my distress at hearing this news by inspecting my salami focaccia. 'Fine. I'm moving to France in a few weeks, anyway. As soon as I get a passport.'

'With what money? You've lost your job, remember?'

'I've got some saved up.'

He snorted. 'Right. From washing dishes in a French restaurant.'

'Well, I do.'

'We should never have let you move here all alone. Your bloody uncle's an idiot, no good to anyone. Too busy prancing around in lycra. I blame myself. We should have kept a closer eye on you. I don't even recognise you anymore.' He broke off until a waitress had set down his coffee. 'You're not on drugs, are you?'

Even if I were inclined to reveal all that had happened in the past eight months, my confession would never be for his ears. I shook my head and took a bite of my now-cold lunch.

We said our clumsy farewells, and I returned home late in the afternoon to find a folded piece of paper slipped under my door. I recognised Sally's distinctive looping handwriting, even though the note consisted only of a single word.

Rooftop

TWENTY-FIVE

STILL HUNGOVER AND SHATTERED BY EVERYTHING THAT HAD occurred in the past twenty-four hours, I drank a glass of water before mounting the curling, cantilevered stairway.

Max and Sally were sitting in deckchairs on the roof. For some reason they both looked surprised to see me but, as ever, Max rallied; he stood to shake my hand with gusto. 'Well, hello there. We're taking in the air. Lovely up here, isn't it?'

I nodded hello. Sally was gazing across to where the sun was dipping behind the elm trees in the Carlton Gardens. Unwilling, it seemed, to meet my eye.

All at once Max's demeanour altered. He clapped a hand to my shoulder and pulled me close, although there was no one else within earshot. 'Mr Orlovsky told us the cops were around at your apartment today? What did they want? Was it about the painting? What did you tell them?'

I tried to placate him. 'Relax. I didn't tell them anything.'

'*What did they want?*'

I was taken aback by the ferocity of his interrogation. 'It's alright, Max. It was unrelated.'

'What, then? Tell me.'

He listened wide-eyed as I explained about the university forms the police had found in the possession of a suspect in the Moonee Ponds killings, how my boss had rung my mother and so on; the whole unlikely chain of events that had led the police to my door that morning.

Not once during my account did he take his eyes from my face, as if scouring it for signs of deceit. Although I was telling the truth, the combination of his zealous interest and my desperation for him to believe me made me edgy.

'Well,' he said when I had finished. 'That's quite a story. And they didn't ask *anything* about, you know, Dora?'

'Not a thing.'

'You're sure it wasn't some sort of trap?'

'Yes. But I thought we were done for. And my father was there, and my aunt and uncle. It was awful. What a day.'

'Where's your father now?' he asked, looking around as if expecting him to leap out from behind a pole.

'He's headed back to Dunley.'

'I see, I see. Sounds truly ghastly.' He paused to absorb all this. 'But well done. Not that I thought you would say anything, but, you know, we have to be on our guard.'

Sally had remained subdued for the duration of this exchange, listening, the toe of one shoe tracing figure-eights in the air. Her exposed ankle glowed in the dusk light. Her calf muscle flexed, un-flexed, flexed.

Max placed a hand on each of my shoulders to better meet my eye. 'Tom.'

'Yes.'

'We did it. I don't think we've thanked you properly. We couldn't have done it without you. We're meeting at Edward and Gertrude's place tomorrow, remember. Five o'clock. We'll split the you-know-what, the proceeds, and make some concrete plans for getting off this island. What do you think of that?'

'Sounds good.'

'It's going to be great. You've got a passport, I take it?'

'Not yet. I was meant to go to the post office today and get the forms, but got sidetracked by the fuss.'

'Oh. Well, not to worry. Get on to that. It only takes a week or two. Best thing to do is stay low until then. Don't splash money around. We'll start packing up. You know what? I am going to fetch us some champagne so we can celebrate. We shall drink to our health.' He dropped his voice to a conspiratorial whisper. 'To our good *fortune*.'

The thought of alcohol made me queasy. 'I'm pretty sure we drank to our health last night.'

'Then we shall do it again. The three of us. Darling, do we still have that bottle in the fridge?'

Sally glanced up, startled. 'What?'

'Champagne. Do we still have a bottle in the fridge?'

'I don't think so.'

'Then I'll go to the bottle shop. I'll be back in a jiffy.'

Sally stood. 'I'll get it, Max.'

Max held up an admonishing hand. 'No. Wait here. I insist. Keep our Tom company.'

He kissed Sally (long, languorously) on the mouth and dashed down the stairs, whistling. Gradually, the sound faded away. A strained silence between Sally and me followed.

'Sally,' I said.

'Don't.'

Although acting on the spur of the moment, I had run this scenario over in my head dozens of times.

I took a step towards her. 'Sally, come with me.'

She coughed over the top of my plea. It was a considerate gesture; an opportunity for her to pretend she hadn't heard what I'd said, a chance for me to pretend I had never said it.

But I couldn't stop. 'Please, Sally —'

'I said: *don't*.'

'Don't go with Max. Come with me instead.'

'What, run away with you? To where?'

'Anywhere.'

She sighed as if exasperated at having to deal with callow boys like me. And I remember noting this, knowing even then it would be an image with which I might torment myself in years to come.

I dug about in my shirt pocket for my packet of cigarettes. I offered her one.

She shook her head. 'I've given up.'

I tried a different approach. 'I know Max hits you.'

'Don't be ridiculous.'

'What about those blood noses you get? I'm not a complete fool, you know. That time you hid from him at my place?'

'Oh God. Not you as well. I'm prone to blood noses, that's all. I've had them all my life. Max would never lay a hand on me. Never has, never will. I'm not one of those women you can project anything onto. I'm not just a screen for your rescue fantasies. Last year a cabal of, I don't know what, gender-studies students accosted me in Lygon Street. Said the same thing. Wanted to save me from myself. Insulted me for taking Max's surname when we were married and letting the sisterhood down. I love Max. I'm married to Max. Till death do us part and all that, things you wouldn't understand yet.'

I was shocked and angered by her contempt for me. 'You know he sleeps with other people,' I said.

She contemplated me, eyebrows arched. 'So do I, remember? But it doesn't mean I love him any less.'

I slapped at a mosquito that had landed on my arm. I took satisfaction from the smear of blood on my palm until I understood the blood was a quantity of my own that the insect had drawn before I realised. 'But I thought we —'

'I'm sorry, but you thought wrong.'

'I love you.'

God, I thought. *How pathetic I sound.* I had sworn not to humiliate myself, yet that was precisely what I was doing. I had become a boy scrambling up the stairs of a collapsing building. Seeking what?

She flinched. 'I know you think you do, but you don't know me. Tom, you're only eighteen. I'm nearly ten years older than you. What do you think love is? Fluffy bunnies? Dancing through meadows? Love is tangled, it's complicated. A dark forest. It's hard to find your way out, nor should you want to.

'You know, last year I was at a party and this awful man with long hair tried to pick me up. He thought he was quite special, assumed I would simply go home with him if he asked. I told him to buzz off, but Max got wind of it and later, when the man was leaving, Max had a go at him. It turns out he was some sort of greasy pop star and one of his minders beat Max up. Broke one of his teeth, gave him a black eye. But Max didn't care. He'd do it again for me. He'd do *anything* for me. And once *Maldoror* is finished, Max will be famous and no one will even remember who that pathetic pop star was.'

She smiled at the memory with satisfaction. 'Love is not always enough, you know. There is always much more. I'm sorry if you got the wrong idea. You and me, it was just a …' Her voice trailed off. She shook her head.

'What? It was a what?'

'Nothing. Sorry. I'm sorry.'

I was embarrassed, furious. This was not the way I had anticipated this conversation progressing. How had things gone so awry, and so quickly? 'Do you even know what happened at Queel's place that night? Do you?'

At this she turned away.

'He murdered Queel? In cold blood. For *nothing*.'

'This is all becoming a bit Freudian, isn't it? Do you wish to win me over or tear him down? Besides' — she tucked a strand of blonde hair behind her ear — 'it wasn't for nothing. It was for everything.'

'He came into the room with a pistol and shot him. Right in the chest. It was unbelievable.' Unconsciously I had made a gun of my fingers, which was aimed at her.

'You were there, were you?' she asked. 'Well, the police think it was one of his mad girlfriends.'

'Yes, you know I was.'

'How did you get there?'

'What? What does that matter? I drove in my car. You were at the warehouse yourself when Max asked me to drive him over to Queel's.'

'Hmm, I don't remember that. Anyway, where is this gun now?'

'Under my floorboards.'

'*Your* floorboards? And tell me, did anyone see you at Queel's place?'

'Well, I hope not. If they had we would have been arrested by now.'

'So it's your word against Max's, is it? Because Max was with me for most of that night. Until he went to that big party up in Drummond Street.'

Although this was hardly a watertight alibi, the hairs stiffened on the back of my neck as I digested the implications of her statement. I stared past her at the tower of the Brunswick Street commission flats, drenched orange in the setting sun. Someone — man, woman or child, I couldn't tell from this distance — stepped onto one of the balconies to shake out a towel or rug.

'But you know that's not true,' I managed to say, and in my stammering voice I detected the dismal wail of a child who realises he has been comprehensively outmanoeuvred.

Sally brushed a twig from her green skirt before turning her gaze — now limpid and cruel — upon me. 'Sometimes you'd do anything for love. Even things you might not want to do. You'll learn this one day.'

My heart felt emptied of blood, my lungs drained of air. How appalling is love: it is almost impossible to judge if someone feels it for you, and yet you know instantly when those feelings are retracted. Almost as if love, like air, is best detected by the lack of it.

'And did you know about Helen? About her girlfriend Pat?'

Sally nodded.

'But you didn't say anything about it when I told you all that stuff about thinking she was my mother?'

She didn't move. I heard footfalls on the outside staircase, and Max surfaced, brandishing a bottle of champagne and three glasses.

I swallowed my anger. I laughed, far too heartily, and held the glasses as Max poured champagne for us. Sally protested ineffectually.

Max held up his glass. He looked from me to Sally and back again. 'My friends. My beautiful friends.'

And we drank.

'Now,' he went on, 'there's one more piece of news we should get out of the way.'

Sally shook her head. 'Oh, no, no. I don't think this is the right time for —'

'Nonsense. Tom would love to hear it.' Max cleared his throat and stood taller. 'Guess what? Sally and I are going to have a baby.'

'Max, we can't be absolutely sure yet.'

'But I'm sure, my love. I truly am. Oh, it's going to be great. All of us in France, our baby …'

Slow as poison, this information moved through me, immobilising first one part of my body, then another. Shock is the absence of emotion — rather than being one itself — in which the world is sucked away or, perhaps more accurately, one is briefly exiled.

I pictured the three of us from a distance. Max, Sally and I on the rooftop. Sally stood clutching the collar of her red jacket at her chin, eyes fixed on the ground, as Max, with one arm draped over her shoulder, threw back his drink with triumph.

And there I was with my glass of champagne, stepping forwards to kiss Sally on the cheek and shake Max's hand. The expressions on our faces were hard to read, and I was too far away to hear what else was said. But there was laughter, Max's laughter, floating forever across the evening air.

TWENTY-SIX

I WOKE AS IF FROM A DISTURBING DREAM, BUT THE DREAM — if indeed that had prompted my waking — was gone, leaving only a faint aftertaste of unease. It was still early. The morning light was only half formed. In addition to the nearby thrum of traffic and the soft sizzle of wind through the peppercorn tree outside my window, I discerned the deep, irregular pant of what must have been a massive hound being walked in the street below. But after a few seconds I realised it was the sound of someone sawing wood with a large-toothed tool.

The noise started, stopped, started again. At first it sounded some distance away, and I assumed a tenant in the block was having repairs done on their apartment. The closer I listened, however, the more it sounded like it was coming from somewhere much nearer. My apartment, in fact. I sat up. Had my father arranged some pre-sale repairs? For some time the front door had been sticking, but I hadn't told anyone about it, so minor had the irritation of this been.

I swivelled around until my feet landed on the cold floor. I was by then positive the horrible sound was coming from close by. My breath quickened and, as on my first morning here, I searched for a potential weapon in case I was confronted by an intruder.

The noise stopped. I was overcome by a terror so acute that it became difficult to breathe. Perhaps it was the sound of a creature, after all? I picked up a mug (empty, save for a soggy crust of mould) and rose to my feet. And it was then I was assailed by the questions one is inevitably assailed by in these situations: Should I call out? Should I attack? Or should I wait out the burglary without revealing myself and hope whoever it was left me unharmed?

Fuelled by who knew what reservoir of courage or foolhardiness, I tiptoed forwards. The intruder had not yet moved into my hallway, as I was yet to hear the squeak of the loose floorboard beneath the carpet runner. This was some consolation. Unless it was someone who knew to avoid the loose board? I drew breath, raised my mug and stepped into the lounge room.

Nothing. No one. The front door was closed, my apartment empty apart from myself.

After a few seconds, the noise started again. It was definitely emanating from somewhere near my front door. I peered through the darkness. Near the base of the wooden door was a glimmer of daylight where there should have been none, a hole at around shin height. As I watched, the hole spread like a puddle, assisted by what appeared to be someone picking away at the crust of wood from outside. Tiny fingers, faintly simian in shape, wrenched splinters away.

I tried to speak but my throat was uncooperative, as was my whole body. After some time (those dreadful, elastic minutes) a head forced its way through, even though the gap was not wide enough for a head. Or not for a human head.

It was indeed a troll-like creature, snouted and bewhiskered, that shouldered its way inside, spitting chunks of wood from its mouth as it did so. When halfway in, it sneered at me, displaying crenellated battlements of broken and bloodied teeth.

'Tom!' it squealed in Eve's unmistakable, high-pitched voice.

'How do you spell murder?'

I woke, gasping for air.

In darkness, I scrambled out of bed and pulled on some clothes. My clock radio showed 1.52 a.m. Spooked by my dream and by what Sally had said earlier, I took the pistol from beneath the squeaky floorboard in the hallway. It was still wrapped in its tea towel. In a sort of grim frenzy I drove out to Eltham, a semi-rural suburb of farmlets and mud-brick houses half an hour's drive away. I pulled up in the car park of some playing fields and picked my way over to the Yarra River's muddy banks. After ensuring no one was around, I tossed the gun into the eddying water at what I estimated to be the deepest part of the river.

Getting rid of the gun didn't give me as much satisfaction as I had hoped, but at least it was out of my apartment. A breeze ruffled the gum trees. A pair of bats drifted across the night sky. I lit a cigarette, smoked it down.

As I drove home, my conversation with Sally looped over and again in my head. Although humiliated, my despair was moderated by a vague gratification at the dramatic turn of events. I had, at least, experienced something adult and important. I imagined how this scene would play out in the movie of my life: a mournful piano motif, tear-stained cheeks, empty city streets. And that hateful obbligato: *What do you think love is? What do you think love is? What do you think love is?*

On my return, I was surprised to see lights on in Max and Sally's apartment. It was past three a.m. I crept over and stood listening at their front door. From within I heard the dim notes of classical music, muffled voices. At one point it sounded as if Max was on the phone. Laughter, then footsteps, the noise of a heavy object being dragged across their wooden floor.

The following day, James banged on my front door. Although it was almost noon, I had only just got out of bed and was standing in my lounge room, wondering what to make of everything. The conversation with Sally, the terrifying dream, and the late-night journey to get rid of the pistol had all combined to instil in me an overwhelming exhaustion.

James swept past me as soon as I opened the door. He reeked of cigarette smoke, liquor and stale sweat; of someone who had been out all night. He was agitated.

'Thank God you're home. Have you seen them?' he asked.

'Who?'

'Max and Sally. They're not here, are they?'

With one hand I shielded my eyes from the daylight flooding the hallway. 'I haven't seen anyone today.'

'When did you last see them?'

'God. What is this? Last night.'

He pulled my hand away. 'I've been over there and no one's home.'

It was too early for this sort of carry-on. I closed the door. 'Perhaps they're asleep?'

He shook his head. 'I don't think so. I knocked very loudly. It's weird.'

'What do you mean?'

He stared at me for a second before flopping onto the couch. 'I don't know. Nothing. Pour me a drink, will you.'

'*James*. It's not even midday.'

'I know, I know, but it's far too late to stop now. I need to get through the rest of the day and the only way to do that is to keep going. Besides, it must be six o'clock somewhere.'

'Where have you been?'

'You do not want to know. Out in the wide, wide world.'

'Don't you want to eat lunch?'

'No. Drink, please.'

I poured him a tumbler of whisky — heavy on the ice — and put the kettle on for myself. I had witnessed James in this kind of truculent mood before, and knew all I needed to do was ignore him for a while and he would settle down. Sure enough, by the time I had dressed and made myself breakfast, he was calmer. He sat smoking while I ate my toast and sipped my tea. I told him about the visit from the police, about lunch with my father; despite the drama of these events, I could tell he wasn't paying attention.

'You know,' he said, 'I drank a bottle of port when I was thirteen because I knew somewhere in the back of my tiny, tiny mind that it might kill me — although that wasn't my intention. I vomited all over our Persian rug that, luckily, was almost the same colour. My parents were away somewhere that year, and my sister never told anyone about it. Bless her.'

I knew James's relationship with his parents to be troubled; we had met briefly once at James's flat, and their affection for him was distracted — more like that of an elderly couple for a pet terrier than middle-aged parents for their only son. The mother wore eccentric, multi-coloured eyewear, the father an expensive-looking leather coat with a fur collar. They oozed money and liberal, arty pretensions; their colognes were interchangeable. I was intimidated by them. Max had told me they were involved in a swingers scene out in the leafy eastern suburbs, that they smoked joints after meals, that their bedside table was piled with erotic art books that he and James used to peruse in the hours after school before the parents returned home from work.

I cleared away my plate and lit a cigarette once I was sitting down again in the chair opposite.

James fished an ice cube from his glass and popped it into his mouth. He crunched on it, thoughtful for a minute or so. 'I was afraid you would all leave without me,' he said.

'What? Why?'

Tears shone in the corner of his eyes. 'I don't know. It's not as if I did much to help with the theft or anything. You drove the car; Gertrude and Edward did the actual painting. Those weirdo Bolshevik twins took the thing. Besides, I think Max is fed up with me.' He controlled his emotions before going on. 'I had this vision of being left here alone while you all lived it up in Europe. What I would do if that happened ...'

'Don't be silly, James.'

'Kill myself, most likely.'

'James. Please. I saw Max and Sally last night. Everyone's excited.'

'Really?'

'Yeah, in fact ...'

'What?'

'Nothing.'

'*What?* Tell me.'

'Sally's pregnant. They're going to have a baby.'

'Oh, I see. That's interesting.'

'So there'll be a baby with us in France.'

James sniggered. 'That fertility dance we did must have worked after all.'

'I suppose so.'

'Well,' he said, 'we are quite the pair of fools, aren't we?'

Disingenuous to the end, I asked him what he meant by this, even though I knew that he was referring to my wasted feelings for Sally and his own for Max. In any case, he declined to elucidate further, and he blew his nose and pulled himself together.

'I suppose they're over at the warehouse,' James said, once he'd recovered. 'We should go around there now. Get our money, our share of the spoils? Isn't that the plan?'

These so-called spoils had become nestled so deeply in the proliferating Russian dolls of complications that I had almost forgotten about them. Despite the abrupt loss of my kitchen-hand job, the money was not as attractive as it had been when Max first broached the plan to steal the *Weeping Woman*. In addition, I wasn't at all keen to see Sally so soon after last night's rebuff. I regretted my outburst, even though we had (superficially, at least) parted on good terms. At any rate, I felt confident she would mention nothing to Max of what I had said.

'But Max told us to come around at five o'clock,' I reminded James.

He waved this away. 'Let's go. Get it over and done with.'

I ground out my cigarette. What difference would it make? I would have to face Sally eventually; it might as well be sooner rather than later. I threw on a coat and opened the door.

Once on the walkway, I was startled by emergency-vehicle lights on Nicholson Street, directly in front of Cairo. I dragged James back, and we hovered out of sight on the landing until I ascertained the flashing lights were those of an ambulance, rather than a police car. Even so, we approached with caution.

A crowd had gathered on the footpath, including the enigmatic New Zealand man and a couple of other neighbours. Two paramedics came along the path wheeling a trolley, on which lay Mr Orlovsky. His trousers were muddy and torn, and his face was as grey as old concrete. He looked awful.

A middle-aged man I recognised as another Cairo resident told me Mr Orlovsky had tripped and fallen on the stairs. Poor Mr Orlovsky was petrified, one of his filmy eyes rolling like that of a dolphin caught in a net. He seemed excited to see me, however, and reached out in my direction. I went to his side. He stammered at me, but the paramedics loaded him into the ambulance before he could get any words out that I understood.

The crowd dispersed, and James and I set off across the park. It was sunny. James hummed morosely as we walked. We didn't speak. When we arrived at the warehouse's battered steel door, it was ajar and rocking in the breeze.

'That's weird,' said James as we mounted the stairs. 'You know how obsessed they are about keeping that door closed.'

The following tableau is frozen forever in my memory, like one of those tenebrous paintings of the Counter-Reformation (by Caravaggio or Gentileschi) in which one can discern the flurry of activity destined to follow the captured scene, as well as everything that precipitated it. A miracle, the conversion, bloody sacrifice, flight.

Upstairs at the warehouse Tamsin and George were slumped at the kitchen table. One of the kitchen cupboard doors was open; the sink was full of dirty dishes.

I took one look at the Bolshevik twins and somehow, before being told any details, I knew what had happened.

'They've gone, haven't they?' I asked.

Tamsin regarded me from behind her greasy fringe. Her smile was more sour than usual. 'Yep.'

Everything was quiet, until George uttered what were among the few words I ever heard him speak.

'Those fucking *fuckers*.'

TWENTY-SEVEN

FOR SOME REASON THE SHOCK WAS NOT AS GREAT AS MIGHT have been expected; it was of belated recognition as much as utter surprise: after all, the clues to a story's end are invariably contained somewhere within.

James groaned and staggered forwards. 'Oh, I knew it. I *knew* it.' He fumbled in his pockets and produced a key. 'The lock to Max and Sally's front door had been changed. I have this key that I swiped from Sally, but it wouldn't work this morning. I tried to get in but ...'

In her faint English accent, Tamsin told us that she and her brother had arrived at the warehouse an hour or so ago. Like James and me, they had been told to drop over for the money at five o'clock but, unable to see any reason to wait, and keen to get their share, they came by earlier.

'We wanted our money,' Tamsin said. 'One o'clock, five o'clock. What's the difference, anyway? But the front door was open and there was no one here. They've left a lot of stuff but most of their clothes are gone; their painting materials are gone. We've been conned. We were so, so daft.'

'Wait a second,' I said, 'this isn't conclusive. We don't know for sure they've left.'

George pushed a sheet of paper across the table towards me. Reluctantly, I picked it up.

'We found this on the floor,' Tamsin said.

It was a crumpled photocopy of an itinerary, prepared by a local travel agent for a Mr Edward Degraves and Mrs Gertrude Degraves. In time, the squiggles coalesced into recognisable words and digits. Passport numbers. A Qantas flight. Melbourne–Bangkok–Frankfurt. Thursday, 21 August 1986, 7.15 a.m.

I re-read it, checked the date. No one said anything. I was horribly aware of James's damp and drunken breathing nearby.

'I heard Sally and Max moving things around late last night,' I said.

'What time?' asked Tamsin.

'Around three a.m.'

'They were probably packing to go to the airport.'

James belched. 'What about Anna Donatella? Is she still in the country?'

'We can ring her at the gallery, I suppose.'

Tamsin and James began to go over it all again, but I couldn't bear to listen. Leaving them in the kitchen, I wandered to the other end of the warehouse.

The place had always been more impressive at night, but then, with afternoon light streaming through the large warehouse window, the trompe l'oeil of the Bay of Naples looked tacky and careworn, no more convincing than one you might find on the wall of a fish-and-chip shop. There were scuff marks where the wall adjoined the floor. Spider webs billowed in the breeze.

Although always chaotic, the warehouse showed signs of having been rummaged through. Scattered here and there on the floor were items that had previously rested upon shelves or windowsills: a bird's skull, an old tram timetable, a Rubik's cube, a pocket edition of Allen Ginsberg's *Howl*.

Edward and Gertrude's bedroom was in disarray as usual, but their dresser drawers were agape and empty. Most of the cosmetics and assorted jewellery had been swept from the top of the dresser. All that remained was a greasy tube of lip balm, an assortment of broken earrings, and a bent and blackened spoon.

Likewise, their studio had been cleaned out. The bottles of pigments and oils were gone, as were the suitcase of materials that had once belonged to Elmyr de Hory, and Gertrude's forgery of the Soutine portrait, which I had liked so much. Blank canvases were stacked against one wall. Crusty brushes and tubes of paint littered the floor.

I ran my palm over the scarred surface of the wooden bench, spattered with its galaxy of paint. I lowered myself into the squeaky wooden chair where Gertrude had often sat to consider her work in progress, and I thought back to the first night I came to the warehouse, and what Max had said about the moon landing: *If people are desperate to believe in something, then they will.*

On the floor was a copy of yesterday's *Herald*. The front page was all about the return of the Picasso painting and featured a photograph of a forensic scientist leaving Spencer Street Station with the package. There was also a reproduction of Tamsin and George's final cheeky note, in which they intimated the theft was merely the first phase of an ongoing campaign for increased arts funding. I found it hard to believe they would attempt anything so daring after this little fiasco.

James stood swaying in the studio doorway. 'There's no answer at Anna Donatella's gallery.'

This was no surprise. 'Maybe she went with them? It hardly matters now, does it?'

James looked devastated, like a freshly orphaned boy. He stared around at the filthy walls and the paint-spattered bench, as if seeking evidence that might refute the hideous betrayal we suspected.

'Do you think they planned this all along?' he asked after a while. The very question (which, doubtless, I would ultimately have asked myself) made me feel ill. It was bad enough to have the future taken away — and in this fashion — but such hacking at the past was too awful to contemplate.

Thankfully, James didn't wait for my response before asking, 'What do we do now?'

I didn't answer. After a while he slumped into the other chair. Tears glistened on his cheeks. We sat like that for ages, not talking, each of us lost in our private worlds.

Ever hopeful, ever gullible, James and I waited for a word (a postcard, an explanatory letter) from them. None came. Their disappearance was as abrupt and complete as death. In subsequent weeks, we learned that Anna Donatella had also left the country, although no one knew where she might have gone. Rio, Paris and Berlin were all touted as possible destinations. Cairo was quiet — downright dull — as if Sally and Max had taken every exciting possibility with them in their suitcases.

I still dreaded arrest over my involvement in Queel's murder. I crossed the road if I saw anyone wearing a uniform; the glimpse of a police car in my rear-vision mirror prompted me to break out in a heavy sweat. Surreptitiously, I replaced the squeaking floorboard in my hall. Several nights a week I woke from violent and visceral dreams — of weird animals, of pistol shots, of windscreens smudged with rain.

As he had threatened, my father put Aunt Helen's apartment up for sale, and I started to look for new accommodation. Packing up a house is always a melancholy process. Although I had only lived at Cairo for ten months, I had in that short time accumulated a variety of mementoes I invested with sentiment and meaning.

There was the note from Max and Sally inviting me to dinner on that first night; some of Sally's records; a collection of T.S. Eliot poems James had pressed upon me; the art-exhibition flyers I had hoarded; matchbooks from various nightclubs — tangible proof I had taken part in the life of the city and had lived as fully as a young man should. These artefacts I bundled and deposited in cardboard boxes, along with clothes, my few cooking utensils and dozens of other books.

James and I spent a lot of time together. Although I felt sorry for myself, I couldn't imagine what it must have been like for him. After all, he had known Max since they were teenagers, and the betrayal he had experienced was profound. We distracted ourselves by playing pool or going to the movies. We tried not to talk of our former friends but, inevitably, our conversation sometimes veered into reminiscence, whereupon one of us would hurriedly (like a pond-skater scrambling to safer ice) change the subject before we went too far. It was easier, perhaps, to pretend the past year had never happened but, alone at night, I thought incessantly of Sally.

The days lengthened as spring gained a foothold. One night James and I were playing pool and sipping some awful homemade grappa at the grimy Double-O coffee bar. We were the only customers, which was fortunate because James was drunk and obstreperous, and it was in such moods he was liable to start fights with strangers.

He hiccuped, mumbled something indeterminate.

'... But it bloody doesn't, does it?'

'Doesn't what, James?'

He slapped the table. 'Kill you. Nor does it make you stronger. That's a lie to make you feel better about suffering. A lie the strong tell the weak.'

Although it wasn't unusual — when he was drunk — for James to launch into monologues barely augured by anything that preceded them, things were deteriorating more quickly than usual. I felt uneasy and began to plot how I might encourage him to call it a night without provoking an argument.

Before I could say anything, however, he lurched from his chair and played his shot, taking no time to assess the spread of balls before doing so. The pool table at the Double-O was so wonky (sloping to the left, buckled felt) that somehow — almost magically — it compensated for the impaired abilities and judgement of the late-night drunk. James was a rotten pool player, but at the Double-O, with enough alcohol in him to render the average man senseless, he often performed with remarkable skill. That night was no exception, and he sank three balls in a row, one of them a tricky cannon-shot, before falling into his chair.

'James,' I said, 'I'm so sorry. About, you know, about Max and everything. I know you loved him.'

He turned his bleary gaze upon me, as if puzzling over who I was and what I might have been referring to. His smile was chilling and the overall effect not only ended the discussion at hand but also indicated, in no uncertain terms, that we were never to speak of it again.

'It's your shot,' he said.

One afternoon, freshly discharged from hospital, Mr Orlovsky knocked on my door. He'd broken his collarbone in the fall, and his recovery was hampered by an infection and other complications that had required him to stay in hospital longer than would normally have been the case.

'Oh,' he stammered when I had opened it, 'I'm so glad you're ho-ho-ho home.'

We exchanged pleasantries and, with some relish, he told me of his medical adventures and expressed amazement at some of the equipment used in hospitals these days. All manner of tubes, machines with flashing lights. He was rather rejuvenated by his stay. The nurses, he told me a number of times, were all very pretty. Even the food was not bad, not too bad at all.

'Now,' he said, 'the reason I have come by is because lo-lo-lo lovely Sally left me a gift for you.'

I reeled. Her name, like an arrow loosed with unerring aim from afar.

'Mo-mo-mo most important, she said it was. Had to guard it with my-my-my life. I was supposed to give it to you some time ago but I was in hospital, so … The trouble is I can't carry the damn thing with this arm of mine in a sling, so you'll have to come over and get it, I'm afraid.'

Tingling with curiosity and dread, I followed him to his apartment. In his dim hallway was a rectangular package wrapped in brown paper and tied with string. It was probably Gertrude's Soutine forgery that I had so admired; she must have given it to Sally to leave for me. I recalled Gertrude's words at our first meeting: *You can have it when we've finished with it.*

I accepted the package without enthusiasm, unsure if I wanted such a potent reminder of that period in my life and the betrayals of which it was so redolent.

When I got home I rested it against the wall in the lounge room and there it might have remained, forever unopened, except for an envelope that slipped onto the floor from where it had been wedged beneath a layer of wrapping. On it was written a single word, in handwriting I recognised as Sally's.

Tom

I sat on my couch hard, as if winded. After several minutes, I opened the envelope and shook free the note within. Although there were only six words written on the sheet of paper, I looked at them for a very long time.

With trembling hands, I set about cutting the string and tearing away the wrapping. It was a warm afternoon. My front door was wide open. James strolled in while I was kneeling on the wooden floor over the torn shards of paper; we had arranged to see a film that afternoon.

He shambled past me and flopped onto the couch with a loud groan. 'What have you got there?' he asked when I failed to respond to his complaint about the unseasonably warm weather.

'I'm not sure.'

By this time I had ripped away a large segment of the outer wrapping and the spongy curatorial paper underneath. It was enough to reveal a significant portion of the painting, and although I couldn't yet make out the complete work, I saw enough to stop me in my tracks.

Stunned, I sat back on my haunches.

James lit a cigarette and waved away the smoke from his face. 'Goodness. That looks like our green friend, doesn't it?'

'Yes,' I said. 'It does.'

Taking greater care, I peeled away the rest of the wrapping until the painting was in my clammy hands — naked, as it were.

It was Picasso's *Weeping Woman* or, at the very least, a version of it. I closed my front door before resting the canvas on a low bookcase and switching on the lights to better inspect it. I turned the canvas over. On its wooden frame were the faded *10F* stamp, the splodge of paint, the twenty-five screw holes.

James said nothing, but I was aware of him observing me. He cleared his throat. 'You don't, by any chance, think …'

'Think what?'

'Well. What *is* that painting?'

I held it in my hands, gauged its weight. 'I don't know, to be honest. You know, the night Max and I went to Queel's place, well, Queel told me he had seen three paintings in Gertrude's studio. I didn't pay much attention at the time. In fact, I've only remembered it now. But what if he was telling the truth? I also remember thinking once that the forgery looked less developed than it had the day before. Maybe they did two copies, and intended to keep the original? To see if they could fool *everyone*? The gallery and their buyer?'

James walked over and inspected the painting as well. 'But why?'

'I don't know. To sell it again? Make more money?'

'Gertrude didn't care about the money. As long as she had some drugs.'

He was right. Never once had Gertrude betrayed any interest in how much she stood to make from her deception; for her it was all about the thrill of the forgery, the contest against those among the art establishment who had spurned her. I remembered a night when we had been discussing the division of money and she had been impatient at the talk of it. I also recalled how reluctant Edward had been to be present when the painting was handed over, and his terror at Eric's presence at the airfield had seemed disproportionate — until now, that is. He knew. He knew we were selling a forgery to Mr Crisp and that his goon would have cut off all our fingers — or worse — had he found out.

'To see if they could,' I said.

James laughed joylessly. 'I guess anything's possible, isn't it. Good old Gertrude. I wouldn't put it past her. She told me she didn't even like the painting that much. You saw it more often than I did. Do you reckon it's the real thing?'

In the weeks I had spent at Edward and Gertrude's studio, I had read through their books on Picasso and learned that he had painted many variations of the *Weeping Woman*, mostly in 1937. The version we had stolen exhibited a frenzied quality that betrayed the speed with which he had completed it. The figure's dark-green hair is combed back hard, the eyes staring in contradictory directions, the purple lips forever open in a gasp. Her tears rest like jewellery on her cheek, and her black tongue, if indeed it is a tongue, hovers between her pebbly teeth. Behind her is a grey, lightly striated wall. If her pinballing gaze could be said to be focused in any one direction, it might be through a black, arched window in the top right corner, through which perhaps lies the source of her grief. The handkerchief clasped to her face is rendered in the same clumsy fashion as the rest of her — as if the scene had been shattered into its constituent parts, then hastily reassembled into a punishing whole. The painting is at once incomplete and crowded with angst.

'The man who checked over the painting for Mr Crisp talked about the connoisseurship of art,' I said. 'He reckoned you have to have a feeling about it, a gut instinct.'

'How very scientific. What sort of feeling?'

'He said you'd know when you felt it. You'd divine its intent.'

'What would this be worth, anyway, if it was the original?'

The figures hovering in front of my eyes were staggering. 'Almost two million dollars. But what would I do with it? I can't hang it on the wall or anything. I can't sell it, can I?'

James straightened up and puffed on his cigarette. 'No, I guess not. But there would be some consolation in knowing you had it. Everyone knows the poof never lives happily ever after. At least one of us would get what he wanted out of this idiotic caper.'

'What do you mean?'

'Well, at least you get the girl.'

I contemplated the painting, the face I had admired for so long in Gertrude and Edward's studio that it had seeped into my dreams. The portrait of photographer Dora Maar, who had attracted Picasso's attention in a Paris cafe by cutting herself while jabbing a knife-point between her splayed fingers, who had the dubious honour of prompting the artist's famous phrase that women were machines for suffering. She was still alive, almost eighty years old and living in the south of France. I entertained a brief fantasy of her and Sally crossing paths — of them strolling arm in arm through a garden blooming with lavender and roses, laughing, exchanging whispered intimacies, a faint piano melody rising and falling on the air.

Still clasped in my hand was the note. I read it again.

I'm so sorry. With love, Sally.

And I stared and I stared, until across my skin swept a shiver, like a breeze dimpling the surface of a lake.

ACKNOWLEDGEMENTS

Although based around historical events and set among actual places, *Cairo* is a work of fiction. One or two of its characters are real, but most are products of my imagination.

Like any city, a novel is made up of many stories, and a number of other books were invaluable in *Cairo*'s creation. At its heart there was, of course, *Fake* by Clifford Irving. Eric Hebborn's *The Art Forger's Handbook* was a goldmine of information on painting history and techniques, as was *Color: A Natural History of the Palette* by Victoria Finlay.

I am indebted to Farah Farouque for the tour of Cairo apartments, and to Michael Varcoe-Cocks at the National Gallery of Victoria for allowing me to inspect the *Weeping Woman*. Thanks also to everyone at Scribe Publications, particularly Aviva Tuffield and Ian See for their tough love and brilliant editorial advice. And last but not least, I would like to thank my beautiful wife, Roslyn, for her invaluable patience and love.

For a very different type of support, I would also like to acknowledge the Australia Council and the City of Melbourne.